Praise for *True Cross*

"In *True Cross*, Pearson writes with his usual idiosyncratic verve."
—*The New York Times Book Review*

"Hilarious . . . Pearson strings innumerable amusing tales. A book that largely succeeds in being line-by-line funny for 255 pages."
—*San Francisco Chronicle*

"Pearson is up to his usual wickedly digressive, grammar-defying literary tricks. The book has to be read to be believed. Engaging . . . corrosively funny. *True Cross* rewards readers with its hilarious detours . . . a strange treat." —*Seattle Post-Intelligencer*

"Very funny." —*St. Louis Post-Dispatch*

"Outrageously funny, in its own dark, leering, crazy way."
—*The Atlanta Journal-Constitution*

"Better than 90 percent of the fiction out there."
—*The Dallas Morning News*

"For those who like their satire neat and with a bite, *True Cross* is sure to please." —*The Roanoke Times*

"Hilarious reading. Pearson spins out stories within stories, painting a detailed portrait of life in a dysfunctional southern community. He writes sympathetically about characters it would be easy to mock, giving them depth and humanity even as he gently satirizes their exploits."
—*The Charlotte Observer*

"At once suspenseful and satirical, gothic and comic—a mix of moods and styles that is, in the end, an unusual tribute to the art of storytelling itself. A book to be marveled at." —*Nashville Scene*

"Pearson knows how to string a tale."
—*Kirkus Reviews*

"A cracker-barrelful of pungently amusing observations and digressions."
—*Booklist*

"Pearson always manages a telling look at human frailty."
—*Publishers Weekly*

TRUE CROSS

T. R. PEARSON

PENGUIN BOOKS

PENGUIN BOOKS
Published by the Penguin Group
Penguin Group (USA) Inc., 375 Hudson Street, New York, New York 10014, U.S.A
Penguin Group (Canada), 10 Alcorn Avenue, Toronto,
    Ontario, Canada M4V 3B2 (a division of Pearson Penguin Canada Inc.) ·
Penguin Books Ltd, 80 Strand, London WC2R 0RL, England
Penguin Ireland, 25 St Stephen's Green, Dublin 2, Ireland (a division of Penguin Books Ltd)
Penguin Group (Australia), 250 Camberwell Road, Camberwell,
    Victoria 3124, Australia (a division of Pearson Australia Group Pty Ltd)
Penguin Books India Pvt Ltd, 11 Community Centre, Panchsheel Park,
    New Delhi - 110 017, India
Penguin Group (NZ), cnr Airborne and Rosedale Roads, Albany,
    Auckland, New Zealand (a division of Pearson New Zealand Ltd)
Penguin Books (South Africa) (Pty) Ltd, 24 Sturdee Avenue, Rosebank,
    Johannesburg 2196, South Africa

Penguin Books Ltd, Registered Offices:
80 Strand, London WC2R 0RL, England

First published in the United States of America by Viking Penguin,
a member of Penguin Group (USA) Inc. 2003
Published in Penguin Books 2004

10 9 8 7 6 5 4 3 2 1

Copyright © T. R. Pearson, 2003
All rights reserved

A portion of this work first appeared as "Dividends and Distributions"
in *Esquire*, issue of June 2001.

THE LIBRARY OF CONGRESS HAS CATALOGED THE HARDCOVER EDITION AS FOLLOWS:
Pearson, T. R., date.
    True cross / T. R. Pearson
    p.   cm.
    ISBN 0-670-03238-7 (hc.)
    ISBN 0 14 20.0478 2 (pbk.)
    I. Title
    PS3566.E235T78   2003
    813'.54—dc21   2002044863

Printed in the United States of America
Set in Janson • Designed by Carla Bolte

for
clan Chadwick—book proud

TRUE CROSS

I

PENGUIN BOOKS

TRUE CROSS

T. R. Pearson is the author of eight novels including *Polar* and *Blue Ridge*, both *New York Times* Notable Books, and the classic *A Short History of a Small Place*. He lives in Virginia.

1 —❧ As housecoats go, it was comely and well crafted. The thing had piping and placket pockets, a stylish drape and a scalloped hem. The collar of it was sufficiently stiff to stand up against a chill, and the belt ran through three loops and had been whip-stitched into place. The fabric was fleecy and gray with scarlet laurel blossoms in the weave along with a manner of foliage Elvin identified as burdock, though I was doubtful that even a shabby robe would come festooned with a weed.

Through Elvin's office window, we could see Erlene out in the cow lot where she served as a housecoat model while she flung corn to her hens. Once Elvin had cataloged for me the sundry virtues of her robe, he brought to my notice a trundle bed in the corner by his sheet stove, had me to know that Erlene sometimes popped inside and loved him up and thereby blunted and salved for Elvin the grinding strain of cattle keeping.

Elvin rose from his chair to show me how Erlene would shuck her robe, lay it back anyway on her shoulders and present herself

4 · T. R. PEARSON

for congress without having to guard against the stray migration of her belt which, Elvin took pains to remind me, had been whip-stitched into place. Then he sat back down and plundered through the shoe box on his desk until he'd found the receipt for that bathrobe and the ticket for the gas he'd required to carry him down and back from Roanoke where he'd bought it.

As was my custom, I refrained from a pronouncement straight-away and occupied myself instead with study of Elvin's documen-tation. I saw on the register tape that Erlene's robe had cost upwards of forty dollars, had been purchased in August at half past noon with cash and for exact change while Elvin hadn't bought his Roanoke gas until December which I hardly felt cause to trouble him to give an accounting about.

Instead I favored Elvin with the slight and colicky smile I'm prone to and shook my head to convey that Erlene's robe was not a deductible item which, naturally, served to render the cost of the gas a personal expense too.

For his part, Elvin shot from his chair and raged about his of-fice. He paused before the lone window and mounted a profane bid to raise the sash, but it was stuck in the slides and resolutely humidified into place. So Elvin put his face to the three-inch slot between the bottom rail and the sill and acquainted Erlene with the news that godless craven sons of bitches had up and taken this nation over and were running it anymore.

By way of response, Erlene flung a fistful of corn in Elvin's di-rection, and he retired from the sill as the kernels clattered like shot against the panes.

Elvin stalked over to his trundle bed and gave the frame a kick. Then he toured the entire office while he sputtered and he swore which, truth be told, was not so terribly much of an excursion since Elvin had framed and built that office where a cow stall used to be. The room was only four strides deep and maybe three strides wide, so Elvin invariably met a wall just as he'd hit prime stalking speed.

I sat and waited him out, occupied myself with perusal of Elvin's decor which was firmly in the local upland workspace tradition—a fair dose, that is to say, of grimy indiscriminate clutter leavened with gaudy religious artifacts and soft-core pornography. The place was littered with ear tags for cows and sacks of galvanized fence staples, half-empty jugs of fly balm and greasy cast-off coveralls. The walls were hung with a decoupaged Bible verse on a slab of varnished cedar, a porcelain likeness of Our Savior with a clock where his sternum should be, a glossy picture of a brunette selling pouch chew with her cleavage and a calendar photo of a leggy bronze thing in a macramé bikini posed before a clump of sea oats with a reciprocating saw.

"Got a good mind not to file. Let the bastards come and get me."

That was pretty much Elvin's quarterly refrain, so I just sat and waited for Elvin to spend sufficient of his ire to see his way clear to drop into his desk chair once again. He was a while, however, in winding down, had a talent for tirades and lurched about for a bit while unfreighting himself of seditious commentary.

I had a handful of clients given to Elvin's strain of indignation, and, like him, they none of them paid any taxes to speak of, earned only enough to qualify for exclusions and subsidies. While his stint as a cattle keeper may have seemed a career to Elvin, year in and year out he was usually on the hairy edge of a hobby. So Elvin didn't really need to deduct a fleecy robe with a whipstitched belt but could have stood instead to have shown a bit more in the way of a going concern.

A cow came to hand as Elvin passed his open office doorway. His herd had to go through the barn to get from the pasture to the springhead, and a heifer paused to look in and discover, I guess, what the storming around was about. Elvin took the opportunity to deride and blaspheme cattle as a species, and, since she was handy for it, he smacked that heifer on the snout, snatched off his cap and popped her which she tolerated well. She rubbed the side of her head on the door frame and indulged in a rumbling bovine necknoise before laying her ropy tongue on the floor and swabbing clean a plank.

Elvin finally wandered over and dropped back into his chair, the one he'd salvaged from the landfill and had proposed to depreciate. It was held together with angle irons and sixteen-penny nails, rode on four scrounged lawn-mower wheels instead of castors. As was his custom, Elvin groaned the way that Atlas probably would were he to ever know occasion to shift the world off of his shoulders, to unkink his achy lumbar and to smoke.

"I don't know," Elvin told me. "I just don't know."

Then he dredged a little phlegm in a fashion that, for Elvin, was reliably punctuational, indicated he was prepared to stray entirely off of taxes and touch, for variety's sake, upon some topic otherwise.

"How's old Stoney?" Elvin asked me.

Now I was acquainted at that time with a couple of Stoneys and had to pause to settle on which one Elvin might be asking after. Professionally, I knew a Stoney who was an exotic dancer in Raphine. She had part interest in a lounge off the interstate that catered to truckers chiefly. She operated a triple-X Web site, sold sex aids through the mail and owned outright a slummy little apartment house in Stuarts Draft.

That Stoney had authentic income and legitimate business expenses, hair about the color of blush wine and surgically cantilevered breasts. She wore around her neck a filigreed locket she'd opened for me once to reveal a tiny photograph of young Sal Mineo sweaty and stripped to the waist.

I decided she was hardly the sort who Elvin was likely to know—a racy female, that is to say, in the 36 percent tax bracket—so I fixed on my fallback Stoney, a neighbor of mine across the road. I was living in a rental on maybe forty acres that cozied up to the national forest, and those evenings I'd stand on the porch to take my Dickel with mountain air, I could sometimes see that Stoney down the swale beyond my drive where he was usually shifting tools out of his van or mucking around in his yard.

As he was a quarter mile or more away, I'd just hear him on occasion, most particularly when one of his cats had made of Stoney sporting use, had sprung out at him and plunged its claws clean through his trouser leg when Stoney would yelp and Stoney would reach to disengage that feline, when Stoney would visit upon it a few choice words of scalding abuse as prelude to flinging that creature overhand across the yard when I'd often meet with occasion to hear the cat a little as well.

I'd made Stoney's acquaintance the day I moved in. He'd dropped by with his mattock in hand both to tell me, "Hey here," and seek my permission to hack at a stump in my yard. Stoney had decided somehow that stump was the remnant of a lightered pine, and he was hopeful of laying a chunk in for the winter. I recall he kindly offered to hack me off a piece as well of what turned out to be weathered white oak with no pitch to speak of in it which Stoney flatly declined to embrace as an authentic fact as Stoney was poorly equipped to retreat from a conviction.

That was the trouble with him chiefly. You couldn't trust anything he said, but not because Stoney was given to mendacity and deceit. He was merely doggedly loyal to his uninformed misconceptions and couldn't be steered with stark unimpeachable proof away from a belief. Stoney had come by the notion that pitted prunes were toxic to most vermin, and he routinely broadcast the things in his ditch to serve as groundhog bait. He was persuaded the framers had troubled themselves to enshrine in the Constitution the right of a fellow who owned more than fourteen acres to urinate in his yard.

Stoney had grown convinced that charcoal insoles improved liver function. He let on to have private reasons to think poorly of the pope, and Stoney claimed to have seen once a science show on public television devoted to the miraculous healing powers of topical kerosene which he had taken to making use of as a balm and an emollient. Stoney, accordingly, tended to be our shiniest citizen about and, with his musk and fossil fuel bouquet, smelled like a flammable collie.

I knew the odd occasion to chat with Stoney when I'd check for mail in my box. We'd yammer at each other back and forth across the roadway, touch usually upon the weather and the prospects of the Braves, and Stoney would favor me now and again with a fresh article of faith. He'd shout out how he'd come by word that fox dander killed head lice or the lieutenant governor's brother had, in fact, been a woman once, but I was rarely tempted to wander across the road for an enlargement which had as much to do with the rotting prunes in the ditch as the strain of talk.

There in Elvin's office I recalled that I had caught a glimpse of Stoney as he'd detached a cat and hurled it just the afternoon before, so I felt reasonably fit to inform Elvin, "I guess Stoney's doing all right."

"ALL RIGHT!" And suddenly Elvin was up again and stalking. "If it'd been me or you, they'd have carried us off in a bucket."

Elvin noticed for some reason that his calendar was two months out of date. He plucked the thing off its rusty nail, flipped the pages over to March and admired for a moment a lithe young strawberry blonde in a translucent thong who was holding an air wrench and draped in compressor hose.

"Things just go his way, don't they? Wasn't even his goddamn car."

I didn't have any earthly idea what Elvin was talking about. "Something happen to Stoney?" I asked him, and Elvin wheeled to gaze upon me as if I'd vented a dose of intolerable wind or poleaxed the merciful Christ.

"You ain't heard!?"

I dropped my head and shook it, allowed I hadn't.

At that time I rarely saw anybody much except for my clients about who had their tax liabilities and simmering civic resentments to occupy them. With no personal taste for country music or NASCAR qualifying, I wasn't ever tempted to ferret out local news on the AM dial, and I'd wearied of the county paper after only a month or two because it was largely given over to grocery ads, undignified birthday announcements, church-league softball scores and forensic descriptions of bridal attire.

From my TV I could come by what was happening down in Roanoke and up in Harrisonburg, watched enough of the nightly network news to gain a sense of the world at large while Peggy, the girl who cut my hair, took such a slew of magazines that every two weeks I enjoyed occasion to refresh my native suspicion that I lived in a country I didn't care to know awfully much about.

I'd hear the sirens, of course, see the funeral processions, the odd plume of smoke above the trees, was aware in a general way of calamities unfolding around me, but I tended to get stale details of them by sheer happenstance and well after the locals had shifted on to fresher miseries.

A year or so previously, I think it was, a pair of gentlemen from town had gotten into an actual gunfight over a woman. They were both of them, to her misfortune, in her kitchen at the time. She was a client of mine. I'd helped her tidy up her late husband's estate and retrench from a few of his more lethargic investments, and she'd never, I'll confess, impressed me as potential gunplay bait.

She was seventy maybe with a taste for embroidered sweaters and treacly gardenia perfume, wore corrective sneakers and trifocal glasses with powder-blue oversized frames. She looked to me the sort of creature far more likely to back her Buick into a fellow in the shopping plaza lot than tempt him to fish his rusty revolver out of his bedside drawer and fetch up in her kitchen to trade live fire with a rival.

And it wasn't like those two suitors were the sorts of local hotheads given by nature to settling their personal grievances with guns. One of them, as it turned out, was retired from the ministry while the other was a lifelong buddy of his who'd been a concrete hauler and who'd traveled with that preacher to poverty-plagued parts of this world to build churches and schools and resurface roadways by way of advertisement for their Lord. To have, then, the pair of them shooting up a local widow's kitchen must have made more of a dramatic sensation than your standard firefight might.

Even still, I heard no breath of news about that episode until probably a half year later when the widow herself touched on it. Since no one was killed or wounded, it never made the TV news, and it turned out I wasn't chummy enough with anybody about to get conscripted into the sort of exchange that had to be common at the time. There must have been feverish local speculation as to what had set those two off, a couple of godly sorts with wives both in the Presbyterian churchyard and long personal histories of sober upstanding behavior, but I wasn't privy to even the meagerest scrap of pertinent talk until I'd inadvertently prompted the widow to favor me with an account.

We were slogging through her medical expenses for the year, and I'd gotten up to make myself some coffee as she was one of those females who'd sworn off cooking of every conceivable sort. So when she'd offer me a snack or a beverage and I'd see fit to accept, she'd stay where she was and point towards the suitable cupboard or the icebox, proved entirely content as a hostess to feature this stripe of self-service alone.

She only ever had decaffeinated off-brand freeze-dried crystal coffee, that sort that tends to taste in the cup like molten galvanized tin, so I was up from the table primarily for relief from that woman's scent and meant to linger before her stove until my head had cleared of gardenias. I plucked a saucepan off a hook on her wall and ran it half full of water, was shifting it towards a burner eye as it drained onto my shoes through a jagged hole in the bottom about the size of a thumbtack head.

That widow pointed out a dishtowel I could swab the floor tiles with and told me by way of explanation, "I guess you got the shot one."

So only then did I hear about the gunfight in that woman's kitchen, long after most everybody else had probably dissected the thing half to death. And I remember my surprise was leavened with a touch of nagging melancholy, sadness over the fact I'd succeeded a little too well at living apart.

"Wasn't much left but the bumpers," Elvin told me as he flopped back into his chair.

"My Stoney?" I asked him, and I'll confess I was pricked and stung and shaken since I'd never, where it came to the company of men, been aiming for unmoored. I'd hoped only to go so far as private, cordial but retiring.

Elvin sucked spit through a tooth gap and nodded. Elvin assured me, "Him."

2 —◦→ As it turned out, I could recall the commotion, had met anyway that rescue-squad boy who raced in his Ford Bronco to most of our local calamities. He had a scarlet beacon on his dash and flashers for his headlights, a siren behind his grille that he could cause to yodel and yip and thereby visit palpitations on the motorists about.

When I'd come upon him, he was spooking an octogenarian into a ditch, had slipped up behind the woman's sedan and ushered her sideways with a squeal. She'd dropped onto the shoulder and had veered down through the rye where she'd snagged on a culvert and come to a lurching indelicate four-point stop. That boy had whipped around her and gone flying past me crowding the centerline, so I'd taken more notice of him than I ordinarily might have since he was as common along our byways as flattened tree squirrels and pavement grit.

Kenny, his name was, and he sort of worked at a local muffler shop, a shabby unfranchised enterprise on the rise behind the Sinclair where they never stocked your muffler exactly but carried one they could make fit. They knew inordinate need for mallets and main force, bent tailpipes with their knees and, as a sideline, replaced windshields for anyone fool enough to let them.

Mostly they sat around unoccupied but for raw unsavory talk of voluptuous TV-starlet anatomy which was hardly so consuming as to forestall Kenny from listening to his scanner. He was privy, then, to news of the bulk of local mayhem as soon as it got called in, and Kenny had an understanding with the Worrell who employed him that he could leave off doing nothing much at that junky muffler shop, race in his Bronco to the site of our latest local mishap and take up doing very little there.

Kenny, you see, was not an official rescue-squad employee but was instead a sort of mascot and hanger-on. He had no training to speak of in first aid or firefighting techniques, had been an unsuccessful candidate for a job with the county police, had proven inept as a wrecker driver for a salvage yard up the gap and so had little but ghoulishness to recommend him. We most of us share in a taste for misfortune as long as it's visited on somebody else, and Kenny was no different, just more vigilant and mobile, a have-rubberneck-will-travel sort of guy.

It turned out Kenny was the first on the scene of Stoney's misadventure. The way Elvin told it, the county police and the rescue-squad boys were otherwise engaged, had raced together to the assistance of a gentleman north of town who had managed to set his draperies alight. Now, of course, that ordinarily would have been a fireman's job but for the circumstances of that man's conflagration. It seems he'd attempted to repair a frayed lamp cord with shrinkable tubing and a propane torch without troubling himself to unplug the thing from the wall.

In Elvin's version, that fellow's wife was plaguing him as he worked, was nattering on about how she would have carried that lamp outside and even then might have used just plastic tape to mend what looked to her hardly more than a harmless scuff on the cord anyway. So she was obliged to endure, quite naturally, a spot of sneering from her husband who turned to gaze on her in such a way as to have her understand that he thought poorly of her electrical expertise. Unfortunately, he failed as he sneered to be duly mindful of his propane flame. It seems he allowed it to dip and wander and set the draperies ablaze.

That gentleman's wife fetched a broom from the kitchen while he called the fire department, and she had successfully swatted the flames out long before the truck had arrived. In fact, she'd chased her husband into the yard and was flailing at him instead, had cornered him down by a stand of crepe myrtles on the border of their lot and was barking him raw with the prickly ends of her broomstraw.

He must have been a pitiful sight crouched there with his arms up over his head and his wife fairly whaling at him with not just a light-duty grocery-mart broom but one of those stout handfashioned items that the Lions Club sold door-to-door. A couple of firehouse boys made a halfhearted bid to come to that gentleman's aid, but his wife turned on them and caused them to know she could chafe them bloody too, so they radioed in for lawenforcement and rescue-squad assistance, recommended they bring out a lasso and maybe a quart and a half of salve.

Most everybody, then, was occupied when Stoney had his wreck but for Kenny who menaced his way across the county in his Bronco and arrived on the scene before anyone else had happened yet upon it. He rolled up on a mangled coupe and a battered Chevy pickup back along an oiled and graveled road in a sunless crease of terrain that was far too steep and gloomy to pass for a valley or a glen but was more in the way of a viny and mildewed crevasse.

That truck and that car had collided in front of a manufactured home, one of those putty-colored houses with plastic siding and a galvanized chimney pipe, with pressure-treated lattice skirting to hide the block foundation piers. The yard was heavily planted with petunias, hydrangeas and daylilies, was fairly choked with sundry ornamental crap—an iridescent gazing globe, a pair of cement geese, whirligigs along the road ditch painted up to look like seagulls, a plastic donkey the size of an Airedale hitched to a little plastic wagon that was asprout with toadstools and prickly broadleaf weeds.

There was a stickwood glider in the yard with a moldy awning to shade it, a birdhouse atop a pole built to resemble Monticello, an elf down by the mailbox and a woodsprite at the wellhead, a fractured speckled horned toad pitched against a painted stump. That front lawn boasted three plywood cutouts of grandmotherly derrieres, a couple of sizable hunks of dangling suet and a trio of folding chairs, each with its webbing entirely rotted through.

It's little wonder, then, that Kenny couldn't locate straightaway the woman he heard crying out for help. "Hey," she said to him. "Come here," and Kenny chose to think her injured, ejected probably from that smashed coupe and shot onto the lawn with seepy tissue exposed and jagged fractures breaching.

Due to an ardent seat-belt crusade on the part of the local police, Kenny had lately been starved for acute life-threatening carnage. He'd seen nothing worse than a scalp laceration for going on six weeks. Consequently, Kenny vaulted across the ditch, raced up between two seagulls and legged it over to where he'd reasoned a pulpy motorist might be, but he found for his trouble just a patch of purslane and a weathered cement gosling.

"Hey!"

He turned to the sound of that woman's voice and spied her across the yard. She was kneeling beside a birdbath, the post of the thing anyway. The bowl had upended and pitched to the ground, and she was feverishly working to raise it. As that basin, however, was concrete and she was decidedly geriatric, that woman couldn't seem to gain purchase enough on the rim to shift it at all.

"Come here," she snapped at Kenny who worked revisions

along the way. He wondered if maybe that woman had been flung clear of that smashed coupe with a grandbaby she'd had charge of who'd ended up beneath that basin, the sort of creature it'd be a benefit for Kenny to help save since he knew for a fact there were females about who might do for a grandbaby saver what they'd never undertake for a boy with just a beacon in his Ford.

So Kenny knelt and Kenny lifted and Kenny freed into the light what proved to be some manner of speckled bunting. With that woman, he watched it twitch and skitter and rise upon the breeze, soar up out of that musty hollow into vineless arid sunshine, but Kenny failed to sigh like she did, and he offered up instead a spot of talk with no moist wonder clinging to it.

"It's a goddamn bird," he told her, and she was prompted to share with Kenny news of how that collision had tipped her basin somehow.

"Jolted it loose," she said. "I saw it from the porch."

"So that's not your car?"

She nodded, though, and assured him that it was, indicated a Ford Econoline van parked over in her side yard and informed Kenny, "He was moving it out of the way."

That was just the sort of talk to touch off Kenny who'd been dawdling there freeing a bird when, in his capacity as an uncertified and ghoulish hanger-on, he should have been over by that crumpled coupe gawking at the driver who, to judge by the devastation, was very probably inside out. So Kenny leaped to his feet and charged towards the road, hurdling intervening ornamental lawn crap, and he peered into that car fully braced for the sight of some fellow rudely sectioned into parts.

What he found instead was oil and coolant pooled up on the floorboard, a chunk of the steering column in the far rear window well, fuzzy bits of liberated upholstery stuffing in the air, chunks of blue-green auto glass on any surface that would hold them, an eight-inch length of timing chain tangled in the torn headliner and the rearview mirror and a couple of radio knobs on the passenger seat. He saw nothing that suggested actual human leavings to him but for what looked a dollop of frothy spittle on the ruptured dash.

Now Stoney, according to Elvin, had been standing all the while on the far weedy shoulder of that gravel road. Kenny had taken him for a civilian who had merely happened by to see what all the crumpled sheet steel was about, so he waved his arms at Stoney and instructed him, "Step on back."

Kenny, after all, had an orange mesh-weave vest in his Bronco console, a brushed-aluminum flashlight with four D-cell batteries in it, insulated steel-toed rubber boots, a canary-yellow hard hat and sufficient acquaintance with three actual deputies to call them by first names. So Kenny fancied himself exalted enough to direct the likes of Stoney just where precisely he'd like him to go stand, and since Stoney was stunned and shaken still, he retreated well into the ditch while Kenny stepped over to check on the pickup driver.

Even I knew it had to be Orville, hardly needed Elvin to tell me, as it was a source of general wonder about that the man was licensed to drive. Orville's eyesight was weak. His hearing was poor, and he was readily prone to distraction which would have been hazard enough on the roadways without the addition of Orville's tape deck. He'd bought that unit at a yard sale and had installed the thing himself, or rather had run wires to the floorboard and had set his deck on the drive-shaft hump where it bounced around as he traveled and routinely shook its connections loose.

You knew you were in peril when you met Orville's Chevy pickup on the roadway and the cab appeared vacant because Orville had leaned down to jiggle a tape-deck wire. Orville was old and creaky and had a nephew at the DMV who let him gaze into the light box and call everything a stop sign, so even once Orville had heaved back upright and trained his eyes upon the road, he was usually a crucial instant deciding which way he might best veer and if that thing up ahead was your vehicle or a milk cow or a bush.

Fortunately, Orville was deaf enough to need his music at full volume, and even I had come by word that a driver would do well at most junctions to pause and listen out for Little Jimmy Dickens on the air. Orville, you see, owned but one cassette, a Little Jimmy compilation, so it was evermore "Bird of Paradise," "Take an Old Cold Tater and Wait" or some similar snatch of nasally backwoods cautionary warbling.

The pickup he drove was held together with scraps of tin patching and rivets, and Orville had had so many dents and dings pulled and pounded from the thing that his truck was comprehensively creased and wrinkled and bled rust from nearly every pucker and seam. That Chevy was awfully ponderous, though, and quite apparently indestructible, since no matter who Orville hit and how, he always drove from the scene.

Orville had even collided with Kenny once, had rammed his Bronco anyway there in the lot of the muffler shop behind the Sinclair. The way Elvin heard it, Orville had thrown a tailpipe and come around for a replacement, had wheeled up meaning to sweep on into the muffler-shop garage bay, but his deck had quit as Orville was beginning his maneuver which had left Kenny entirely equipped to welcome the sight of Orville mangled.

According to Elvin, Orville's pickup was unserenaded as Kenny approached it. The engine was idling. The radiator was spewing fluid through a crack, and there wasn't any trace of Orville above the dash there in the cab which must have served to quicken Kenny's hopes for ghastly human carnage. He'd rolled up after all on a virgin wreck, the first man on the scene, and he'd met so far with just a speckled bunting. So Kenny was spoiling for the sight of rended flesh and giblety effluvia, but soon enough he got instead the sound of Little Jimmy Dickens.

"'I'm in Love Up to My Ears,'" Elvin told me. Then he described how Orville had laid his knobby hand upon the wheel to hoist himself full upright into view. As was his custom, Orville gunned his engine and proceeded to back up. He eased around that spot of crumpled bother in the roadway, parked on the far shoulder, flung open his door and climbed out of the cab.

"Come out of nowhere," Orville shouted, declaring it generally into the air.

By now, of course, Kenny was irate, and he screamed at Orville, "Who!?" which won him a jerk of Orville's head towards Stoney in the deep weeds. Stoney who nodded. Stoney who raised his hand.

Stoney hadn't, as it turned out, gotten ejected the way most motorists tend to. He'd failed to pass through the windshield or shatter his skeletal structure on a door stanchion.

"Popped out," Elvin told me, and he troubled himself to mount his trundle bed, leaped daintily off it and lit with a thump on the rough-hewn office planking which I watched him at in the company of a bull calf in the door. "Lost a little spit. Landed right there on his feet. Didn't break so much as wind."

Even Orville had scraped a knuckle and bumped his forehead on the wheel, but Stoney had come out just like he'd gone in.

"Lucky," I said, and Elvin moved accumulated phlegm. He swung his head from side to side as he apprised me of his view that there was only so much luck to go around.

Elvin had come to believe that Stoney had long since used up his good fortune and was dipping into everybody else's to get by which proved outrage enough to make a man stalk, so Elvin embarked on a circuit, ranted his way through a couple of orbits before he paused at the window sash.

Elvin grappled with the thing to no effect and laid his cheek upon the sill to acquaint Erlene with the news that there were bastards in the landscape content to poach a fellow's good luck and employ it as their own.

Then together me and Elvin watched a salvo of feed corn sail our way across the cow lot and rebound sharply off the panes.

3 —◦→ Early on I'd had a pet to serve me as a consuming distraction, so I'd paid but marginal notice to Stoney off across the way and had met no cause to come to think of him as blessed and charmed. He was just the guy with the van and the cats and the ditch full of pitted prunes, the naphtha bouquet and, to judge by his habits, a bladder the size of a nuthatch.

I'd had a dog back then, a mongrel pug I believed I had adopted, though it turned out I'd abducted him instead. I had visited Manhattan on a winter package—airfare, a midtown hotel, complimentary continental breakfast (a hard roll and the *Daily News*)—and I'd passed the bulk of my weekend walking the city in a wind off the river that was steady and brisk, the way I recall it, and ever so achingly cold.

I came across that dog in the forties just outside of a Dodge dealership on Eleventh Avenue. I'd been wandering back in the icy shade of sooty West Side warehouses and emerged into tranquil sunshine at the cross-street traffic light where a derelict corner building did duty for me as a wind block, so I'd lingered to warm myself and unconstrict.

Like with most far West Side midtown streets, there was no foot traffic much. A jolly lunatic up the block was singing loudly in his shirtsleeves. He'd married a jingle for a fever-blister ointment to a hymn about the glorious wonder of the virgin birth. A woman across the avenue offered to service me for fifteen dollars, drew open her fun-fur coat to reveal a lilac bodice underneath which prompted me to study a pair of paper boxes by the lamppost—one for real-estate circulars, one for continuing-education brochures—and I feigned interest in the details of a Yorkville fixer-upper while enduring speculation as to how I might be hung.

I only saw him just as I was contemplating full retreat, spied that dog on the walk in the lee of the lamppost in a band of sunlight, right between those paper boxes and the curb. He was no bigger than a rabbit and sat with his stubby back legs askew to permit his belly to rest on the cement. He was not by any conceivable canine standard the least bit becoming, was collarless and filthy and punishingly fragrant, had the strident savor of a herd of goats. Once he'd turned his runny eyes upon me, I took him for forlorn, thought him destitute and cast out in this world.

I kneeled to offer my hand for a sniff, and he gave it a thorough adenoidal once-over without bothering to shift off his haunches and rise entirely to his feet which should have brought to my notice the fact that he was tubby for a stray, hardly looked to have gone without a square meal lately. I offered him a breath mint—the only foodstuff I had on me—and he eyed me the way a man who offers a dog a mint deserves which I elected to take for a sign of uncommon intelligence on his part, and I decided on the spot he was just the sort of creature whose company I could probably abide.

By any measure, my personal pet-owning history was already rather deplorable. As a child, I'd had a beagle who'd disappeared in the Kitty Hawk surf, had charged out into the breakers after a stick I'd thrown there for him where the undertow had sucked him clean away. We'd replaced him with a chow that I'd backed over in our drive. I was twelve at the time and had no business behind the wheel of our Newport which most parents would have offered up as arid philosophy, but I'd provided mine a lifeless carcass for a visual aid.

I'd once given our Siamese cat a bath in the toilet bowl which had served to leave her lemony fresh and consumptive, and I'd killed off countless hamsters and gerbils by way of shiftless neglect.

Even recently, I'd continued the trend with a mutt from a shelter in Roanoke. I was living at the time in the suburbs and working days at the professional park, and that dog had sensed that I was not good management material. He failed to come home one night after I'd owned him a couple of weeks, proved to have moved in with my neighbors, had slipped inside through their cat door, and I didn't mount much of an effort to take him back. I liked to think I knew a canine bid for asylum when I saw one.

This creature, however, in the band of sunlight hard beside the lamppost was a different case, I told myself, and seemed to need salvation. I chose to believe that the cruelties of the city had ground him down and there was destiny at play in the fact I'd run across him. I fully embraced the notion I'd been dispatched on a progress, had gotten routed down chill and desolate cross streets and out into the sun to have put in my way a thing that I could save.

He proved passably cooperative, didn't bite me anyway as I drew him by his forelegs out where I could gain some purchase. I saw fit to lift him without proper leverage from my legs which was when I discovered that he was awfully dense for a wayward urchin and pretty alarmingly aromatic up close. He smelled like a blend of hot asphalt and spoiled macaroni salad, and he was greasy enough to lubricate me everywhere he touched, slickened up my hands and forearms and stained my topcoat to the lining.

I cooed and burbled in a bid to put him at his ease, but it turned out he was not the sort inclined to agitation, was incapable, really, of elevated spirits of any kind and was given instead to bouts of wheezy ennui. He dozed off there in my arms before I'd covered half a block even though I was panting and lurching and having to shift my grip upon him due to how he traveled like a sack of sand. He only roused himself awake once I'd crossed Seventh Avenue since, apparently, he'd not visited midtown proper for a while and was pleased to meet occasion to soak in a change of scene.

Now my hotel was a sort of Quality Inn with urban airs and pretensions. The lobby was hung with chandeliers and appointed with clubby paneling. There was a liveried doorman and uniformed bellhops, clerks with brass name tags and a concierge at a seemly mahogany station between two Chinese palms who saw to the wishes and needs of the guests all throughout the day.

A redhead was on duty when I brought in that dog who I'd taken already to calling Lincoln after the nearby tunnel. Quite naturally, he set about perfuming the lobby straightaway, and the concierge shot up from his chair and raced headlong through his foliage so as to step up and acquaint me with hotel policy on pets. He wore a jangly gold bracelet and sported a skimpy manner of goatee, a little rusty wisp of hair beneath his lip and in his chin cleft, and he wagged his finger at me as an undue irritant, so I stiffened and planted and gave that fellow cause to understand that I was hard set to shampoo Lincoln in my sink.

He waved over three bellmen who saw me roughly into the street. A chambermaid packed my suitcase and brought the thing down to me, was kind enough to direct me to a car-rental agency in Portuguese, I believe.

The rental agent only had a subcompact she'd let me take one way, a puny contoured two-door built in, I think, Malaysia. It had no options and no features, tires the size of dinner plates, an ungodly citrus scent that Lincoln shortly swamped and thwarted and an engine a thief with a crescent wrench could have spirited off in his arms. Turbulence from passing traffic shoved us off onto the shoulder, and I got all but stopped in Allentown by the onset of headwinds.

Lincoln traveled well. That's what I told myself anyway when he failed to spew nuggets or gnaw the floormats, neglected to void on his seat. For a considerable while he just sat and looked at me, wheezed and wafted and gazed intently at the side of my head until I'd allowed him an airing at a rest stop north of Harrisburg where he made extravagant water while I explained to a state patrolman how I'd come by cause to walk my dog on a nappy bathrobe belt.

Now if I'd not been flush with righteousness and self-congratulation, I probably would have noticed early on that Lincoln was unhappy, that country life at my rental house adjoining the national forest didn't impress him as an improvement on Eleventh Avenue. I went blindly ahead, though, and tried to make him out to be my pet. I bought him toys, a fleecy bed, a few greasy pig ears to chew while I waited for him to warm to me and become a little cordial, meet me evenings at the door to have a romp out in the yard. He remained, however, listless and decidedly lethargic, sat nights with his ample belly resting on the front-porch planking and proved content to watch me toss his squeaky ball out on the lawn.

Lincoln reliably evacuated in the kitchen twice a day, urinated so on the metal works of the glider on the porch that the rivets scaled with rust and the whole contraption seized up fast. I could hardly for the life of me get him out into the fescue. He far preferred man-made surfaces—the porch, the steps, the walk, the drive. I never found a packaged dog food he would eat with any relish, kibble with lure enough to keep him from plundering through the trash at night.

I happened to have a local veterinarian for a client. Not the good one trained at the state university, the young man with manners and grace, with the spotless clinic, the coed interns, the laundered dungarees. I got instead a courtesy discount from Victor by the landfill who'd received somehow his schooling quite entirely through the mail. Victor operated out of a glorified car shed at the back of his lot with his wife for his receptionist and assistant. She mostly sat in a ratty upholstered chair at a table by the door smoking Kools and watching daytime television.

Victor tended to see those animals that had passed beyond the healing reach of conventional veterinary medicine. He was like those herbalists people go to once the chemicals have failed them, and he'd known just enough flabbergasting success to guarantee a clientele. I'd heard talk that Victor had once cured a failing Hot Springs Pekingese of what was routinely a mortal liver complaint with an elixir made from cider vinegar, lacquer thinner and rye, and around Easter, when resurrection was quite naturally in the air, there was widespread local mention of the goat Victor had saved.

Apparently that goat had lapped up a good half gallon of antifreeze and was well on its way to being killed and poisoned when Victor showed up to scour clean its organs with a hose. I'd heard he introduced the nozzle into that goat's nether gland and left the spigot open until water had shot out if its nostrils which had struck me at the time as anatomically unlikely. I had to think there were ducts and byways, valves and vessels and canals that a stream of water couldn't back up through.

I'd been assured, however, that Victor had sluiced away those coolant toxins by three different local men who'd shown me each a different goat.

So Victor's practice was devoted to hopeless cases and economizers like me, and I sat in the car-shed waiting room with Lincoln on my lap while Victor treated a ferret in his consultation cubicle, dosed it for galloping vermin anemia with what smelled

like a marriage of blackstrap molasses and fingernail-polish re-
mover. Victor presently emerged in the company of the woman
who'd brought that ferret to him, and the thing was artlessly swaddled along its trunk in sticky reeking gauze. Victor nodded my way
and got arrested by the sight of Lincoln who was sitting on my lap
with his belly resting on my upper thigh.

"Goddamn, Paul," Victor told me. "I didn't know you had
a . . ." And here Victor subjected Lincoln to a spot of contemplation, looked to me like he was running through his options in his
head. It was a quarter minute later and with palpable misgivings
that Victor finally elected to tell me, ". . . dog." Then the woman
with the reeking swaddled ferret charged me to inform her how in
the name of Christ I'd tempted a muskrat and a groundhog to
mate.

I'd come hoping for a poultice or some manner of elixir, any
sort of treatment, really, I might visit on my dog to make him
more agreeable and loving. I'd half convinced myself that he was
down with some affliction, a parasite or blood disorder that had
muted his zeal for life, and I was prepared to believe a cure would
serve to win me his affection. As it turned out, he did have whipworms and a colony of ear mites along with a violent native objection to anal thermometers, but his disposition failed to improve
even once he'd gotten dosed.

He stayed sullen and listless no matter how I tried to perk him
up. I bought him endless treats and toys and worked most evenings to amuse him, would prattle gaily at him and toss his ball out
in the yard, but he'd just watch me from the porch with his paunch
resting on the planking unless, of course, he'd elected to swab his
ruby member instead.

I only saw him truly excited once. A buck had strayed into the
yard, and the sight of him set Lincoln aquiver, brought him entirely to his feet. He warbled a little and looked from that deer at
the edge of the lawn to me in a way I found articulate and inquir-

ing. Lincoln seemed desperate to come by word of what manner of beast it might be. Then he scampered, I'll call it, directly to the door and flung himself against the stile until I'd opened the thing to let him into the house.

From then on, whenever he'd step outside he'd walk to the lip of the porch and gaze out over the landscape after a fashion I found expressive. Most dogs would have sniffed the crisp mountain air and surveyed the terrain with something, I'd think, in the way of a raw and predatory thrill, but Lincoln subjected the far horizon to a baleful brand of perusal and would evermore vent a manner of snort touched plainly with despair.

If he could have talked, I'm sure most days he would have asked me the same question: "Where in the name of sweet creeping Jesus are we?"

It took me almost three months to figure him out, but I finally pegged Lincoln for an unregenerate urbanite. His preference was for gutter grit, cornerstones and drainage grates, a general dusting of boiler soot and rats by way of fauna. He'd developed a gastronomic ardor for putrid trash-barrel cuisine, a fondness for the prevailing westerly breezes off the Hudson that bore with them rank Meadowlands swampiness and sulfurous refinery stink. He welcomed the bracing features of year-round al fresco living, the exposure and the foraging, the filth and the neglect. Unimproved cement for bedding. Instead of moonglow, vapor light.

That anyway is what I saw clear to make myself believe. I came home one evening to find an appalling stool sample on the linoleum. Lincoln had moistened it with urine in order, I guess, to keep it fresh, and I was swabbing it up with some paper towels he'd dumped out of the trash when it occurred to me I'd probably done that creature a disservice, had selfishly torn him away from the simple existence he'd likely grown to love.

He was being just then disconsolate upside down on the settee, and I like to tell myself anymore I offered to take him home, but the truth is I grabbed up a fistful of scruff and showed Lincoln those paper towels, provided that he was gazing through his nostrils at the time. Then I hauled him directly out to my Cavalier sedan in the drive and rode him in the trunk about as far as Hagerstown where I stopped for gas and felt contrite enough to hoist him out.

We didn't hit Manhattan proper until a little after midnight, and once I'd pulled to the curb at Lincoln's corner on Eleventh Avenue, I reached across to open his door. I nudged him firmly off his seat.

At an all-night Pennsylvania diner, a man at the counter beside me ate a leathery minute steak while acquainting the waitress with bunion cures. At a service station in West Virginia along towards 5 A.M., a woman down the island gassing her Pinto saw fit to detail for me instances of heartache she'd endured at the hands of her ingrate son.

In the dawning at home, I came upon Lincoln's ball out in the drive, plucked it up and took it across the dewy side yard to the fencerow where I threw it over the neck of the meadow and deep into the woods.

4 —•❧ So Stoney was hardly more to me than a fellow across the way who served some evenings as part of the panorama. Of course, once Elvin had told me how he'd cheated death in a mangled coupe, I did pay for a time more heed to Stoney than normally I might have, even probed him a little one afternoon while I was out checking my mail.

Stoney had set up a rig in his yard and was turning threads on a pipe. He was lubricating the cutting blade by drooling onto the works as I called out to inquire how he was faring. Stoney wiped his mouth on his coverall sleeve and glanced up and down the roadway before seeing clear to let me know, "All right."

Then Stoney wondered if I'd heard about that woman from Nevada who'd gotten lost for two full weeks in a cavern there. She'd survived, it seems, exclusively on a diet of foraged bat guano and had developed as a consequence a capacity for radar, could drive anyway in her Reno neighborhood with both of her eyes clapped shut.

As commentary goes, that seemed to me sufficiently vehicular to supply me leave to touch on Stoney's wreck. I had to wait, though, until Stoney had fairly exhausted a line of speculation devoted to the sorts of feces he might eat.

"I hear Orville got you." I just blurted it out while Stoney was inhaling.

"I don't believe," Stoney told me, "I could choke down much of anything out of a cat."

"I hear Orville got you good."

"Yeah," Stoney allowed. "He was jiggling wires. I never heard him coming."

"They tell me you ought to be dead."

Stoney shrugged. Stoney nodded. "Went out the window somehow. Insurance is fighting me on it. I might want to be dead in the end."

At that moment, I didn't see before me a man disposed to feel lucky. Stoney laid back his head and peered forlornly up into a sugar maple. He sighed. He winced. He muttered. "Little Jimmy Dickens," he said.

Naturally, it occurred to me that Elvin might have been wrong about Stoney, had maybe sized him up through the lens of his own frustrations since if Stoney, in fact, was charmed, he truly didn't seem to know it.

I swung shut my mailbox door and told Stoney merely, "Well," which I had come to know as the back-hollow version of *arrivederci*, and I turned and headed towards my house, leaving Stoney as I'd found him—drooling, that is, lubricationally on the blade of his pipe rig.

For a couple of months thereafter, he hardly troubled my thoughts at all. I'd see Stoney around on the roadways or wandering evenings in his yard, and I never met temptation to construe him fortune's favorite, decided Elvin had been guilty of misbegotten peevishness. Then, however, by chance I happened to hear of

Stoney at some length from those sisters who ran the remnant shop where the rolling mill used to be.

One of them was widowed, and the other had suffered grave disappointment in love. I'd been told the spinster sister—who everybody called Miss Addie—had been betrothed in her youth to a fellow from up the valley who, in courting Miss Addie, had grown keen on her sister and had married her instead. Now that's just the sort of circumstance to make for undue friction in a family, but apparently Miss Addie and Cora, her name was, had ironed their troubles out. Miss Addie, anyway, had largely suppressed her rancor through the years and was given in her spinsterhood to but odd fits of sniping, most particularly when Cora gloried in the memory of her husband with moisture enough to render herself a galling provocation.

That gentleman had not, apparently, turned out to be much of a catch. The way I heard it, he was prone to a species of bourbon-heightened shiftlessness and was evermore selling off trinkets and heirlooms to come by pocket money.

It seems he'd pawned off Cora's mother's silver a serving piece at a time and had traded her cut-glass turkey platter for a Remington revolver which, in high spirits one afternoon, he'd beaten a cousin senseless with. He'd once settled a wager with a matching set of mahogany hassocks that Miss Addie and Cora's great aunt had done the close work on herself, had unloaded item by item the lawn equipment in the garage and had even swapped out once the culvert at the end of the home-place driveway for a chunk of cured ham and a fifth of Colonel's Pride.

Furthermore, he was famously quarrelsome even in his sober moments and had hardly ever had a kind word for Cora at home or out in the world. So Miss Addie knew ample cause to resort to prickly skepticism whenever Cora grew misty on her late husband's behalf. Once a year at Easter, Cora carried lilies to the graveyard which served to ensure a bilious sisterly rupture every spring.

Ordinarily, though, the two of them managed to get along after a fashion and made for lively company when I'd swing by to reconcile their books. Their shop was one of the few around that turned a thriving profit almost in spite of the way the two of them operated the place. They'd never really given the building a proper scouring and fumigation after they'd leased it from the family that had owned the rolling mill, so there were husks about and moldy grain and no practical end of mice which teemed in the walls and nested occasionally in the bolts of fabric. It wasn't uncommon for browsing customers to root out cause to shriek.

But the squalor and the vermin were offset by the deep-discounted prices, so that store was generally crawling with local seamstresses as well. The patrons, by my best measure, fell into two distinct categories. The larger was given over to the Simplicity-pattern set, those ladies who stitched for themselves the manner of frocks that proper women wear when their bridge club meets or their organs fail and they're due to get interred.

The other sort was afflicted with wholly unfettered improvisational flair, women who shared among them an avid taste for appliqué and no personal editorial sense when it came to lace and piping. They were reliably partial to fabrics of a pattern and a style best suited to bordello draperies or bridesmaids' gowns. Consequently, they rarely competed for merchandise with the Simplicity ladies, but that did little to dampen the traffic in searing mutual disapproval.

Probably, but for the mice, that store would have seen a criminal assault or two since the air in that place was frequently thick with corrosive antipathy. Some customer in a crinoline frock that looked to belong in a mausoleum would run up on a patron in rhinestone-encrusted jeans and the hint of a rodeo clown in her family woodpile, and they'd exchange the sort of sneers that might well have escalated but for the punctuation of a vermin-induced shriek.

So the rodents made for defusing distractions, and Miss Addie was the one who killed them. She could hold up her end of a conversation or conjure a price by the yard while drumming the life from a mouse with the fireplace shovel she kept for that purpose after which she'd pluck the carcass up and fling it out the door.

The day we spoke at length about Stoney, I'd seen a woman in the store, a creature unfamiliar to me fingering percale across the way. Both statuesque and comely, she was decidedly out of keeping with the degraded local standards for allure. Rangy women in those parts were given to looking underfed, were commonly sinewy and stark with the species of flinty features that the Holy Father might have fashioned with a honed camp ax.

That woman, however, testing the feel and finish of percale was tall and yet voluptuous after a fashion, had curves anyway instead of angles and counted among her prominences bits of anatomy other than her collarbones and nose. Moreover, once she'd shifted around to permit me a full look at her, I saw she was authentically pretty instead of "handsome," they liked to call it, which seemed to mean symmetrical and bordering on pleasing and was never locally applied to men.

Cows could be handsome, furnishings, the occasional half-ton truck and sturdy females with nearly all of their teeth and the merest hint of a waistline.

That woman, however, was attractive in a conventional sort of way though she was hardly dressed to draw attention to it. She had on dungarees and boots that looked to have honestly seen a paddock, a sweater frayed and oversized and given up on by some man, a little lip gloss by way of cosmetic adornment and a clip to stay her hair that she'd piled on her head in a fashion that, since it was careless, proved beguiling.

Now at the time, I was widely known to be involved with a lady from town, or rather she was involved, and I was more ensnared and tangled up, but nonetheless I hardly felt that I could just come out directly and ask Cora and Miss Addie who the woman across the store might be. I had reason to know that word of my interest was sure to travel and range and would, doubtless, reach my lady friend at last.

So I elected instead to indicate that creature across the store and wonder aloud if maybe she wasn't that legendary wayward Ogden fetched up after all this time to shop for percale. Everybody knew the Ogdens had suffered a daughter to run away. By all accounts, she'd fallen for a Pentecostal Republican functionary in spite of the fact that she came from a clan of hardened Roosevelt Democrats.

As I understood it, her parents had tried to accommodate her at first, had opened their home and attempted to soften their hearts to their daughter's boyfriend, but after he'd eaten their pretzels and cheese puffs, two helpings of Stroganoff and a heaping bowlful of Mrs. Ogden's nectarine cobbler, he'd troubled himself to lambaste the New Deal and the Great Society both prior to laying waste to the Ogdens' representative in Congress who they had actively canvassed for and helped elect.

Understandably, Mr. Ogden had felt sufficiently provoked to volunteer a snide assessment of supply-side economics, and he and his daughter's Pentecostal Republican functionary boyfriend had gotten into a lively colloquy about the Reagan years which, thanks to the neighbors one door up, had involved a deputy at length.

The Ogden daughter's response to the turn of the evening was icy mortification, and she surrendered herself to that functionary out of embarrassment and spite. That, anyway, was the prevalent regional interpretation, and that girl shortly saw fit to lacerate her mom and dad outright by helping her fiancé, he was by then, elect in South Carolina a Holy Rolling primate to the Senate.

The way I heard it, that daughter was effectively dead to those Ogdens after that. They chose to consider her brainwashed and abducted and mourned her with nearly the pitch of grief they'd lavished on Hubert Humphrey.

I'd personally seen enough Ogdens to know they were rarely statuesque, were squat as a rule and oftentimes ungainly, so snorting dismay from Miss Addie and Cora was just what I'd expected, and they assured me together the percale woman was a Hooper from out the pike.

It was Cora, I believe, who clucked and who contributed, "Poor thing."

"What?"

"Stoney threw her over," Miss Addie informed me. "I don't know that she'll ever get past it."

"My Stoney?"

Cora and Miss Addie both nodded while that Hooper across the way uncovered a mouse and dispatched it with a casual backhand flick which made do, for me at least, as an additional allurement.

Then she caught us looking at her, turned to ask after a price, was fingering anyway a fold of percale in an inquiring fashion when she spied us in unvarnished study of her which made alarming inroads into that woman's composure. She seemed to sense that we had lately been dissecting her, appeared doomed to believe it was all people did when they saw her anymore.

She looked at first like she wanted to say a thing but only vented a moan instead. Then she released her percale to fall and charged directly out of the store.

Even based on first impressions, I could hardly help but find that Hooper of an appreciably higher caliber than Stoney, more woman than his small-bore charms had any right to lure. She was lovely and stylish in her way, was willowy and enticing, while Stoney could boast just indifferent hygiene and an overabundance of cats. I must have been looking a little lost for a romantic rationale since Cora and Miss Addie threw in to volunteer an explanation.

"It was four or five years ago," Cora informed me and then yielded to her sister who patted my knee and added, "He had a lovely head of hair."

My own hair had never been lovely exactly, but it was once thoroughgoing. I could part it and comb it, cream-rinse it, blow-dry it, have it styled every couple of weeks as opposed to the sort of trim I got from Peggy at the time which was brief and trifling, pitifully custodial.

"Blond," Cora told me, and Miss Addie, by dumb show, described a crop of locks any woman with fingers would have been eager to touch.

"My Stoney?"

I pictured the man in his camouflaged Browning cap, had met with occasion to see him lift it to blot at sweat or scratch. He had scant sprigs of dingy tow-rope-colored hair, freckled patches of scalp and a hatband line impressed across his forehead.

Cora and Miss Addie both threw in together to tell me decisively, "Him."

5

—⋙ I'd suspected from the beginning that she wasn't remotely my type, but I'm powerless against those women afflicted with an appetite for me, run across one every other decade or so. She'd gotten my number from her postman who I'd helped with his return, and I'd met with her one evening to sort through her allowable expenses.

She was just at that time in the last convulsive throes of a divorce which had been, as those things go, particularly sulfurous and nasty and, by all rights, should have put her off of men. Once, however, I'd laid out for her a tactic to employ to shift state liability to her future former husband, she'd closed on me and, in a show of ardent gratitude, had shoved her tongue into my ear canal.

I'd recognized that she was in a fragile emotional state, suspected her divorce had likely shaken her confidence as a woman and had left her unsure of her standing as an object of desire. So I doubted her a victim of my personal magnetism and assumed she was only lashing out at her husband as best she might which meant my job, both as a man and as a professional tax preparer, was to offer by way of response mere flattered restraint.

My aim was to hold out the promise of a dalliance between us but only after her matrimonial acrimony had fully ebbed, and I had even manufactured a rather graceful recitation couched to make me seem intent upon what was most fair for her. I was polishing it and punching it up, rehearsing it in my head, while I swabbed the woman's tonsils down and shucked her from her blouse.

Once we were grappling on her throw rug in our underthings, I attempted to convey a sense of my misgivings to her. I eyed her anyway in a fashion intended to tempt her to know that I was hardly in the habit of trading vital fluids with my clients which, if blessed with a gift for clairvoyance, she might well have taken in.

We'd graduated to frank indecorousness by the time her daughter joined us. She'd gotten roused, I guess, by the sound of grown-ups frolicking on the floor. We were formally introduced. She was three years old and went at the time by the name of Dinky. She wore a flannel nightshirt and carried a grubby plush toy the color of slate. The thing was mangy and misshapen, separating at the seams, had probably started out a walrus but had come to look a slug with teeth.

The girl stuck a nappy fluke in her mouth and subjected me to clinical perusal.

I usually know quite enough trouble, even when fully and decently dressed, dredging up some scrap of agreeable talk to visit on a child, so I was comprehensively speechless in my undershorts on the floor.

At length, she asked, "What's that?" and pointed to a scar below my knee which supplied me occasion to talk about the barbed wire I'd run into, to speak of the stitches and the antibiotics I'd required. We examined together a grainy birthmark on my upper thigh and were distinguishing on my boxer shorts the schooners from the sloops when that girl's mother finally snatched her up and carried her back to bed.

So I met with the opportunity to undo what I had done, should have pulled on my trousers and buttoned my shirt, perched primly on the sofa from where I could best have favored Dinky's mother, upon her return up the hall, with a performance of my graceful recitation. But I just sat where I was and gazed around to soak in the decor which itself would ordinarily have set me scrambling for my pants.

The woman had amassed a telling assortment of cat-related items, figurines mostly that cluttered the tabletops everywhere I looked. She had a clock with a cat-tail pendulum, cat tapers on the dinette, a tabby fashioned in stained glass that dangled from a window casing and an actual feline skulking about in the bowels of the house. I'd yet to see it but had dislodged stray nuggets of litter from my rump.

The place was awash in the cloying aroma of rose-hip pot-pourri, and in midgrope that woman had troubled herself to put on a recording. She'd sought out in her collection and had loaded in her deck an item given over entirely to the stripe of musical stylings routinely piped into your better professional parks.

From there on the floor in my undershorts, I could see her magazines. Her clear preference was for the cosmetological choices of movie starlets—the conditioners they were partial to, the lip glosses they used, the astringents they employed on those rare days when they were blemished.

There was a Bible on her coffee table and an Episcopalian study guide devoted exclusively to the Book of Matthew, a blown-glass trinket that looked like a Manx captured in defecation and a jar topped off with butterscotch candies, the balance in peppermints.

Above her sofa she'd hung a soft-focus photo of sun-kissed meadow flowers with a scrap of vaporish New Age doggerel printed across the sky, and while I was trying to extrapolate what the poet might have meant, she slipped up on me and called out from the near end of the hall.

"Paul, darling," she said, and I turned to find her in scarlet lingerie, a sheer one-piece ensemble that was brief and plunging both. It was just the sort of boudoir-wear that, if I'd given it to a woman, I'd have fully expected a kick in the stomach by way of recompense. I remember wondering if, in fact, that little satin number was the sort of item a serious student of the Gospels should wear.

I might have even wrestled with my itch to recitate for those few seconds before I got stirred enough to cast off my misgivings. I do clearly remember sitting there on the rug in that woman's front room wondering how I might rise to my feet while retaining some scrap of decorum. An aroused man in boxer shorts with sloops and schooners in the pattern can't help but look like a baremasted dinghy once upright and afoot. So I was weighing my alternatives when she took the merciful course of retiring out of view along the hallway.

She had lit candles in her bedroom, bayberry and sandalwood, which offered vigorous competition to the rose-hip potpourri. I joined her on the mattress where we had a sort of chat, aired anyway between us a regular bouquet of disclaimers intended to confirm that we hardly ever did what we were about to do. Then she dabbed jasmine oil on my temples and licked my sternum clean.

Her name was Mona which is lovely in its fashion and wouldn't have troubled me at all but for the fact that my father's mother's sister had been named Mona as well. She was a sizable homely woman with chin whiskers and phlebitis. Each time she grinned, she revealed a piece of bridgework a blacksmith might have made. Unfortunately, my client Mona proved doctrinaire in bed. She insisted I call out her name while performing various intimate duties, so I got a lesson in the alarming turns a train of thought can take.

When we were done, she praised me inordinately, rehashed the congress between us and spoke at length of those maneuvers I had managed to best effect. I made a feeble attempt to steer the conversation back to taxes—tried a little joke, as I recall, about graduated rates and revenue streams—but she pressed on with talk of Tantric positions she wanted us to try, both eventually and (I divined by her tone) in the very acutely near term.

Afterwards, she fried me sausage patties and made me toaster waffles, and we sat and chatted like people acquainted in a meaningful sort of way. Mona had lately read of the benefits of supplemental niacin and could very nearly recall a virtue or two of the stuff outright. She went hunting for the article but failed to come across it. Instead she returned with a photo album full of snapshots of her child.

The thing opened with that girl as a greasy newborn fresh out of the womb and carried her up through various holidays and sundry unsightly rashes, culminating with a picture her mother had taken only the previous week. Portions and pieces of that child's father, quite naturally, figured into some of the photos, and without fail Mona pointed out Larry, his name was, wherever he showed up.

Apparently, Larry was a loving and a conscientious dad, and Mona took pains to catalog for me the man's endearing qualities as I flipped through that album and ran across Larry's elbow, Larry's cheek, Larry's trousered thigh with his baby daughter perched upon his knee. Mona struck, however, the sort of tone when speaking of Larry's grace notes to suggest they weren't remotely compensation for the fact that the man, at bottom, was one of Satan's minions.

Mona played for me a recording she'd bought on the recommendation of a TV hostess, a curious assortment of songs performed by a Florentine tenor who'd been born deaf but had regained his hearing in a freak Vespa accident. Apparently, to judge by his musical choices, he'd been born tasteless as well which had survived his scooter crack-up unaffected.

Mona skipped through to the final cut, a treacherous medley that was equal parts Puccini and Neil Diamond. I managed to endure the thing politely for a while, succeeded at looking (I'd like to believe) persuasively entertained right up to the "Cracklin' Rosie" portion of the enterprise. Even then I avoided withering study of the stereo speakers, pretty well stifled a wholly involuntary acidic snort and kept myself from glancing at Mona in any telling sort of way by shifting about to contemplate my socks.

They lay on the rug in the front room just shy of my scruffy Nubucks, and I could see that they were each pilled up and gauzy at the heels, poor specimens for a tax preparer to shed in a client's house and hardly so swell as the Gold Toes I'd been partial to in Roanoke back when I'd been more dapper and authentically employed.

So other than mild sartorial recrimination touched with musical revulsion, I had truly awfully little on my mind when Mona looked over to alert me to an upcoming medley passage and caught me in rapt study of my socks.

She decided I was planning to tug them on my feet and leave, was sorry I'd ever shown up at her house and yielded to her advances, didn't much care for children and positively hated her decor, had found her even naked in candlelight overfed and unexciting and so had pretended to discharges as a courtesy to her, would rather eat a bowl of dryer lint than toaster waffles and sausage, detested her Florentine tenor, her haircut, the woodsy scent of her eau de cologne and would have surely been out the door already and halfway to my car but for the galloping onset of paralyzing regret.

She never said as much exactly. Instead she delivered herself of a noise that proved articulate and pointedly expressive. It was one of those noises common to people who get the wind knocked from them, a startled squeak in the throat that tends to suggest they had hoped to go on breathing.

Once I'd heard her, of course, I looked her way and took in her plaintive expression which induced me to wish I'd steered clear of her house and had avoided her advances, served to remind me I'd never known much personal use for children, found sausage indigestible and took a bleak view of Neil Diamond's hair. I realized I wanted to smash all of Mona's cat figurines with a hammer, doubted any woman should wear lingerie in fluorescent kitchen light or drain a man in one long rigorous session of all of his amorous juices. She looked to me far too old for bangs and smelled faintly of car freshener, and I felt anxious to take a hammer to her Florentine tenor as well.

So for a moment we were probably verging on uncanny agreement, and if I'd answered Mona's necknoise with a rascally smile and a shrug, I have to believe I might have gotten pretty cleanly away. Unfortunately, I wasn't remotely prepared to own up to being a lout, so I put on my best bewildered expression and inquired of Mona, "What?"

She spoke and blubbered both at once, stood gurgling in her scarlet teddy which proved far more disturbing a spectacle than a serene half-naked woman simply sporting lingerie in unbecoming kitchen light.

I did what men do in such circumstances. I stepped over and clutched her to me and made the manner of noises meant to confirm the groundlessness of her fears which, I'm sorry to say, were largely fueled by repeating breakfast sausage.

By the time I woke up the next morning with Mona's cat grooming my scalp and her daughter (a filthy gray fluke in her mouth) eyeing me from the foot of the bed, I was full in the steely relentless grip of paralyzing regret.

It seems this life is chiefly timing, the preponderance of it bad.

6 — ❧ About as soon as I was able, I cobbled up a feeble justification and went scouring after a fashion for Stoney's Hooper out the pike. I had no clients in her direction but had stopped her way at a yard sale once where I'd bought a book and a slotted spoon and had coveted an ashtray, a shallow slab of pewter in the shape of Tennessee. I told myself I should have snatched it up. I hit the road to seek it out.

In those parts, a yard sale was hardly an occasional affair touched off by a spot of domestic industry. Throughout the rest of the nation, I have to imagine, when people clean out their basements, tidy up their garages or prepare some dead uncle's bungalow for show, they end up with the sort of detritus apt to get marketed on their lawns throughout the course of a weekend until the dump opens on Monday.

That variety of commerce makes for a fair bit of healthy retail tension since rummagers and scroungers who stop by to browse are doubtless animated by the fear that those treasures they fail to ferret out—a hand-illuminated Magna Carta, an old tube sock full of Krugerrands, baby Elvis's teething ring—are doomed to get shoved in a hole come Monday by a landfill motor grader.

Where I lived at the time, however, the yard sales ran a different course, were reliably open-ended and ongoing. A fellow would set up sawbucks on his lawn, lay a plywood tabletop, and his wife would freight the thing with hideous gimcracks from the house along with battered flatware and coffee mugs, grimy cruets and tumblers, toasters from the chrome age, handbags and crushed fedoras, bowling gear, the odd shoe tree, spark-plug wires and air filters, trailer balls and harnesses.

Customers would plunder through the stuff from Friday noon to Sunday evening when the proprietors would drape a sheet of plastic over their merchandise, anchor it down with hunks of cinder block and close business for the week. The following Friday they'd peel the sheeting back and offer their rubbish afresh, what of it that hadn't been lost to the wind or weathered beyond recall.

So local yard sales resembled proper regulated business, just without the troublesome paperwork, the hours and the roof.

Readily enough, I found the place where I'd bought my book and spoon, and I joined three Saturday-morning rummagers sifting through the goods. I turned up straightaway my ashtray with its four-dollar sticker on it which had struck me previously as a little steep. I might have paid that for one of the glamour states, say, Florida or Nevada, but three dollars seemed more fitting for narrow homely Tennessee.

I was smoking at the time. Not heavily, but I was tired of dipping ashes in my palm. I'd hit upon the fact that those occasions I was blue, feeling weary of this life and crowding close upon despondent, there was nothing that quite revived me like a couple of Chesterfields. Standing there at that sawbuck table of crap on that front lawn up the pike, I could picture myself on my glider with my Tennessee ashtray, saw me flicking a Chesterfield down to the coal, grinding the butt in the Cumberland Gap.

The proprietress was sitting in a dinette chair with a hickory stump for a table which was crowded with a saucer of dairy-case biscuits, a roll of antacid tablets and a Mr. Coffee that was plugged by way of a drop cord into the house. She was talking on a puny violet cell phone to what turned out to be her sister who she called, by way of a sibling endearment, a "lying alky tramp."

The sister, apparently, was trying to borrow money to pay for repairs to her car and was swearing that this was the last loan she ever intended to draw. Naturally, the proprietress was put in mind of several other last loans she'd drawn which she went to the trouble to enumerate for her sister. There'd been going-to-California money, molar-extraction cash and an instance of tattoo arrears. The proprietress, apparently, had advanced her sister a wedding-gown down payment that had passed through her fiancé's gullet in the form of applejack, and she'd personally made up the bail short-fall for the fiancé after that who, from what I could hear, was dodging Richmond warrants in Costa Rica.

Now that proved, as a strain of talk, more than the alky tramp could bear, and she gave herself over enthusiastically to indignation. I could hear her shrieking out word that she'd paid for all of her tattoos herself, and the tooth she'd had pulled was abscessed and a danger to her baby which reminded the proprietress of the lawyer she'd hired to get the father served and sued.

I made out not to be listening, feigned interest in a piece of dented enamelware until that proprietress saw fit to interrupt her family business and ask me, "What is it, hun?"

"Take three?" I showed her Tennessee and picked significantly at a spot of corrosion, tried to insinuate the thing was probably not even worth four bucks pristine.

She did me the good grace of pausing to think before she told me, "Naw."

Then she went back to her lying alky sister's fiduciary history while I fished out my wallet and laid the full four dollars on the table. That woman gathered up the bills as she spoke into the phone, touched on night-school tuition she'd forked out for a class that had gone unattended, diaper money she'd put up that went instead for rum.

When I failed to retire across the lawn but just stood where I'd been standing, she troubled herself to tell me that she didn't give receipts and then went back briefly to sniping about an additional fiancé before I'd prompted her, by lingering still, to inquire of me, "What?"

I had, of course, expended no little thought on how I'd ask after that Hooper. As an authentic local businessman with legitimate clients about, I felt confident I could convey by my tone I had business with the woman which was at variance, it would seem, with what I conveyed by the rest of myself.

That proprietress watched me speak and then entertained a query from her sister. I could hear but the tinny chirp of her voice over that violet cell phone.

"Some guy," the proprietress told her. "Looking for Maud."

The sister made a remark that caused the proprietress to peruse me up and down as preamble to saying into her cell phone, "Uh-uh."

Ordinarily, I would have been acutely sensitive to that brand of exchange, would have assumed that they were gauging me for Hooperworthiness and were finding me underqualified and wanting, but I was far too distracted on this occasion to notice or to care.

Maud. Maud Hooper. Somehow that name seemed awfully right to me, and I was busy savoring it and rolling it around in my head. It impressed me as sturdy and noble, entirely fitting for that brunette. I could imagine her the namesake of some ancient August Hooper who had dressed ghastly wounds at Chancellorsville or invented the butter churn.

Better still, I didn't seem to be related to any Mauds, had taken a moment to scour my lineage and had come up agreeably empty. No whiskery aunts, not even so much as a far-flung lumpy cousin.

"That way," the proprietress told me, pointing down along the road before her house. "Turn at the sycamore. Look for the barn and the ponies."

I could hear cackling from the both of them as I headed for my car.

Trees are not a particular interest of mine. I tend to draw the line at knowing pines from hardwoods, so I didn't manage to turn off at that sycamore right away since it hardly distinguished itself from the oaks and the poplars. Instead I motored on past it a time or three and got useful help at last from a gentleman grubbing weeds in his yard.

Maud's ponies, as it turned out, were warmbloods. Her barn was an equine palace. The thing had cupolas and turrets and multiple weathercocks, a dozen stables with plank Dutch doors, fresh siding and trim paint. I could see a part of the house beyond it on a rise in a thick stand of trees.

I left my Cavalier on the edge of the gravel road that fronted the property, hopped over the ditch and parked myself against a run of fencing—the horse-country board sort painted white, even on the underside.

Maud Hooper had what was known in those parts as an executive estate, a show spread largely given over to meadows and manicured pasture with thoroughbreds scattered about for ornamentation and effect. The paddock was surfaced in groomed imported loam instead of the local clay, and the boulders along the driveway and the side shoots and the lanes had been spaced and positioned with excruciating precision.

Like with most executive properties, there was no implementa in sight. No mowers or tractors or shovels or rakes, not even an upturned wheel barrow. They were all packed off in a shed somewhere and only met with the light when in use. In the hands of a staff, I felt certain. Hondurans, more likely than not, since that estate looked better tended than local help was usually up to.

Maud Hooper had a garden on the hillside between her fine barn and her house. It had been laid out and planted on the order of one of those lush Provençal plots—leggy wind-bent clumps of flowers among bee-plagued banks of lavender, a rusty sundial, a rickety willow bench. That garden had a fraudulent air to it, the vague reek of studied neglect, had probably been designed by a landscaper with a magazine photo to guide him there in a run of country most decidedly not Provence.

The house looked authentic enough, what I could see of it back in the trees. It appeared to be one of those boxy Federalist piles with beveled clapboards and fluted casings. The roof was slate. The guttering burnished copper. I could readily imagine the pedigree of the furnishings inside.

On the rebound from Stoney, Maud Hooper had married a Gaithersburg attorney who had rated from Cora and Miss Addie hardly more than curdled smirks. As it turned out, I had run across him personally before, had recognized him from talk at the remnant shop as the fellow from the Citgo who'd rolled up on me at the pump island and had directed me to move my car.

I'd just gassed my Cavalier and was heading in to pay when he whipped in snug behind and motioned to me out his window, waved me over so curtly I thought he was in some manner of distress.

Once I'd reached him, he said, "Third subhead and then straight to provisionals," which I was dutifully laboring to digest until I noticed his cell phone earpiece.

He showed me his palm by way of a sign I should wait for his regard, and presently he deigned to tell me, "Pull up, sport." Then he tapped his watch face and glanced, I felt, derisively at my car.

He was perched in a spanking new off-road Euro touring beast. Champagne on the outside, aromatic leather within. For the price of one of his alloy wheels I could have had my engine rebuilt. I took occasion to subject him to a spot of study. He was weedy and bug-eyed, Barbour and Lands' End from the door panel up. He smelled of Cubanos and aftershave. His hair was impeccably parted. I detested him instinctively, resented him outright, dropped my jaw and told him sweetly, "Sure."

By the time I'd come out with my receipt, he was well into his fill-up. He proved to be half a foot shorter than me, wore proper trousers with cuffs and that variety of loafer with tassels and too much taper for human feet. He leaned against his fender well and barked in strident legalese while I paced my breathing in hopes of staving off an aneurysm.

I was put upon to wonder what the creature I imagined Maud Hooper to be could have possibly seen in that Gaithersburg lawyer to have brought her to yield herself to him or what, for that matter, she'd plumbed in Stoney beneath his fabulous hair. So I was ruminating and lounging against the woman's painted fence when she led a saddled horse from the barn and they both took notice of me.

I gave a little wave, a conflicted salute, less a greeting than a brand of spasm, and she studied me for a moment before she bothered to lift her hand. Then she drew her mount to a boulder by the paddock, climbed up on it and gained the saddle from there.

Her ride was a massive bay, and she was easy and natural upon him, comely in her stretchy pants which, given the general play of gravity, impressed me as a triumph. I looked on as she put that bay through its paces, sent it prancing across the pasture, sailed handsomely over a hummocky creek and galloped flat-out to the far fence. She rode like she'd been raised to it, plainly wasn't one of those women who'd come to horses once her bonds had matured and her marriage had grown stale.

She glanced every now and again my way, stayed conspicuously mindful of me as she cantered and galloped and trotted that horse back and forth across the pasture. Accordingly, I knew reason to think she'd venture over at length, that I would finally pique her sufficiently to rate some sort of earshot encounter, so I felt sure to have need of an effervescent nicety in time.

I applied myself to the manufacture of a clutch of the things straightaway and was soon enough armed with a chirpy remark on the fine turn in the weather which I shored up with a compliment on the charms of that Hooper's estate. I was presently prepared to touch upon the splendors of her garden, quiz her on slate as a roofing material, ask after the strain of her pasture grass. I felt competent shortly to let on to have stopped for a look at her fencing, hoped to convey that I was a landed squire with livestock to close in.

As was my custom back then, I took pains to practice and hone my spontaneous banter, and I'd persuaded myself I was reasonably well equipped for an exchange by the time that Hooper had reigned her bay around to canter towards me. She was halfway across the pasture before I'd bothered to consider the general tone her end of our chat might take. So the woman was bearing down upon me by the time I'd calculated that no matter which frothy scrap of talk I visited on that Hooper, she was all but certain to tell me, "You're that creep from the remnant shop," back.

Now that proved just the sort of prospect to undo and rout my pluck, and I suddenly found myself with little available spit for palaver, guessed I was moist enough to probably only tell her, "Yes."

Consequently, I undertook a renovation of my options as I watched that Hooper approach me up the gentle pasture slope. Somehow, even with all of my forethought and my appetite for rehearsal, ungainly improvisation was still the meat of my repertoire, so I was hardly shocked to find myself in flight across the ditch and heading at a trot for my sedan.

I might even have managed a tolerably ignominious escape if my Cavalier engine had fired up straightaway. Instead the thing dieseled and sputtered as prelude to a spot of arid grinding, so I was sitting there still when that mounted Hooper arrived at the pasture fence.

Together she and her bay both glared at me. Then he pitched his head and snorted while, for her part, she colored from the collarbones up and drew breath in such a way as to signify she'd pegged me for which creep I was from where.

7 —⟶ It wasn't the hair exactly, I came to find out, though the hair plainly hadn't hurt. Instead Stoney's allure had largely hinged upon his brooding reaches, those nooks in his psyche that women had chosen to take for mysterious. As I came to understand it, Stoney had once been moderately unchatty and had known a preference for Clubman talc instead of kerosene which had allowed him to pass for contemplative while agreeably aromatic, and that sort of thing beneath lustrous tresses will oftentimes make for girl bait.

Stoney, moreover, enjoyed the benefit of living in a run of country where men, generally speaking, did service as semidomesticated oafs. The local crop cherished their socket sets, chain saws and acetylene rigs, wore steel-toed boots and mesh-weave caps, hunted deer drunk every fall. They owned reversible blazers for proper occasions, gave their women friends kitchenware for Christmas, cultivated intimate knowledge of byzantine remote-control functions and stored their significant personal documents on the dashboards of their trucks.

For his part, Stoney was certainly handy and had an Econoline van full of tools, featured insulated coveralls as a staple of his wardrobe, was hardly ever out of his Red Wings or terribly far from his Browning cap. His personality, though, ran counter to his sundry surface features, and what women expected from looking at Stoney was rarely what they got.

Though Stoney never told me exactly what he worked at for a living, I met with cause to suspect he functioned as a manner of helpmeet for hire. Countless wives in those parts were saddled with husbands quite useless around the house. They were either too weary from working for pay to leave the settee on a weekend or could hardly be counted on to burrow out of the cemetery. So their mates were left to put up with seepy faucets and blistered paint, puckered linoleum, chalky tub grout, dinette chairs with spindles unglued, spongy bug-eaten porch planks, clotted downspouts, balky windows and doors which they'd raise a futile fuss about for maybe a year or two.

Then Stoney would finally get summoned in, the fruit of exasperation. The wives would threaten to call him, and the husbands with breath still would tell them, "Go on."

Accordingly, Stoney probably took a fair amount of fire. As the stand-in hired to address some long-neglected household complaint, he doubtless heard much of the scalding talk the husbands would have rated if they'd not been dead already or off gainfully engaged. Stoney, after all, went around disguised as a common lumpen male, and local women had surely long since come to the unified conclusion that they were just as well served to visit their ire on one man as another for all of the meager edifying good it was likely to do.

So Stoney would absorb on behalf of his gender a stinging salvo or two, and only once the women who'd hired him had exorcised their indignation would he set about giving them notice of the rare manner of creature he was.

He'd browse their hutches and china cupboards, admire their crystal, the odd piece of Spode, was evermore prepared to touch upon the frailties of the Sun King, Nelson's daring at Trafalgar, Rodin's genius with raw stone. He was passably conversant in Chippendale and late Victoriana, could regurgitate the triumphs of the Gemini space program and call up more than a Virginian had much right to know of scrimshaw. He spoke a little Esperanto, could tell quartzite from basalt and was sufficiently acquainted with the Boxer Rebellion and the Mesozoic Era to hold forth on either one at numbing length.

Stoney was solidly versed in the mating rituals of the tufted up-land grackle, could duplicate the knot employed by Cantonese rugmakers, was equipped to discourse on the difference between a mousse and a brandade or catalog the various gases in the atmosphere of Venus, and he was routinely prepared to apply to whatever artwork hung at hand Sir Kenneth Clark's principles of painterly perspective.

Stoney, you see, was a devoted educational-TV viewer back in the days when educational TV was, in fact, educational. The way I heard it, Stoney made do for years with an aerial strapped to his chimney stack and so was blocked off by the mountains from very nearly every station except for Richmond public television. Consequently, he grew accustomed nights to dropping onto his couch and suffering himself to get rigorously informed.

He'd watch shows about rocket propulsion and joinery, shows about reptiles and spelunking, shows devoted to the satisfactions of amateur philately. Stoney would take in tips for braising stringy troublesome cuts of meat, imbibe the architectural curiosities of the Minoan kingdom, welcome acquaintance with the social customs of Maldivians. As I understand it, he even sat through the occasional British costume drama, the odd operatic performance and hand-wringing civics debate.

Moreover, Stoney was given at the time to a public-television demeanor. He was reliably subdued and exhibited a preference for earnest measured chat, strands of talk embroidered with anecdote and peppered with stray facts that Stoney would set off each from the other with interludes of rumination. Ordinarily when local men fell silent, they were either fast asleep or orchestrating the discreet release of noxious gastric vapors. Stoney's lulls, by comparison, seemed altogether steeped in philosophy.

By the time I met Stoney, he'd long since traded up to a satellite dish and was under the sway of twenty-first-century educational fare which is frequently a blend of visual dexterity and breathless misinformation. So the Stoney I knew was chattier, in fact, than the bulk of local guys and had a particular interest in morbid statistics and sensational criminal cases. He was keen as well on the general topic of global calamities—volcanic eruptions, meteor impacts, wildfire and tectonic shifts—and he knew a fondness for fatal unforeseen domestic misadventure, the sort of story that ends with a furnace explosion or a grandmother smothered by her cat.

For me Stoney did service as a cultural barometric device. I'd run across him and tolerate the news at his disposal, endure all manner of pseudoscientific revelations, celebrity gossip, scraps of shrill political propaganda, talk of the latest air disasters and venomous Indian Ocean eels. Stoney would usually bring up details of a surgery he'd lately seen on the channel devoted to invasive procedures, would invariably speak of some documentary he'd sat through at least part of (the life and times of Diocletian, a Mandrell Sisters retrospective), and he could prattle at greater length about prevailing weather patterns than I could usually tolerate with grace.

In fact, the Stoney I came to know was just precisely the sort of fellow no amount of lustrous head hair could have helped.

But I had evidence he'd been otherwise from assorted females about, women I could tempt with mention of Stoney to quivering nostalgia, the brand of longing men will display once they've cast back to recall their perished spaniels, their El Caminos, their youthful willowy physiques.

Aside, however, from topknot fuzz and a rusting aerial in his weeds, I can't say I detected much in the way of the previous savory Stoney. Moreover, those occasions I'd trade chat with him when I checked for mail at my box or suffered Stoney to visit chatter upon me at the luncheonette in town (which he frequented for the barley soup while I favored the turkey hash), I don't recall he ever exposed me to anything beyond his shallows, ever supplied me incentive to think he'd not been always what he was.

The presatellite Stoney, the Stoney of the lapsed deliberate charm, remained, in fact, at odds for me with the Stoney across the road until one evening when Stoney decided to move a bureau to his basement and came over to conscript me into the enterprise.

You see, we were both of us single men with no help around the house. No wives, no strapping children, no convenient blood relations in any shape for shifting furniture, hauling trash or grubbing stumps. Stoney had an aunt in the area who drove her Chrysler out from time to time, a rather thick unsightly woman who'd sit with him in the yard where she'd complain about her ailments and her far-flung thankless children and would as soon have roofed his house as helped to shift a chest of drawers.

For my part, I had employed a local gentleman for a while who specialized in yard work but was willing for a bonus to assist me on the property with four-handed bits of business. Buster, he'd had me call him, and he was industrious after a fashion, most particularly off the clock at night. Buster, as it turned out, divided his time between yard work and marauding, would cut a lawn in the afternoon and then return in the small hours to steal the mower, the edger, the wheelbarrow and anything else that might be about.

As business plans go, it was a little shortsighted. Once Buster had spirited off my Snapper (which was dinged and rusty, evil to start and might have brought twenty dollars), I declined to buy a new mower but hired a boy with his own equipment. So Buster effectively stole himself out of a job.

My replacement yard man had a pickup with which he pulled a low-slung trailer to haul his tractor and his trimmers, his gas cans and his broom. He was efficient and serious, kept scrupulous records and offered proper receipts, was far too much of a lawn-care professional for supplemental furniture shifting.

Out of necessity, then, Stoney and I had cultivated an understanding, were agreeable each to be called upon to do service as ballast and brawn. Early on I'd brought in Stoney to help me move a cast-iron sink out of the middle of the back-porch floor where the previous tenants had left it, and he'd come to aid me in the assembly of an entertainment center once it had arrived in far more pieces than I'd been led to think it would.

Stoney owned a proper set of tools. He had a craftsman's intuition and a knack for digesting instructions indifferently translated from Chinese. For my part, I'm about as handy as a practicing Orthodox Jew, so while Stoney worked to piece together my entertainment center, I stood by attempting to hand him whatever he failed at that moment to need.

Over time, I'd worked myself into deep neighborly arrears since Stoney was entirely wanting in custodial impulses and so rarely had much cause for me to help him at his house. I was, then, awfully quick to agree to help Stoney move his bureau and tried to steel myself as we crossed the road for the squalor I felt sure to meet.

Stoney was grubby and fragrant, with an unlicensed landfill for a yard, so it stood to reason he probably didn't trouble himself with housework. He had, after all, his TV to watch and his avocation to tend—scattershot interests to give himself up to briefly and in sequence, convictions to rotate, facts to mangle, half-truths to recite. I couldn't imagine he'd know much occasion to scour and vacuum, to tidy and dust.

We paused, I recall, on Stoney's front porch while he described to me the bureau he was meaning for us to carry down his narrow basement stairs. Stoney informed me he'd taken the drawers out and had measured the thing for fit, spoke of how we'd best negotiate the jog in his back hallway, touched on the pivot we'd need to manage once we'd gained his basement landing. The whole time he talked, Stoney held his rickety luan door cocked open, so I was treated to an aromatic and acclimating view of his living room.

By the time we stepped into the house, I felt prepared to face the clutter and was effectively inoculated against Stoney's bachelor musk which had smelled on the porch like last week's socks perfumed with last night's shortening and had the same sour bouquet on the inside, just bolder and staggeringly worse.

The state of Stoney's front room constituted a more severe assault on order than I'd anticipated from the porch. To say the place was messy would be like holding the *Hindenburg* out as singed. That room was choked and clotted and stoppered with stuff—piles of desiccated *Times-Dispatch*es, unruly heaps of bulk mail and coupon sheets from the grocery mart, saucers and tumblers and encrusted flatware, jackets left to lie where they'd been unzipped and sloughed off, liquor boxes stuffed full of plastic sacks that Stoney seemed to be hoarding, joint-compound buckets fairly bristling with kindling, empty milk jugs by the gross, a hummock composed of dryer lint and toilet-paper tubes.

But that stuff, even taken together, hardly touched in magnitude Stoney's accumulated periodicals which were ranked about the front room in columns and piles and mounds and clutches, were rolled up to fit between stair-rail pickets and broadcast indiscriminately across the floor. They were simply everywhere anything else had failed somehow to be.

As we were living just then in the age of the complimentary trial subscription, Stoney seemed to have multiple issues of most magazines on offer. Newsweeklies, fashion glossies, assorted trade publications, dry scientific quarterlies in nearly every conceivable field. He had sporting rags by the bushel, monthlies devoted to haute cuisine, to quilting, to cosmetology, to exercise and rapid weight loss, to organic gardening, to recreational boatbuilding, to peerless inner Tantric peace.

But they were all overwhelmed and swamped by that species of magazine devoted slavishly to the habits and hairstyles, the tattoos, the piercings, the heartbreak, the criminal indictments, the surgical enhancements, the narcotic dependencies, the nuptials, the bliss, the trial separations, the charitable work, the staggering talent, the precious toddlers and home decor of what passes anymore on this earth for celebrities.

My thoughts went immediately to the integrity of Stoney's house, most particularly to the strength and construction of Stoney's floor joists and his decking. I feared that my weight added into the mix might spoil the equilibrium, and I'd end up on the basement floor entombed in *Vanity Fair*s. For a moment there, consequently, I couldn't bring myself to move. I stood just inside the front door and watched Stoney stalk across the room. He plucked up what turned out a scrap of chipmunk and a gristly nugget of squirrel, told me, "Goddamn cats" as he made for the front porch to toss them into the yard.

In his absence I detected three actual felines lounging about the room. One was dozing on Stoney's hutch shelf atop a stack of grocery-mart circulars. Another was upended in the turntable well of Stoney's console stereo, while the third was perched on a sideboard hard by Stoney's kitchen door, fully awake and engaged in licking its nether reaches clean.

Just above that cat, cocked a little crookedly on the wall, hung a reproduction of a painting that I couldn't help but notice. The thing was oddly shaped, about two feet long and maybe ten inches high, and was laminated onto a plank with beveled edging. The hues of it were elegant and unexpected in a place like Stoney's front room. Ambers and chestnuts and deepest maroons muted, I figured, by varnish. It looked a picture, from where I stood, of a man on horseback having a parley with a cow.

I was prepared to ask Stoney about it, but he was loitering on the porch. I could hear him informing a cat, I reasoned, how very pleased he'd be if the nugget of squirrel and scrap of chipmunk would get left just where he'd tossed them. Typically, of course, there's no profit much to be had from instructing a cat, as cats seem to tolerate instruction poorly, and ever so shortly I heard Stoney shout out, "Hey" and "Hey!" and "HEY!!" after which he stalked down the front-porch steps and, by the sound of things in the yard, loosed an acrimonious dose of abuse on the run.

So I was left, for the moment, on my own and stepped over as best I could to have a closer look at Stoney's painting. There was a modest network of footpaths through the clutter in Stoney's front room. The main route ran from Stoney's chair to the kitchen and back hall, but I detected a branch—constricted and much more lightly traveled, obstructed even a little by a year's worth of *Argosy*s tipped across the way—that circled the settee and put me within arm's length of the sideboard where I endured the brief and passing scrutiny of the feline there which interrupted its bunghole grooming long enough to glance my way.

The man on the horse turned out to be Saint George in ebony armor who was caught up in a bid to slay a rather exceptional dragon, a beast that looked like an enormous dachshund in an ill mood and with bat wings. Saint George had run his lance into that creature's mouth and driven the tip of it out the back of its head which pretty well served to account for that dragon's pitch of irritation.

They were battling, the two of them, on a corpse-strewn piece of real estate. The ground was littered with torsos, human appendages, heads attached to stumps of necks in various stages of putrid mortification. There were heaps of skulls and bones picked clean of sinew and of meat, a ropy string of large intestine, a few wall lizards, several conch shells carried in somehow on the tide even though the shore looked a good half mile removed there in the background.

Off to the left was a village by the water with palm trees and turrets and crenellated fortress walls. Two ships were heeled over under sail out in the harbor, and a virgin (I assumed from my days as a Bible-school scholar) occupied the far-right margin of the painting. She wore a luxurious gown, a tiara and an expression on her face that suggested she hardly meant virginal purity to serve as her life's work.

That painting was identified along the bottom band as a sixteenth-century Carpaccio, the original of which was hanging in some *scuola* off in Venice. Straightaway I was prepared to take the thing for a diverting curiosity, a holdover from Stoney's public-TV years, until I looked around to see what other art he might have hung and found nothing but more of George, his steed, his lance, his punctured dragon, that virgin, those skinks, that carnage, those two ships under sail at sea.

He had smaller versions of the entire painting plus assorted details and blowups tacked and taped to the wallboard all around the room. They weren't nearly as apparent and conspicuous as they previously must have been, had gotten over the years concealed in part by influxes of clutter, were half hidden behind lampshades and stacks of yellowing newsweeklies, were sooty and cobwebby, curled and puckered, peppered with mildew.

What struck me was that they made do as essentially one thing, one item of rather intense and wholly uncharacteristic study which hardly suited the Stoney I knew who tended to skim and flit. My Stoney could be depended upon to shift among his interests, was famous about for encyclopedic enthusiasms that raged and flagged, but there on his walls was evidence of a steady devoted Stoney, a fellow content to lend his full regard to one thing for a while.

Stoney came in off the porch and caught me ruminating at his sideboard. I'd licked my finger to rub at what had looked a stain on Stoney's painting, a stubborn umber streak that proved a splash of dragon's blood.

"Hell of a thing, ain't it?" Stoney waded my way as he spoke, blazed a route past a heap of *Scientific Americans*, sidestepped a pillar of woodworking catalogs. "Went over and had me a look at it."

Stoney joined me at the sideboard and swept the cat before us to the floor.

"Venice?" I asked him.

Stoney nodded and described in appreciable detail a delectable sandwich he'd eaten in a café at the airport in Milan.

"But . . ." And I do believe that's just about all I managed to get out as I pointed first to the painting before us and then to the versions and details of it attached to the wallboard throughout Stoney's front room. I was hoping to hear of the riveting charms that picture held for Stoney, or of the spell anyway the thing had undeniably cast upon him which was a bit of a trial for me to even conjure and imagine given that indiscriminate nattering was all I'd ever known from the man.

Stoney subjected that painting to a thorough once-over as if he'd walked blindly by it for a while. He soaked in the carnage, the virgin, the harbor, the town, pointed out assorted painterly details.

"The real one's big," he told me. Then he grinned and tapped on George's ebony armor. "Who is that?" Stoney asked me after which he stepped aside so I might lean in close and meet with cause to say.

Until then, I'd spent but fleeting and meager regard on George himself. He was hardly more than a pasty head poking just clear of a breastplate, and, upon inspection, he didn't look terribly saintly or heroic. His nose was sharp and oversized. His chin was puny and receding. He had a very unfortunate head of frizzy blond hair and an expression in his eyes that took me back to my days in the office park in Roanoke. There was a touch of chilly officiousness in his glare as if, while passing his morning in dispatching that dragon, he was thinking already of accounts he'd reconcile come afternoon.

The resemblance, though, proved remarkable once I'd weighed his features together. I loosed a snort in recognition. I turned and informed Stoney, "You."

8—✒ We would have ended up out in Williamsburg or down on Ocracoke if I hadn't gone and opened my mouth. Mona had been agitating for us to take a trip somewhere together, had been clipping magazine travel stories and sending away for brochures, but I'd put her off throughout the spring (tax time, don't you know) and had stalled her with talk of extended filing well into the summer. She was not, however, the sort disposed to shelving an idea.

We had become a couple due largely on my part to rank procrastination. I'd entertained early on intentions of laying my frailties out for Mona, of presenting her with assorted of my shiftless qualities so she might see cause to throw me over for a better man. By the time, however, I finally got around to ticking off my flaws, Mona was blinded by affection and comprehensively enthralled. I outlined for the woman sorry episodes from my past that featured me as charmless, dull and callously self-serving which Mona elected to counter with news of rather deplorable bits of business in which Larry, her future former husband, had behaved far worse.

I even trotted out in time a regular enormity once Larry had proven a challenge to outlout. I confessed to the cat I'd had put down for no defensible reason. He hadn't been old or ailing or actually even, for that matter, mine. A neighbor who'd transferred overseas had left the creature in my care. It turned out he did most of his sleeping while I was off at work and passed his nights howling and darting and tattering my sofa arms which earned him a trip to the animal clinic where I'd intended to have him declawed but opted instead, on a whim, for euthanasia.

On a postcard to his owner, I did him in with a liver complaint.

That proved the sort of sorry episode to give Mona authentic pause. Instead, however, of throwing me over, she invited me to Christian worship. She planned to pray for my salvation. She intended to make me whole.

Now I had noticed her Bible and study guides, her religious tracts about the house. Mona's way of saying, "Praise Him," in a low and swampy whisper once we'd finished with lovemaking had struck me as a trifle odd until I'd flattered myself to believe that she was speaking of little Paul. We'd certainly never talked of Jesus which seemed appropriate enough since we were routinely guilty of unsanctified fornication.

So Mona caught me unawares and exacted a pledge that I go with her to church which seemed harmless enough at the time since, once I'd ably resisted salvation, I guessed Mona would probably feel justified in giving me the boot. I usually spent my Sunday mornings with squabbling politicians or watching grainy footage on the Hokie coach's show, so I was prepared to welcome the chance to see what decent people did.

Mona, as it turned out, didn't attend a local conventional church but worshiped instead with a splinter congregation, a pack of evangelical Episcopalians who'd broken with their brethren in town and met Sundays in a storefront about halfway across the county. It seems the place had been a hair parlor some years back, had a linoleum floor and a water-stained drop ceiling. It smelled faintly of jojoba tempered with mouse urine and proved capable at full capacity of the acoustics of a number-ten can.

Mona had come to those Episcopalians long after their contentious split with the more traditional arm of the church in town. The way I heard it, cracks in the congregation had initially shown themselves when the right reverend of the unified Episcopal church had renovated a parsonage bathroom and finished the raw parsonage basement space at building-fund expense. The congregation had approved the outlay with near unanimity, and the trouble only started once the reverend had an open house to show off the refit.

Now no right-thinking tithing Episcopalian was prepared to begrudge his preacher much in the way of modern domestic amenities. It turned out, though, that reverend had tinkered with the plans he had submitted, had dropped a cupboard from the basement to accommodate a wet bar instead. Apparently, as wet bars go, that preacher's was elegant and swanky. It had recessed lighting and brass accents, a refrigerated wine-storage system, a copper sink and granite counter, etched glass in the cabinet doors.

Anybody who cared to could see past that glass to the bottles of liquor on the shelves, and not just sherry and bourbon and applejack—spirits a man might justifiably soak fruitcake in or take in a toddy for a cold—but provocative recreational bonded alcohol. Schnapps of various flavors, half-gallon jugs of vodka and gin, two shades of rum, grenadine, Jose Cuervo Gold.

The reverend was quick to point out the accoutrements and pricey construction items that he'd determined, in the spirit of fairness, to pay for from his own pocket. He'd gone with a low-slung toilet, a platinum bathroom chandelier, had opted for European hinges on all of the basement cupboard doors, and he allowed he'd reimbursed the entire expense of his swanky wet bar which, for the bulk of the congregation, was all that needed to be said.

There proved, however, to be constipated Episcopalians in the mix who'd preferred the parsonage spartan and didn't much care for their toilets low-slung. They couldn't see why a bachelor reverend should have any call for a rumpus room or be saddled with need to decide nights between tequila and iced tea.

So those parsonage renovations led directly to nagging congregational unrest. Committees met and factions hardened, and the general tone became unchristian as Episcopalians endorsed their preacher or agitated to replace him with a holier and less thirsty sort of man. Those moderate sensible Episcopalians content to allow their preacher a drink far outnumbered the stodgy variety and worked to frustrate them at every turn until tensions had escalated and quarrels had gotten commonplace.

A pitched battle broke out when a narthex window shattered and had to be replaced. The glass had featured angels and lilies of the valley, a primitive homespun rendering of the Annunciation which the hidebound minority vigorously agitated to get supplanted by a window depicting various lurid apocalyptic scenes. When they were thwarted and overwhelmed by a vote of the membership, their leader and chief scold—a Delp who shortly became their preacher—took his pack of ardent followers and withdrew from the church.

Mona had started attending services well after they'd claimed their storefront. They'd been divorced from the mother church a couple of years by then and were attempting with ever-so-meager results to raise money for a sanctuary, held bake sales and yard fairs, quilt raffles, car washes and had put together funds enough to construct the sort of shed that might hold the tools required to build a sanctuary with. So they'd come to consider their storefront something less than temporary and had fixed it up to look a little like an actual church.

A couple of the brethren with very nearly the skill for it had constructed a riser for that Delp to pace along with a pulpit and a sort of high altar (a table underneath a satin sash). The congregation sat on pews made from pressure-treated planking, hammered together quite plainly without lumbar support in mind, and a solid bit of money had gone for fancy religious accoutrements—candlesticks and collection plates, an ornate platinum cross, an incense burner that close quarters and local fire codes prevented from getting much use. That Delp wore a surplice with a cassock beneath it, sported a Roman collar even though he wasn't, in fact, ordained. He stalked and preached in front of a sizable graphic painting of crucified Christ with His wounds and His thorns and His display of beseeching forsaken anguish.

Some neighbor of Mona's, a widow up the street, had fetched Mona away one Sunday to the evangelical Episcopalian service once she'd noticed that Mona's souring marriage had left her sullen and blue. My understanding is that Mona was raised in the Moravian church which, as denominations go, is tuneful and famously festive at Christmas but about as feverish and fanatical as swim class at the YMCA.

It's no wonder, then, that Mona got a charge out of that Episcopalian service, came away enlivened, palpably refreshed and stirred. That Delp, as it turned out, knew a considerable gift for testifying, was loud and twitchy and antic in ways Moravians never were, but he observed throughout the hour sufficient Episcopalian rituals to render the experience a curious blend of high-church ceremony and lowbrow Holy Gospel literalism. I don't imagine Mona could have known more unalloyed surprise if she'd met with a Passover clambake or a spot of Baptist interpretive dance.

My own hour with the evangelical Episcopalians in their storefront turned out to be painless and moderately entertaining. That Delp seemed to recognize that I was fallen and trained a fair bit of brimstone on me, laid out the full range of torments most blasphemers were likely to meet with in hell. He stole glances my way while traveling back and forth across the riser, looked me over pretty sternly when visitors got invited to stand and withdrew the communion wafer from me when I was slow to take it, when I failed to drop my jaw and stick my tongue out in good time.

I'd only paused because I'd never seen a church wafer quite like it. The thing was toasted on top and perforated, sprinkled lightly with salt.

The congregation turned out to be comprised of abject strangers to me which I counted as about the only blessing that Sunday morning brought. I didn't work for any of them or know so much as one in passing, so I didn't expect to meet occasion to explain my holy rolling away. People tend to want their book-keeper to be honest and discreet. Decent and God-fearing are probably welcome traits as well, but unbridled rapture is likely to seem an accounting complication, so I gave thanks for Episco-palians I'd never set eyes on before.

Accordingly, I was feeling satisfied by the time that day had ended. I'd come out of that storefront wholly unaltered but for a sciatic complaint which left me essentially the same sorry speci-men I'd been when I went in, only gimpier and a little less worth having. Even now I'm ready to think that Mona was set to throw me over, had exhausted her options for lifting me up to her per-sonal standard for men which is to say I doubt she was aware of the romantic implications of even makeshift storefront-church atten-dance. You see, once word got out that we had been to services to-gether, we might just as well have been joined in wedlock by the pope himself.

By Wednesday, everybody knew we were a doting couple. That, anyway, is what people stopped to tell me on the street as prelude to offering congratulations and voicing their approval. When I'd balk at the news and try to stammer out a contradiction, I'd ever-more earn by way of reply, "Hear you two went to church," which got tossed out like a chunk of unassailable concrete proof that Mona and I were bound up to each other.

Even that lunatic Tucker woman out the gap, who raised foxes for their urine and openly boasted of cordial relations with Mephistopheles, stopped me in the co-op to inflict her blessing on me and confide she'd never known much use for Mona's future ex.

Churchgoing, of course, had only served to alter local perception. I was still tepid about Mona and ambitious to get tossed aside, and I'd acquainted Mona with quite sufficient of my peccadilloes, had exposed her to enough of my governing frailties to have dampened her ardor for me. So we'd gone into that storefront sanctuary shaky as a couple and had come out an hour later not remotely better off. We should have parted on the sidewalk which, as things presently played out, was our last tidy opportunity to be finished with each other.

When nobody knew about us, it would have been inconsequential to split. A little regret. A little sadness. A touch of acidic recrimination. But once word got out that Mona and I had worshiped in public together, we suddenly had an entire county to disappoint.

There I'd gone and laid the groundwork for my personal shiftlessness, had very nearly won Mona to a low opinion of me when people about began volunteering flattering contradictions, claimed for me virtues and allurements that I've simply never had. Mona heard I was good with children and held her daughter especially dear, got wind of local kindnesses I never had committed, was told of wealth and holdings I had not accumulated, witticisms I'd failed to utter, derring-do I'd not performed, princely favors I could not recall so much as contemplating.

She went daily out in the world and got a gilded version of me that I had to work ceaselessly to try to tarnish and undo. I was subjected, quite naturally, to the same sort of frothy piffle about Mona, but, unlike her, I'm the ilk who's usually given to knowing what he knows. As advocates go, the locals were a silver-throated bunch, had been reared in the Old South fashion to a knack for flowery insincere charm. Even the grubbiest and least socialized back-hollow hovel dweller among them could usually cobble up a compliment with enough atavistic skill to ensure that the fraudulent bits—the seams and rivets—hardly showed.

It seems Mona preferred the falsely perfumed and rumored version of me to the rank one I'd established in the flesh. She was probably weary and beaten down, couldn't face another stab at romance, and there I was handy already and enticing enough, I guess, to tempt Mona to settle for me in spite of myself. So I had another reason to be suspicious of organized religion and cause to resent the drift of popular local thought. I knew our neighbors were pimping for us in the spirit of self-interest and regional matrimonial socialism. Why, after all, should Mona and I be better fixed for mates than they were or enjoy finer prospects than they'd ever verged upon for bliss?

Finally, when the Headley sisters let me know that they were wounded, I had to face up to the fact that I was pretty well ensnared. Those Headleys were single girls, or rather borderline spinsters with scant prospects, who were in the habit of encouraging suit from every available unattached man. By "encourage" I mean they would giggle and flirt and wear scads of eau de cologne. They once had me over to prepare their taxes even though they lived on family holdings and there was hardly anything for me to do. They served me tea and made me a sandwich—smoked tongue and iceberg lettuce—which tasted intensely like Shalimar on wheat.

They weren't forward, really, or desperate but just pathetically ready for love, and when I ran up on the pair of them in the grocery mart one day a month or so after I'd been to church with Mona, they threw in together to snub me in a corrosive sort of way, snorted both and wheeled to concentrate on the margarine as I passed. Those Headleys caused me thereby to know that I was unavailable to them which meant I was either spoken for or dead.

So we got locked together, Mona and me, by public acclamation which is not, at bottom, very much like love. When everybody, though, assures you that you're one half of a couple, it becomes a bit of a chore to even convince yourself you're not. Straightaway Mona embraced the consensus and went blind to my flaws, chose to overlook our general unsuitablity for each other.

And that essentially is how we fetched up in a gloomy Venetian guildhall to take in Stoney's painting of Saint George. Mona had suggested Williamsburg with Ocracoke as a fallback option, and I'd countered with the Doge's palace, al fresco dining on Torcello.

Mona, you see, had once happened across a pouch of photographs while hunting rubber bands in a sideboard drawer. They had turned out to be pictures of Mona and Larry's honeymoon in Venice which Mona had sifted through and volunteered the odd remark about. The photos themselves were unexceptional Venetian-tourist-board fare—the boat-littered sweep of the Grand Canal, the Zattere in twilight, the Rialto bridge, the public gardens, a produce vendor in a *campo*, San Marco pigeons, sunless *calli*, Diaghilev's ornate tomb.

In among them was but one snapshot of Mona and Larry together taken, plainly, by their gondolier. It seemed he'd triggered the lens before they were quite posed like they'd intended, before they'd set their grins and fallen gaily into each other's arms. Instead they were sitting slightly apart in the gondola's stern with a gaudy maroon throw across their laps. They looked to be in a scummy side canal, and Larry was pitched forward, had an arm raised and his mouth dropped open, appeared to be instructing that gondolier to not, *per favore*, push the button that gondolier had pushed.

For her part, Mona was gazing at the side of Larry's head and not in a fashion ripe to be taken for loving.

As she worked her way through the photos, Mona touched on quarrels they'd had, meals they'd eaten, sights they'd seen, rubbish they had purchased. She described their dingy hotel room and gave a general account of Venice as a place Larry had tainted for her, a city her honeymoon trip had comprehensively served to sour and spoil.

I'd stored that information away and had never guessed I'd

need it until Mona brought out the brochures and hotel flyers she'd sent off for, a real-estate pamphlet listing condos to let at Nags Head and Kitty Hawk which had prompted me to ask if we could go to Venice instead.

Mona was supposed to remind me that she and Larry had honeymooned in Venice. She was supposed to argue for the solid historical value of Williamsburg followed maybe by a few days on the Outer Banks where we'd suffer the green flies and fight the undertow. I was prepared to be contentious, was primed to insist on Venice and then wring from Mona an explanation of her reluctance to travel there. I hoped to prompt her to dredge up Larry and his husbandly offenses so that I might pronounce them trifling and not, as husbandly offenses go, bad.

Then we would argue, I hoped, and Mona would know sufficient exasperation to invite me to haul myself off her sofa and evacuate her house.

But Mona only said, "Venice," softly and with a dreamy descending lilt after which she indulged in a spot of reverie before gazing at last upon me a bit moistly and with a wholly unnerving smile.

"You know," she said, "it is time I put Larry behind me."

Dinky just then was coloring on the foyer floor, was sprawled there with her crayons and her half a ream of printer paper. She was big on trees and cows and houses, the occasional economy sedan, and the odd item that she evermore called "Daddy"—a thicket of lines marked down so forcefully the paper usually tore.

"Sweetie," Mona said, "how would you like to go on a trip, way over the ocean?"

The child dropped her crayon to the floor and gave the offer some thought before she opened her mouth and shrieked in a way that was not exactly joyful.

9—➤ I had visited Venice before and had never actually hoped to go back, had been traveling in the company of an acutely unbalanced young woman who, on the way to the Lido, had climbed the boat rail and jumped into the lagoon.

I was on my postgraduate tour of the Continent at the time, was sleeping in hostels with other postgraduates from all around the world and the occasional (usually German) geriatric flower child in barracks rooms that evermore stank of feet and indigestion. To save money, I took only coffee for breakfast and ate apples usually for lunch, passed my afternoons touring galleries, lounging in parks, on esplanades where I read fat Russian novels and labored over journal entries, a mix invariably of bombastic self-pity and meteorology.

It seems although I was lonely and bitter and cruelly misunderstood, I could readily tell a zephyr from a homely freshening breeze, distinguish cumulus clouds from banks of fleecy cirrostratus.

My taste at the time ran towards the sort of young women who impressed me as mentally unwell. Zany would do in a pinch, but I knew high spirits were usually temporary and found I preferred those females touched with clinical psychosis to the ones with half a bottle of Bordeaux in them. There was something about the emotional volatility that stirred me. Truly erratic girls, after all, were sure to punish men like me, so I could have the female company, the odd display of affection and still meet with ample occasion for lonely and bitter and misunderstood.

I'd met Sophie in Paris. I was sitting in the Luxembourg Gardens on a dreary afternoon, was waiting for five o'clock when the hostel would open, was damp from a persistent drizzle which I'd cobbled up already cunning scraps of lyrical prose about. My thoughts were running towards the hot tea I'd have in the hostel common room, the dry socks I would change into, the sweater I wished I'd worn, lacerating phrases I'd employ once journalizing about my mood when I caught sight of Sophie across the way dancing on the grass.

You weren't, of course, supposed to even walk on the grass, much less caper upon it, so straightaway she attracted a couple of gendarmes from opposite ends of the park. They came running at her blowing their whistles in a kind of accidental rhythm that she adjusted her movements to and kept time with. She was graceful after a fashion, appeared to have a bit of training, unlike the general run of folk inclined to spontaneous open-air dance.

Each of the officers grabbed an arm, and they screamed at her as they hustled her off the grass, supplied her (I guess) an education in the sanctity of fescue. Once they'd turned her loose on the cinder walk, she laughed and pirouetted away without the first trace of embarrassment or that strain of humiliation that would surely have plagued me for several weeks thereafter. That's when I knew she was my sort of female provided, of course, that she wasn't just drunk.

She made her way to me which I was given, back then, to laying to my personal magnetism. Truth be told, aside from a filthy gentleman with clumps of matted hair, I was the only other civilian in that end of the park, certainly the only other fellow about with cigarettes and English, and I was pretty much hers once she'd poked me in the shoulder, raked her hair out of her face and told me, "Hey."

Sophie had a private room in an actual hotel, was making her way across the Continent on her father's AmEx card. She claimed to hail from Vancouver when she didn't claim to hail from New Orleans instead, and she could recite a good half dozen sonnets by Edna St. Vincent Millay, the poet laureate of the lonely, bitter and cruelly misunderstood.

Our first two days together we passed in philosophical conversation which I would punctuate with the occasional thwarted sexual overture. Thwarted not because Sophie was prudish or didn't think of me in that way, but more on account of the fact that she was certifiably batty, and it's an awful tall order to seduce a lunatic. They're distractable, given to wayward and untimely shifts of interest, prone to fits of unchecked palaver, bouts of weeping, sudden deep sleep.

I'd be right there in the middle of a tender enterprise, the sort of undertaking I felt sure would melt a saner woman, when Sophie would rail against deconstructionists, light a cigarette or snore.

You couldn't legitimately have a female like her, not in the way that men tend otherwise to have women, could never be sure she'd settled on you, convinced herself you'd have to do. Sophie's ilk didn't tend to give off mountain-fresh domestic musk, the powdery scent of clinging resignation that issues usually from a woman who's thrown her lot in with a man. With Sophie's sort, a fellow was almost certainly never to meet the moment when, persuaded he was adored, he'd smugly ask himself, "Now what?"

We weren't planning to go to Venice, but once we'd missed the train to Berlin and felt the need still to put the rigors of Paris behind us for the weekend, we took passage on the Orient Express with Sophie's father's credit card and would have known occasion to wake with the rising sun on the causeway into the city if we'd ever, in fact, gone actually to sleep.

Instead we drank between us three bottles of criminally over-priced champagne while Sophie read aloud to me excerpts from a Venetian travel guide. Even at the time I could tell she was unhappily surprised by the cruel and bloody history of the place. Sophie nosed up bits about flayings and gibbets, ceremonial beheadings, inordinately ghastly mercenary wars. She lingered, I recall, over news of the antique republic's common practice of binding up its enemies, attaching them to stones and sinking them in the lagoon.

I suppose Venice was sinister for her by the time we finally reached it. When we came out of the train station, Sophie looked undone there on the plaza, and she fairly led me a chase through the city in the general direction of St. Mark's Square. I followed her down *calli* and *rio terre*, along *fondamente* and *salizzade*, through *campi* at a trot. She made out to be excited, innocently charged by the beauty of the place, but even I could tell she was manic and agitated. She squirmed away from me when I'd catch her, laughed in a desolate sort of way.

We followed what signs there were high on the puckered stucco, obscured by café awnings, overgrown with bougainvillea—AL'ACCADEMIA, PER RIALTO, PIAZZALE ROMA—their directional arrows pointing usually nowhere much. We spilled out at last into Saint Mark's Square by sheer happenstance. The orchestras at Quadri and Florian were jousting back and forth across the square. They played show tunes at each other, the odd French cabaret song, cantering versions of Verdi overtures. I tried to get Sophie to settle in at a table for a coffee and a little open air, but she was twitchy still and too wrought up to sit. We threaded our way through the tourists, drove pigeons before us, declined special bargain tickets to various glassworks on Murano and finally paused for a moment at the base of a column by the water's edge, the one with Saint Mark and his crocodile high upon it.

I can't say what her affliction was exactly. Sophie was jumpy and anxious, peered about at the knots of tourists as if feeling hemmed in. I tried to soothe her, held her hand for as along as she'd allow it, invited her to tell me what her complaint might be, but she only responded by indicating points of interest to me—the Salute, the Redentore, the public gardens down the way. She'd interrupt herself now and again with laughter of a semihysterical sort, that brand of cackling that's ordinarily a ready substitute for tears.

I wasn't equipped to help her, had no firm idea what to do. I come from an uninterrupted line of ruthlessly sane people. We Tatums have always been dull and steady. We plod and grind along as a rule. When I was a boy, we had a neighbor who was famously disturbed. She couldn't seem to get out of her stained and dowdy housecoat for weeks on end and would wander the neighborhood in it calling for Everett, her cat, a creature not terribly likely to stray from her house.

Everett was nappy and stitched together, had button eyes and a scarlet felt tongue. He'd been lovingly manufactured in Taiwan. One of us kids would usually get sent to fetch him and bring him to that woman to prove to her that he was safe, was found. Whichever adult was handy usually steered her towards her house, my mother often who'd chirp at that lady as if she were a child, ask her simple-minded questions, carry on about the weather as a lubricating distraction until they'd gained the woman's drive.

I was told her affliction had something to do with her faithless cad of a husband, with a stillborn baby, financial disappointments, corrupted genetic chemistry. Even as a boy, I could tell from the stink it had something to do with gin as well.

So I tried with Sophie what I guessed my mother would have tried. I went giddy over the lavish facade of the Palazzo Ducale, brought to Sophie's notice a line of cumulonimbus over the sea.

She laughed, I recall. I believe it was meant to be laughter anyway, and then Sophie stood and said, "Oh, Paul," in a despairing sort of way and turned towards the lagoon as a water bus came warping in on the chop.

I followed her on board, and we took a bench together up in the open bow. I'd half decided by then, in the ignorant way that men come at such things, that Sophie was probably only suffering through a spot of hormonal upheaval, the onset likely of a thermonuclear monthly. I'd seen milder cases in other of the lunatic women I'd dated, so I decided to take my usual course of action in such matters. I lightly stroked her downy forearm and apologized for being a man.

In fact, that and the freshening salt air seemed to placate her a little, and she appeared calmer to me as that boat made calls along the *riva*, looked to have vented a bit of anxiety and even managed to smile my way as we turned away from Venice proper and made for the Lido across the lagoon. I volunteered to hold Sophie's rucksack once she'd set it on the deck. I took it onto my lap and watched as Sophie stepped onto our bench seat from where she crossed with a smile to the boatrail and leaped into the water.

I hardly knew what to say, partly because I was shocked and stupefied but also because I was armed with only wretched menu Italian. So I could order my water *gassata* and ask politely for a check, but I was ill prepared to inform a swarthy *vaporetto* captain that a girl I'd, in fact, only met a week or so before and who was probably more than a little out of her mind had, without so much as a crumb of collaboration on my part, mounted the rail and jumped into the lagoon.

I seem to recall I managed to get out a "Hey, *signore!*" or two, and I undertook what I intended for a spot of articulate pointing which had the effect of bringing the conductor, I guess he was, onto the deck. In another time and place, he would have been the sort of fellow likely to swab your windshield and pump your gas.

His uniform fit him like sacking, and his forays out among us to open the rail for passengers at the various scheduled stops he'd treated, I'd noticed, like irritating unwelcome interruptions in his wheelhouse conversation with the captain. A tourist, then, bobbing not even accidentally in the lagoon but as the result of a willful and calculated act appeared to strike him as an instance of wholesale effrontery.

Consequently, once that gentleman had joined me at the railing, he passed a minute or more yelling at Sophie in scalding rapid-fire Italian, and a couple of passengers threw in to bark at her a little themselves. While the captain slowed the engines, he chose not to stop them entirely, and I could only look on as Sophie dropped quite steadily astern. Nobody threw her a life ring or offered to jump in and save her.

They'd seen before I did the blue police boat racing Sophie's way. It was tiny and cobalt with CARABINIERI stenciled on the transom, sat low enough in the water to allow for the mate to reach in and grab Sophie's arm. He yanked her onto the deck as if he were landing a carp.

Our captain revved the engines, and we continued to the Lido. The conductor snarled a few choice words my way before retiring to the wheelhouse, and the rest of the trip I suffered the odd burst of passenger commentary, got the feeling people thought I'd driven Sophie to a decadent American prank. Once we'd touched at the Lido, I endured vigorous encouragement from the crew to haul myself and my two rucksacks off their boat.

Accordingly, I failed to head back and track down Sophie straightaway. Instead I wandered around the Lido for, I guess, an hour or two, called at several crap emporiums where I bought millefiori trinkets, had a gelato and a coffee, walked over to the beach. I'd never seen the Adriatic which proved about as still as a pond. The shore was largely deserted but for a little boy sitting in the surf, I'll call it, and a sizable woman in a rubber bathing cap and a swimsuit with a skirt. Mostly she stood in knee-deep water surveying the horizon. Every now and again, without warning, she'd squat and struggle gamely back up.

During my return across the lagoon, I thumbed through Sophie's guidebook for any suggestion as to where a tourist who'd jumped from a water bus might end up. I found out where to go if my pocket was picked or my hotel room was burgled, and once I'd strung together guidebook phrases enough that spoke, more or less, to my situation, I approached a policeman who was smoking a cigarette and idling by the Campanile.

He tolerated me in silence as if I were making a sort of sense, but once I'd introduced him to my *indisposta umida amica*, I got stranded and had to search around for what I'd hoped to say next. He took occasion to relieve me of my guidebook, just reached over and removed it from my hands. He examined the thing and gave his head a disapproving shake.

"Now," he said, shoving the book back at me, "your friend is sick because she is wet?"

As it turned out, he had a cousin in Chicago and an uncle in Anaheim, a childhood friend on the sales floor of a Baby Gap in Houston. He had flown to Atlanta once and toured the Southeast on a bus, told me he never again hoped to meet on this earth occasion to eat a cubed steak.

I shared with him a version of what had happened on the boat in which I was kept by main force from diving in to rescue Sophie. He was polite enough to nod and smile and tolerate me at it as he walked me to the waterfront and up along the *riva*. He put to me questions along the way, probed me first for information on the marital status of a starlet he'd read about in a magazine before moving on to the reliably deplorable prospects of the Cubs.

We turned up a little side canal where three bright blue boats were moored and entered past a massive mahogany door into the *carabinieri* station where we were met by a sergeant, I guess, at a lavish high altar of a desk. My policeman informed him in some detail of my situation, and they enjoyed a rollicking laugh together at, I had to think, my expense. I was handed off to another officer who escorted me sternly up the stairs in his peaked hat and his monstrously fussy *carabiniere* uniform. Like the rest of them, he looked to be bucking for Central American despot.

I was left a considerable while alone on a bench in an upstairs hallway. The place was gloomy and ancient with terrazzo flooring, flaked paint on the walls, rococo plaster cornices fleecy with dust. I was aware from down the corridor of what I thought a radio, could hear the sweet high voice of a woman raised in song, and a quarter hour or more had passed before I knew the voice for Sophie's. She sounded to be working through the entire Cat Stevens catalog.

A man finally showed up and sat down beside me. He wore a rumpled dress shirt and a tie. He shook his head and smiled at me in a kindly sort of way, said something in Italian that I didn't understand, offered me a cigarette which I saw fit to decline. Each passing *carabiniere* saluted him and asked politely after his day in such a way as to persuade me he ran the place and mattered.

With his spotty English and my deplorable Italian, we managed a sort of murky glancing communication between us. We both fell silent and listened together to a stanza and a half of "Peace Train" as preamble to a labored piece of business about the *ambulanza* he'd called, the variety of *dottore* he'd elected to dispatch Sophie to see.

At length, he tapped me on the shoulder, fondly I thought, familiarly anyway, and assured me that Sophie was *completamente pazza* which, by Socratic inquiry and guidebook consultation, I discovered to mean "quite mad."

I unzipped Sophie's rucksack and showed him her passport, her traveler's checks, her lumpy cosmetics pouch. Remarkably enough, he seemed instinctively to know that I wasn't bound up to Sophie, had no authentic claim of ownership or lawful cause to be consulted, that I was just some guy who'd come along to Venice on a lark.

He stood and plied me with a mournful wince, offered me his hand. I rose to take it as he told me, "The women. *Belle misterie*."

Addled like I was and even ashamed a little already, I believe I nodded and said to that gentleman, *"Oui."*

He left me there, retired down the corridor with Sophie's rucksack in hand, was serenaded along the way by a reedy medley of "Wild World" and "Morning Has Broken."

I sat in the afternoon sun on the Zattere. I took an evening train.

10—→ She screamed, Dinky did, as we lifted off at Dulles and didn't leave off screaming until we were well east of Newfoundland. For my part, I was so busy stifling homicidal urges that I hardly knew occasion to fear, as was my custom, for my life. A man can't hope to fret about turbulence, read peril into flap adjustments, actively agonize over the quality of oversight at Boeing when he's sitting alongside a shrieking child he feels an itch to kill.

An ever-changing cadre of flight attendants kept stopping by our row to see what might be done to soothe and silence Dinky. They offered her apple juice and saltines, candy and roasted nuts, tried to pin platinum wings on her smock front and help her color in her book, but Dinky responded with piercing wails, told each of them in turn, "NO!" So soon enough even the cabin crew, those thespians of the skies, couldn't effectively hide the fact that they'd prefer her limp and lifeless.

The sentiment seemed to me fairly unanimous in our congested section of coach except for Mona who was busy reading the in-flight magazine. To be fair, she would occasionally nearly leave off altogether in order to tell Dinky, "Now, honey," in a vaguely scolding tone. Chiefly, though, she devoted her attention to a profile of a former CEO who'd purchased a monastery near Medford, Oregon, where for an enormous fee civilians with disposable income and guilt could wear homely friar's robes and embrace vows of silence for seven days a throw. They could garden and meditate, sleep on a pallet, enjoy slimming spa cuisine.

Mona saw fit to read aloud passages to me when Dinky was searching for breath, scraps usually of the inspirational philosophy of that former CEO who, I reminded Mona, had run a company that made exploding light-duty trucks. By then I was hoping for multiple engine fires or simple hydraulic failure. I certainly didn't imagine that things could possibly get any worse which was just about when I caught my first whiff of dinner. A cart came wheeling out of the galley with a stewardess on either end, and there at the first they'd trouble themselves to ask after passengers' entrée choices, but by the time they got to us—a full six rows back—there was only one item left: gumbo with Cajun rice on the side, composed salad and flan.

The aroma of that meal was dicey enough with the foil still on the plates, but uncovered the reek of it proved debilitating. Most particularly for Dinky who, felled by a blend of exhaustion and disgust, collapsed onto her seat and went to sleep in among her scattered Crayolas. The passengers around us took time out from dining to applaud.

Mona had moved on in her magazine to a story about a sheriff in Arizona who happened to be a grandmother with both a prosthetic foot and an indefensibly sunny outlook. Mona shared with me nuggets of the woman's worldview while she (I could hardly believe it) ate. And not just the flan which I'd sampled and found marginally inoffensive, but the composed salad too with its radish curls and its desiccated carrots, the Cajun rice with its saline overlay and flecks of who knew what. Mona even ate the gumbo, lapped it up with her stubby spoon and insisted, when I asked her, that it was savory stuff.

I poked at my little tub of it but failed to break the skin that had formed over the surface in the pestilential cabin air. I could make out machined nuggets of what looked to be potatoes along with chunks of a pinkish shrimplike substance that, at thirty thousand feet, was as close to the ocean as it had ever been.

Instead of dining, I offered my tray to a stewardess wandering the aisle. I traded it in for a fistful of vodkas that she'd been reluctant to give me until I'd reached over and threatened to shake Dinky awake.

So I drank steadily for an hour or two and watched on a tiny seat-back screen about eight inches from my nose bits and pieces of maybe a half dozen movies. There was an uninvolving melodrama, a pair of humorless comedies (one cobbled up to bore adults, the other designed to benumb adolescents), a bewilderingly inaccurate historical saga in which Napoleonic French aristocrats sounded a little too frequently to hail from Santa Monica, a feature-length cartoon about a philosophical mosquito and a space opera in which Martian colonists traveled at light speed between planets in what looked like gym bags with external plumbing.

The last time I'd flown overseas, a screen had scrolled down from the ceiling, and all of the passengers had been obliged to suffer through the same film at once which had instilled a kind of unity there in the shank of the fuselage. We'd banded together like galley slaves under the lash. Anymore, though, transatlantic flight resembled a night at home in front of the television. I could channel-surf and eructate, get liquored up and fall asleep, stumble to the toilet with my pants unfastened in my stocking feet. I had every little thing a fellow might want except somewhere to put his knees.

I dozed off and awoke as the sun was rising, to find Mona intent on her screen, captivated by the uninvolving melodrama. She was

gnawing a thumbnail and blotting her tears with the nasty under-
belly of Dinky's garden slug with teeth.

◦⊖◦

At Mona's insistence we took a water taxi instead of the airport
ferry and so straightaway got a taste of the quintessential Venetian
experience—stark romance joined inextricably to ruinous expense.
Mona spoke her brand of Italian to the water-taxi driver which was
very much like my brand of Italian only less self-conscious and
louder. She showed him a brochure for our hotel which touched
off a soliloquy, prompted him to gesture and hold forth in an animated sort of way on the topic, I'm prone to believe anymore, of
the inaccessability of our lodgings.

He let us out in a side canal, pointed up a narrow *calle* and directed us to go (as best I could decipher) straight. We ended up
walking around for probably three-quarters of an hour. Mona
anyway and Dinky walked while I slogged along with the luggage,
followed them in and out of *campi*, up dead-end alleyways and
back and proved helpless against the memories of my previous trip
to Venice when I'd chased a lunatic down (most likely) some of the
same streets that I'd returned to as a dumpy balding porter.

For the eqivalent, as best I could calculate, of thirteen dollars
and change, a North African gentleman selling ladies' handbags
off a blanket agreed to escort us personally to our hotel. He even
carried Mona's cosmetics case the entire fifteen yards, set the thing
down on the lobby landing and told me, *"Voilà!"*

The place was full of jolly Bavarians, fairly crawling with them,
and I have to think they'd claimed the choicest rooms. Ours
turned out to be cramped and gloomy with a view of a seepy copper downspout, with laminated Titians on the walls that looked to
have been place mats once and a Eurotoilet I was a full ten minutes
figuring how to flush. The beds were soft. There was no—Dinky
informed us—television, no minibar or electric shoe buffer, scant
towels and one chair.

We did have a filthy Venetian piebald cat for an anxious couple of minutes until I'd managed to drive it back out of the window onto the neighboring roof.

We took a sort of vote on what to do as Mona was a democracy enthusiast in theory. I was all for sleeping for a couple of hours and rising refreshed for dinner. Dinky came out pretty strenuously for going directly back home while Mona suggested we troop outside and have a look at the Grand Canal which is what, once the votes were tabulated, we ended up having to do since, in practice, it turned out Mona operated as a junta of one.

Worse still, she proved the sort who has to go in everything—museums and churches, retail enterprises of every kind and any other unquantifiable attraction charging an admission fee. So we hardly ever ended up where we'd set out to go since Mona was given to darting in doorways and falling into ticket lines. She'd leave me and Dinky waiting at one storefront after another while she browsed and bought and waved occasionally through the window glass.

Dinky, for her part, threw most days a couple of fits an hour, usually when I was tending her while Mona had gone off to shop. Even the Italians, who are famously sympathetic to children, would take in Dinky's outbursts—the stomping and the shriek-ing—and favor me with conspiratorial *morta bambina* looks.

As the week wore on, Dinky's native vinegar ebbed a little, and her fits grew briefer and noticeably anemic around the edges. Except, of course, at dinnertime when she would unfailingly mount a tirade which led us to take the bulk of our meals in assorted hotel restaurants where the staffs were accustomed to insufferable chil-dren from all around the world.

I never actually mentioned to Mona that I'd been to Venice be-fore, given the acutely unflattering circumstances of that particu-lar trip. So I was obliged to put on a regular air of stark bedazzled wonder as we came across storied Venetian sights that Larry had ruined for her and that I, in fact, had usually seen already. We did,

I recall, one afternoon round a corner at a canal which brought us hard by the *carabinieri* station I'd visited previously. The trio, I guess, of blue police boats tethered at the landing put a look on my face that Mona couldn't help but take notice of.

"Sugar?" she said and subjected me to diagnostic perusal.

I thumped my belly and mustered a necknoise, informed Mona, "Clams."

Truth be told, I'd altogether forgotten Stoney's painting. There towards the end of our stay, I was in such a fever for our trip to be over that I was consumed with marking the hours and counting down the meals. By then, of course, Dinky had decided that she didn't want to leave. She'd grown partial to boat rides and had developed a fondness for chasing pigeons, had come across a cookie she doted on, a fruit juice she could stand to drink. Since the place was carless, she could run through the streets antagonizing the locals, and I think she relished the chance to inflict misery on a fresh wait staff each night.

So as I became more excited, Dinky got freshly peevish and ill, and we passed each other there on the final day before our departure. By then I figured we'd gone in just about everywhere there was to go, and I recall we were wandering in an out-of-the-way and rather shabby part of the city, had lost the trail of some glassware store Mona had decided she simply must visit on the recommendation of the night clerk at our hotel.

Somehow, after a week of staring up at the thing on our ceiling, Mona had developed an affection for the ghastly blown-glass chandelier. It was blue and peach and misty white with snaking arms and knobby protuberances, and, in Mona's defense, I have to allow it was almost hypnotically hideous.

She'd concluded she required just such a fixture over her dinette at home, and the clerk, as it turned out, knew a man with an unfindable fixture shop.

Once we'd passed the same church a half dozen times, we

stopped to reconnoiter by a canal which had been dammed up and drained for dredging and repairs. A couple of guys in coveralls were standing doing nothing much shin-deep in fragrant estuarial muck. Condemned to go back to a place where there was not such lovely swill, Dinky set up a fuss canalside that was laced with revulsion for me, and I was entertaining *morta bambina* looks from sundry passersby while Mona was scouring about, apparently, and spying an attraction.

"Come on," she told us and pointed to a sign beside a door advertising an entrance fee of five thousand lire.

There was no clear indication of what we were buying our way in to see. The building was a grimy pile of a place and looked, like the rest of Venice, to be actively disintegrating and more than a little out of plumb. I paid a gentleman just inside the door, a fellow in a dandruffy blazer, and followed Mona through heavy draperies into the dimly lit interior.

At first, I couldn't see anything at all. I ran into a bench, I think it was, and barked up against a tourist, a stout woman who reproved me in some throaty Slavic tongue. Then Dinky jerked loose of my grip and went scampering across the room towards a niche where she'd detected somehow venerated leavings.

Out on Torcello, Dinky had happened onto a dried-up corpse, the shriveled remains of some saintly fellow laid beneath glass in a sanctuary floor. So you couldn't just see the gentleman but could tread on him as well which struck Dinky as impossibly delightful. Since then, she'd demonstrated a gift for nosing up holy relics, could sense them somehow back in their sanctified reaches and airless shrines—teeth and hair and scraps of bone, dehydrated organs, the occasional entire goodly soul reliably bejeweled and frequently in acute need of dusting.

I like to think Dinky recognized in the body parts about a brand of ecclesiastical impulse to tear the wings off flies, break open beetles just to see the buggy gunk inside. There was something faintly cruel and morbid about that cherished human litter that couldn't much help, I guess, but charm a latter-day American child. She was exposed, after all, back home to carnage on the television along with the arid pieties that pass anymore for evangelical worship, but not until Venice had she met with ghoulishness sanctioned by the church.

A girl like Dinky could spend the balance of her Sundays with storefront Episcopalians and never know occasion to see a rib from Saint Stephen or a splinter of the Virgin Mary's femur.

So Dinky got wind of a bone about and ran off to turn it up while Mona and I waited in the gloom for our pupils to dilate. Once I could see, the place didn't look much like a chapel to me, had more the feel of an ancient Moose lodge with its benches and its lectern. What light there was shone onto paintings high upon the walls, and not the sort of paintings we'd waited in lines all over Venice to see—cityscapes mostly with monstrous frames populated by countless hatchet-faced Venetians. These were something else, something plainer and better and more worth wanting to see.

I know now we were in the Scuola di San Giorgio degli Schiavoni, some sort of Dalmatian guildhall from the sixteenth century. I know now I first saw Saint Jerome leading a lion by a tether, know now I turned and caught sight of Saint Tryphone exorcising a demon, but I knew even at the time once I had shifted yet again that I was looking at Stoney's dragon, at Stoney's pasty officious Saint George.

"Oh," I think I managed to say and with more fervor than Mona had heard from me in all the museums and galleries and in front of all the paintings we'd seen.

"What?"

"Remember that guy I told you about? Came all the way here to see a picture?"

Mona paused for a moment to mull upon the matter. I could sense she didn't recall him as she nodded and told me, "Yes."

"This is it."

It was arresting, was six or eight feet long, maybe four feet high. It was painted on board, I think, and heavily varnished so that the scene had a rich amber glow to it even under those feeble lights. The thing fairly vibrated in a way that the bulk of the art we'd paraded past hadn't which failed to prevent Mona from opening her guidebook and studying that instead.

She read me scholarly scraps about the history of Slavic peoples in Venice, about Vittore Carpaccio who'd been hired to dress their guildhall up. Then Mona labored through a description of everything that I was seeing—the carnage, the dragon, the maiden, the fair knight, the walled town on its hillside, the ships out on the sea. She identified the other saints in the other duller pictures, read aloud how the wainscoting had been crafted from Dalmatian mahogany.

I was, I guess, too caught up in the curiosity of the moment to muster my usual pitch of exasperation with Mona. As she prattled on about various insignificant architectural details, I tried to digest the string of events that had put me in that place which even at the time I felt to be more than a little wondrous. By all rights, I should have been watching a woman in eighteenth-century garb make lye soap in a tub in Williamsburg, or at the very least I ought to have been browsing at that moment through an array of unspeakably tasteless Murano chandeliers. Yet there I was standing just where Stoney had probably stood, taken, I'll confess, with the painting that had snared him.

The bluff serendipity of it all dazzled me a little, and I became a bit effervescent as a consequence. So Mona would visit on me a snatch of unilluminating guidebook prose, and I'd bring to her attention painterly triumphs and deft artistic touches which she'd very nearly endure before she'd read at me again.

I could hear the gentleman in the dandruffy blazer speaking, I had to assume, to Dinky. He seemed to be telling her, "*Basta! Basta! No no no no no,*" in response to the way she was pawing sundry of their artifacts. I assumed, then, we'd shortly get ushered out into the swampy afternoon, so I pointed out flaxen-haired George on his mount and told Mona, "It's Stoney all over."

Now the resemblance in Stoney's copies had been curious enough, but in the original it was spooky and unnerving. The determined set of George's chin, the unaristocratic nose, the workmanlike cast of his near eye as he ran that dragon through. That George was a miraculous facsimile of my neighbor across the way who I'd seen in the selfsame attitude with the indentical expression while cutting threads into a pipe on a spit-lubricated rig.

For her part, Mona made a show of studying that painting, told me, "Uh-huh, uh-huh," as she contemplated George. And I recall it wasn't until we were well away from that Dalmatian guildhall, after we'd given up looking for the chandelier shop and had visited a naval museum, after Mona had bought a crushed-silk scarf and a pair of slingback shoes and we were taking Campari like worldly people at a café on the *riva* that Mona finally troubled herself to inquire of me, "Stoney who?"

11 ⟶ As it turned out, she was probably a virgin only incidentally since that dragon, my research revealed, had not been observing a strict virgin diet. By all accounts, he'd started with livestock—goats most particularly—and had graduated in time to young adults sacrificed by lot. So the ground in that painting was chiefly strewn with odd scraps of luckless teens.

More to the point, she was a princess, daughter of the king and queen of Libya or Chamonix or the upper Schonberg Mountains, depending entirely on which version of the tale you chose to read. She had a name even every now and again—Cleodolinda—and for some reason she'd seen fit to face her doom as dragon fodder in her bejeweled tiara and her wedding gown.

George, legend has it, was a soldier of fortune, a knight-errant for hire who'd been scarce through the years while that dragon was feasting on mutton and unmoneyed youth. The man, however, had left off slaughtering infidels and plundering empires of their riches so as to gain a spot of royal favor by interrupting that reptile's lunch. George went at the creature like maybe he'd lanced a dragon or two before.

His expression was what stuck with me, was what popped into my head when I'd entertain stray thoughts about that painting. He had a look of calm and bloodless concentration on his face, gave off the air of a fellow engaged in a routine piece of commerce, suggested most anybody might lay waste to an ill-humored oversized dachshund with wings if equipped with a sound work ethic and a smattering of soldierly skill.

In every version I read, George was said to have "transfixed" that dragon as opposed to having skewered it and run it through. Then he led it into town with Cleodolinda's girdle for a leash and lopped off the creature's head in front of the grateful citizenry. The stories invariably ended before he drained the royal coffers and deflowered the princess and various of her comely appreciative friends which I had to imagine my own sort of George would have probably gotten up to.

"Oh yeah?" was all Stoney could muster when I told him I'd seen that painting, and as comments go it was wan and ever so slightly perfumed with pity as if I'd confessed I'd married his ex-wife.

I rattled on about the thing, was standing there just alongside my postbox with a welter of bulk-rate rubbish in my hands while Stoney was scouring for something in his junky Econoline van, was poking through a bucket with a length of galvanized conduit. I described to Stoney how I'd come across that painting, emphasized the happenstance and the underlying wonder in the fact I'd even seen the thing at all which yielded in turn to an interlude of art appreciation that consisted of regurgitated assessments I had read.

Stoney neglected to contribute to anything I had to say. He merely stood there looking at me and rubbed his conduit as I spoke. I could hear his callused skin upon the metal. Just before I'd started in, Stony had been replete with chatter, had held forth for some few minutes about a wondrous bit of business he'd gotten wind of on the television.

According to Stoney, a naturally occurring enzyme found in tiger shrimp had visited second sight on a fellow passing through Savannah. Upon polishing off his seafarer's platter, he'd called a busboy over to instruct him where his sister could locate her missing cat. It seems the creature had inadvertently gotten shut up in a car shed, had been waiting out a chipmunk by a barrel of scrapwood when the owner had left for a weekend of court-ordered community service and had brought down his car-shed door with the cat and the rodent still inside.

Stoney claimed that the restaurant patron had even conjured the address, had identified the shade of satin enamel on the carshed siding, was aware that the chipmunk had met already a fairly ghastly end and proved capable of speaking in detail of that carshed owner's offenses. He told how that fellow had quarreled and fallen out with his fiancée and had stopped by her place to bust up a bedroom suite she'd plagued him to buy which had earned him one hundred hours spearing trash along a freeway. And this all from a guy on his way to Clearwater who'd just stopped in Savannah for lunch.

Stoney had expected me, I have to think, to marvel along with him, to wonder what secrets the enzymes of other crustaceans might possibly hold, but instead I'd forged directly into talk of Stoney's painting on the pretext that the way I'd blundered across the thing was strange as well, maybe not shrimp-clairvoyance strange but curious nonetheless.

So I stood there by my mailbox spilling talk in Stoney fashion and allowed him hardly space enough for more than his "Oh yeah?" as I visited on Stoney the Georgiana I'd accumulated.

Only later did I notice he'd neglected to enthuse, had endured me in silence but for the rasp of his palm on his galvanized pipe.

Stoney, after all, had allowed his clutter to swamp his reproductions, had largely permitted his periodicals to eclipse them from his sight, so I should have recognized that painting had ebbed a little in Stoney's regard which would naturally have steered me towards some speculation as to causes, would likely have led me to wonder if he'd just wearied of the thing or had soured on it for some definite and telling personal reason.

At the time, though, I was far too grippingly preoccupied with me to have any unemployed regard to lavish upon Stoney. I was busy parroting art-historical appreciations, mangling technical painterly phrases I had picked up on the Web, waxing bombastic on the warrior saint as a potent Christian icon and unfreighting myself of impressions I'd come away from that guildhall with. I topped the whole business off by declaring that painting "powerful" and "electric" and then fell briefly silent for stirring dramatic effect.

Stoney took occasion to nod my way and smiled at me in a fashion. It was a brief sort of grin I see anymore as touched with a vague strain of sorrow. Then he lifted his cap and clawed a little at his freckled scalp. He shook his head and snorted. "Don't I know it" was all he said.

II

1 —⟶ Cora and Miss Addie had pretty well gotten the entire business wrong, most everything anyway except the hair. It turned out Stoney had never wooed that Hooper, had never properly won her and so had failed to enjoy the standing to leave her a wounded husk of a thing. They'd, in fact, met cause to come together and occasion to drift apart but hardly in the way those remnant-shop sisters had laid out and promoted.

There was a lone uncompromised speck of truth at the heart of what they'd said, but Cora and Miss Addie had larded it over (in accepted local fashion) with rumor and groundless elaboration, with hearsay thrice removed that they'd collected like magpies over time and had freely offered as fact. I'd been by then in that territory long enough for ready skepticism. I had endured all manner of gospel that had turned out largely chaff, and I'd discovered the trick was to sift in repose through the details and accusations in hopes of separating the unassailable truth from the falsehoods littered about.

Most proved simple exaggerations, lies primarily of degree. Local tramps were given more men friends than any woman could possibly pleasure. Tightwads had dazzling riches socked away in wall cavities. Children of townsfolk who'd left to make their way in the wider world proved routinely instrumental in celebrated national triumphs, made contributions that tended to bear up poorly under scrutiny.

The daughter of Riddicks out the gap had reshaped federal banking standards by, as it turned out, dating a congressional aide who'd helped to type the legislation. The son of a widowed Merriman had made a feature film, or had kept anyway a junior executive producer in bottled water, while the nephew of a Crandle woman at the nursing home in town had been crucial to the intergalactic success of an unmanned deep-space probe by delivering gaskets to NASA in his Federal Express truck.

Beyond the exaggerations, most stories I heard got corrupted by imported details. Even the liveliest yarns were prone to bland and static intervals, and no prattler worth his salt could help but add a little spice. So the Hagee from up the ridge who'd led an uneventful life until he got mauled and dispatched by a black bear he'd run up on was often saddled in the telling with the frailties of a Gable who'd been notorious in those parts for his unchecked volcanic temper and who'd once throttled a beagle to death when it had barked more than he'd liked. The result was a conflated Hagee who'd plainly had it coming, an improvement on the one who'd simply smelled of fry grease in the woods.

Naturally, the logical course of action would have sent me across the road to rap on Stoney's rickety luan door and ask him about Maud Hooper. In that world, Stoney would have had me in to perch amid the clutter while he favored me with bluff unvarnished facts. We lived, however, elsewhere, so I didn't go to Stoney but circulated instead among a pack of relative strangers to him who'd heard what they'd heard, knew what little they knew, said whatever popped into their heads.

I chose to start with Elvin in his fragrant cow-stall office, dropped by on some tax-filing pretense and thereby invited from him a rather involved fulmination that set out with the IRS but soon enough played raking fire on various government irritants from unseemly army-procurement expenses to alpaca subsidies. Erlene dropped in to berate Elvin over an errand he'd failed to run. It turned out she'd dispatched him some hours before to pick up an ointment for her, but he'd stopped off at his office on his way out to the car to log on and check his e-mails and had gotten, he claimed, "hung up."

Even I had known occasion to glance over Elvin's shoulder and soak in the general flavor of his electronic correspondence. He might have sent out noble missives and wholly innocent inquiries, but he got back penis-enlargement offers and randy come-ons from nubile teens who gave themselves out as "HOT!HOT! HOT!" and "Oh So Barely Legal!" Erlene was quick, then, to rise to a pitch of evolved aggravation since she had to know Elvin had put off driving in to fetch her ointment so as to free himself up for a spot of amateur gynecology.

Accordingly, they barked at each other before concluding somehow between them I had acute need of seeing Erlene's rash. Fortunately for me, it was on her foot, though she gave me a bit of a fright by shooting a hand up underneath the hem of her quilted housecoat in pursuit, as it turned out, of a stray and incidental itch. Then she kicked off one of her terry-cloth slippers and shoved her nasty foot my way, indicated what looked a fungus bubbling up along her instep and wondered of me how she'd possibly contracted such a thing.

Involuntarily, I identified pertinent evidence in my mind. Those flimsy shoes made for excursions from bedside to commode and hardly intended for everyday barnyard wear. The chickens, the guineas, the peahens, the goats, the cattle Erlene wandered among while effectively unshod and careless of their leavings. The personal cleanliness that was appreciably south of godliness for Erlene and the elixir I'd seen her and Elvin both use for occasional scourings— a blend of two-cycle gasoline on whatever grimy rag came to hand. It was a marvel to me that Erlene had somehow avoided whipworms and pinkeye, a regular holy wonder she had only a rash.

I subjected her affected instep to a spot of somber study. "Can't imagine," I told Erlene, and she and Elvin wagged their heads as they couldn't between them figure where those pustules might have come from.

"Crusty too," Elvin informed me and poked Erlene's foot, was motioning for me to unfurl a finger and jab that rash as well when Erlene unbelted her housecoat and whipped the near flap open so as to show me on her midriff a brace of inflamed cysts. She had to hike up some sort of underwear to put the things on view, a variety of bodice with gusseted seams, with reinforced strap ends and grommets. It looked like something a doughy chorine might see need to resort to, most particularly if she were doing double duty as a lawman since there was no way on God's earth that garment wasn't bulletproof. Erlene required both of her hands and brute force just to hoist it up her rib cage, and I was standing there stunned and overcome by the flesh that she'd unleashed when I heard Elvin behind me say with virtually breath alone, "Oh, baby."

Now there I was in between Erlene with her robe half shucked already and Elvin making noises like he meant to get loved up, and I could readily imagine the grim force the two of them might inflict on a bystander in harm's way who intervened in an embrace. It was self-preservation, consequently, tempered with disgust that spurred me to ease backwards out of Elvin's office door where I stepped blindly into the cow pass, found what felt two quarts of flop and then turned and punted a Rhode Island Red as I staggered towards the barnyard.

Erlene, apparently, was not in the proper temperament for a cuddle and instead routed Elvin from his cow-stall office and drove him towards his Plymouth, charged him to ride directly into town and pick her ointment up. By the time he got under the wheel, I was almost turned around in the drive, was working my Cavalier past a couple of Elvin's tractor carcasses when I heard Elvin cranking his Duster over with what sounded meager spark. The thing grumbled and sputtered and failed to fire, and I was easing towards the road when Elvin called me to duty by slapping the wheel and venting obscenities.

While I'm hardly much of a man in any traditional sense—don't hunt, don't fish, don't tinker as a rule with balky small appliances, have yet to own a chain saw or wire a table lamp, couldn't replace the workings of a toilet on threat of violent death—gender imprinting has left me mindful of my obligations, and I recognized once Elvin had slapped his wheel, was aware once Elvin had sworn, that I had a responsibility to join him at his quarter panel and gaze at his Plymouth engine as if I knew how one might work.

In truth, I was about as likely to locate Mona's G spot as diagnose Elvin's internal-combustion trouble, but I felt enough of an atavistic chromosomal pull to shut off my Cavalier and rendezvous with Elvin. I rested a foot on his front bumper. I yanked at a belt. I jiggled a hose.

As Elvin removed his air-filter housing, he spoke to me in some detail of the carburetor trouble he'd lately been suffering through with his Duster, proceeded as if I had some notion of what a carburetor did. I listened and nodded and spat a little as Elvin laid out for me the procedure he needed my help with to bring his Plymouth engine to life. I was to pour what turned out to be ether into an intake valve while Elvin turned over the engine from the passenger compartment where the windshield, I figured, and the upraised hood would protect him from the explosion.

I tried to make out to be an altogether unfit ether pourer, but Elvin allowed the accelerator required his special feathering touch, and as he slipped beneath the wheel and drew, I noticed, the door shut behind him, Elvin suggested I might want to juke back a little once I'd uncapped that ether and poured.

Consequently, I drove Elvin to the Rexall in my Cavalier and eventually carried him, ointment-laden, back out to his farm which afforded us occasion to speak at some appreciable length about Stoney, provided Elvin anyway the chance to fulminate further over Stoney's galling luck, the bulk of it having been cobbled up by Elvin and imagined.

Elvin resented Stoney for triumphs Stoney had never known, advantages Stoney had not (as far as I could tell) enjoyed, breaks and dispensations Stoney had never actually met with, special treatment there was precious little chance he had received. And but for Stoney, Elvin insisted, it would all have gone to him which made do as cause for heightened vinegary aggravation since Stoney had failed to impress Elvin as remotely the sort of fellow who'd be likely to savor his blessings and appreciate his luck.

"Different with me," Elvin allowed as we rolled into town and eased to a stop in front the hair academy to let a woman cross the street. "I wouldn't be looking no show pony in the gullet." And I'm a little sorry to say that, though Elvin was no Aesop, I'd lived in those parts long enough to readily know what he meant.

"Hey, doll," Elvin called out the window to that creature as she passed, winked at her once she'd glanced his way, showed her his cracked and pebbly tongue tip, and she failed for some reason to close on Elvin and flail at him until she'd drawn blood. Instead she smiled and giggled, flushed a little, told to Elvin, "Hey."

Elvin cut me a glance and purred in a fashion, gurgled that is, in such a way as to oblige me to picture him and that woman in the altogether up to indecorous overtures on Elvin's trundle bed.

"Got her some knobbies," Elvin assured me and unfurled again his tongue, flapped the thing around in such a way as to make himself revolting.

I turned the whole business to profit, however, by bringing

Stoney's Hooper up, invoked her on the grounds that she was a female who had her some knobbies as well. Oddly, though, Elvin couldn't seem to place that Hooper at first, was more intent upon grappling with the news that he was now obliged to count a woman among Stoney's prodigious unwarranted blessings.

I assumed Elvin's world would sour further once I'd described her to him, had laid out her comely attributes and enticing personal flair, but once Elvin had conjured that Hooper and had recalled just who she was, he seemed relieved that it was her and not the sort of local female he was geared to find bewitching and chock-full of wiles and charms like that lady who'd crossed before us and would be Erlene in fifteen years.

And that brand of thinking was hardly confined to Elvin exclusively. Maud Hooper's allure proved not to count with the bulk of men about who confessed to me a preference for the local strain of female. Sturdy sorts, most of them, hale and God-fearing, resolutely unstatuesque and capped off with scant exception by whatever ilk of coiffure was least suitable for their features and their builds.

So their appeal, in part, was due to the hair academy itself, a combination barber-beautician-cosmetologist training ground located in an unsightly fabricated three-tone sheet-steel structure that had started life as a muffler- and brake-repair shop. The place was situated there in the prime business block on the site where the old jail had burned, was located between the luncheonette and the Christian stationery store (the office goods weren't born again, but the owners surely were), and in fair weather that academy operated with its four bay doors upflung which permitted passersby a view of neighbors and acquaintances in various undignified stages of tonsorial renovation.

I kept the books for the gentleman who ran the place. He'd gone to barber school in Georgia and had worked in three- and four-chair shops all around the South. He had a cousin in our county who he'd swung by to catch up with along about when that muffler and brake garage had been offered for sale. As it turned out, Brady, his name was, had been nursing for some years a dream of running a body and paint shop as he preferred to barbering the satisfaction of pulling dents, the smell of Bondo and Clear Coat.

Consequently, Brady bought that four-stall sheet-steel garage in the middle of town and was trying to work out financing for the equipment he'd require when his cousin got laid off on a slow-down at the paper plant and wondered of Brady if maybe he'd teach her a little barbering on the side. Since she'd put him up and fed him, he didn't charge her for instruction, but when a couple of her friends came around to study styling with him as well, he got tuition out of them, schooled them on his cousin's children's heads, and was highly recommended by those friends to friends of theirs.

The local thinking was, as far as I could tell, that while the economy might fluctuate and sag and thereby close out shifts at the factories about and make employment scarce, hair would continue to grow at a regular rate and have need of being trimmed. Brady's students harbored dreams of running unisex hair salons, of opening up shops in trailers convenient to their homes. Like the bulk of people who'd only ever hired out for regular pay, they put inordinate stock in the romance of self-employment, weren't prepared to believe that being your own boss when the bills are coming due can mean little more than having yourself to blame.

While Brady was giving instruction to the friends of his cousin's friends, he took to noticing the common state of vehicles in the area, remarked that they were most of them rust-eaten from road salt, were dented and were dinged, and what repairs had been made on them were usually rude and amateurish—brushed-on paint, unsanded epoxy, the occasional duct tape.

Now some men might have read that as a cry for body work,

but Brady proved more sensible and realistic in his thinking. He recognized that a man with a Geo Metro for a family car was very likely unsusceptible to the romance of motor travel. The more a fellow like Brady looked around, the more he was sure to see that the county was filthy with boxy subcompacts and rickety half-ton pickups mended with ungainly spot welds and patched over with galvanized tin. Clearly drivers about were not prone to spring for detailing and fresh lacquer, probably only hosed their wheel wells out once a year or so.

So Brady reconsidered his options, weighed the car-owning clients he'd never see against the potential stylists who were flocking to him already, and he gave over his ambition for automotive body work, determined to content himself with a hair academy instead.

Brady got the proper licenses, the certificates he required, and he bought up chairs and cabinetry from defunct barbershops about which his enrollees failed to take for a brand of pointed career counseling. The students supplied their own shears and scissors and combs, paid a Barbasol allowance along with a daily supplement for boxed chicken and coleslaw from the luncheonette. They brought in magazines for customers to thumb through while they waited, tidied up evenings and were waiting already come morning when Brady rolled up.

At three dollars and a half for a man's haircut and four dollars for a lady's do, that hair academy attracted a reliable stream of specimens willing for the most part to accept whatever style was being inflicted. The students usually had a pair of cuts to practice every day, one in the course of the morning and the other throughout the afternoon, so a customer might get a feathered shag or a razored Eurofringe depending on when exactly he showed up.

The uninitiated would usually go to the trouble to describe to the barbering students precisely the manner of trim they intended to leave that academy with, and the students would evermore look to be soaking all the instruction in which Brady insisted on as a re-hearsal of hair-professional people skills. But once a customer had laid out his caveats, had described just what he wanted, he'd sit back underneath the cowling, doze a little and get what he got.

On a piece of Formica in a picture frame out by the entrance-way, Brady would write every morning in grease pencil the featured hairstyles of the day, and people about who were getting a little shaggy and unkempt would consult that Formica and decide what they were willing to tolerate. It probably needs to be said that the area natives could, most of them, trace their blood back to the Borders and the Highlands, to the Hebrides and Orkneys which, generally speaking, ensured they were ill-tempered drunks and mercilessly tight. Consequently, hair-academy prices proved powerfully seductive and tended to trump the risk of a couple of weeks' worth of unsightliness.

The effect locally of near-universal hair-academy patronage could be, given the cut on offer, creepy and unsettling. I was new to the county, had only recently thrown over my job in Roanoke and moved with my meager furnishings into my rental house by the woods when I happened to visit town for some shopping on Dorothy Hamill wedge day.

I'd stopped in at the grocery mart and was searching, I recall, through margarines and spreads after a pound of actual butter when a woman shouldered me aside so she might snag a brick of cheese food. I turned to glare at her, was culling through my arsenal of snippy remarks, when I became so alarmed by her coiffure that I couldn't find breath to speak.

She was a ponderous thing, squat and round, probably grand-mother vintage, and her wedge looked severe and lopsided, left off well above her ears and was about as becoming on that woman as antlers would have been. I assumed she was out on furlough from a state facility, just stood there and gawked at her, watched her fling her cheese food into her cart and bark out a heyhowdy to a woman up the way choosing among yogurts. *Her* wedge was even briefer, less symmetrical, more abrupt, and I could see beyond her a creature opening cartons and inspecting eggs whose own wedge, though slightly fuller, was no more of a success.

I had a moment there of panic, a spot of palpitation and regret over having thrown over a salaried actuarial career, a house in a settled neighborhood in a handsome Roanoke suburb, a life of cozy tedium and unregimented hair in order to move to the country and end up in the dairy aisle of the damned.

Soon enough, though, it got to where I rarely even noticed that half the people I'd run across on any given day were sporting artless variations of the identical coiffure which I soon enough understood to be the consequence of thrift instead of a symptom of collective derangement. We all, however, occasionally ran across motorists from the interstate who'd come off for gas at the Cavalier or lunch at the Tastee Freeze and clearly didn't know quite what to make of the hair that they were seeing, were usually already a little stirred up in advance of the coiffures.

Our signs out at the highway junction were not terribly current, I'll call it. The fuel prices listed on the Cavalier billboard were a decade out of date, and the Tastee Freeze had, in fact, burned entirely to the ground but for the garbage-bin corral and the drive-thru menu. Worse still, some civic booster had gone out to the exit ramps and painted over the proper distance to town on the signs at the ramp bottoms leaving people to think that gas and food were only just ahead when, in truth, we were a full three miles due west of the interstate which qualified more as a side trip than a simple highway stop. As a rule, then, motorists tended to be aggravated already before they'd discovered that gas was hardly a bargain and there was no fast food about.

A fair number of them invariably tried to make do with a meal at the luncheonette which looked from the outside quaint and appeared inviting. Inside it was dowdy and tended to smell of an unappetizing blend of wild-cherry urinal freshener and scorched green beans. Martha, the lone waitress, tried to compensate for the failings of the place—the stink, the glacial service, the tissuey napkins, the balky air-conditioning, the singing of the fry cook who improvised his own salacious lyrics and belted them out to the tunes of Methodist hymns—by calling the customers "sugar" and "honey" and pointing out the tea urn so that, once they'd been neglected, they could refill their tumblers themselves.

If the food had been digestible or even inoffensive, most everything else at the luncheonette might have served as local color, eccentricities that, like margarine pats, came gratis with the meal. There were only, however, a couple of menu items with any savor. I was partial myself to the turkey hash which was served with a coddled egg, and I could tolerate the batter-fried chicken about once a month or so as it was tasty but inordinately lubricated. Otherwise, except for the icebox pies, there was not much on offer to eat, not anyway for regular humans with common sensitivities. The Brunswick stew was cayenne-heavy. The veal cutlet was gristle-bound. The halibut came with fries and coleslaw and systemic freezer burn. The rib eye showed up gravy-swamped and as toothsome as tassel loafer, while the barley soup Stoney doted on tasted like liquefied salt lick.

The hamburger arrived on loaf bread. The pork chop was mostly bone, and the meat loaf was so cornflake-padded it should have been served with milk and toast. The luncheonette featured assorted sandwiches—pressed meat primarily and yellow mustard—and hot dogs that were probably half pig snout and half Red Dye #2. For dessert, in addition to store-bought pies, customers could know the chalky indulgence of bargain-brand ice milk washed down with strong boiled coffee that was somehow never fresh.

So a regular luncheonette patron could have made an authentic career out of steering uninitiated drop-ins away from menu pitfalls which induced us to opt as a civic service to clear up instead the hair. As chores go, that was far less complicated, required but two quick words even on those days when the coiffures in question were little shy of alarming.

I can recall enjoying a spot of hash at the counter on bouffant Thursday when the luncheonette was studded with women whose locks were all upswept and heaped. A man and his wife claimed the stools alongside me. They both had carcinomic tans, looked to have holidayed down in Florida and were heading north back home. I failed to intervene as they consulted the menu, as they ordered from Martha the clam fritters and the chicken fingers Kiev. I made no comment once their meals had arrived and they'd actually tasted the stuff, didn't trouble myself to inform them that, despite what they were hearing, singing bawdy improvised Methodist hymns was the fry cook's leading skill. I did pass them dispenser napkins they could spit their food into.

I didn't, however, speak to the pair of them until they'd noticed the hair about. The wife was the first to look around as a distraction from her fritters. She'd shoved her plate as far away from her as the counter would allow and had passed a few minutes in fruitless attempts to lure Martha with a glance before turning, exasperated, to take in the sort of people who, equipped with local knowledge, would still eat in such a place.

There was a creature down from her with a beehive, a girl who worked at the savings and loan and made do for that woman as an object of almost hypnotic study until she'd noticed another creature across the way with her hair all gathered and teased and heaped to even less beguiling effect. From then on, the bouffants fairly leaped out at her and were just about all she could see. I watched her as she swiveled on her stool and took them in, as she elbowed her husband and brought the bewildering wealth of them to his notice.

That luncheonette looked a regular Love Canal of ill-advised

dos, the site of an inexplicable concentration of beauty-shop offenses, a world of bobby pins and Final Net with no sign of a
prom. I allowed that couple up from Florida to scan the place from
end to end, sat by as their mouths sagged open and they cut
glances at each other before I knocked on the Formica with my
knuckles to gain their notice, leaned in conspiratorially, told them
lowly, "Barber school."

About the only thing Elvin turned out to actually know about
Maud Hooper was that she refused to patronize Brady's hair academy, drove instead clean up to Manassas three or four times a year
for a trim. Elvin informed me that, for his part, he'd as soon drive
to Milwaukee for beer, and once we'd parked in front of the Rexall and were walking towards the store, Elvin assured me with the
certainty common only to hairless men that it would take an extravagant fool to pay full retail for a styling and a bit of a dope to
drive two hours to pay it.

Elvin told me he'd once thrown a little business the hair academy's way, apparently back when he'd still had sufficient wispy
thinning topknot tufts to persuade himself that they required occasional proper barbering. "Got me a girl up from Blacksburg,"
Elvin said and then paused there at the landing where the Rexall's
newspaper boxes were chained and locked up each to the next.

He smiled as he cast back and recalled, I figured, the feel of the
woman's fingers on his scalp. "Flattop day," Elvin told me a little
more dreamily than it rated. "I was a few bristles short of a butch
stick, but she didn't let on to care."

Then Elvin winked at me the way he always did when he was
saying one thing about a woman and thinking something else.
Elvin, you see, was essentially a hound without portfolio. He
didn't chase women that I know of, didn't slip around on Erlene
who would surely have presented Elvin occasion to discover if a
man could indulge in wayward romancing unencumbered by his
entrails. Elvin often suggested, however, with the tone that he

took and the quality of his leer that he was harboring scandalous thoughts about one female or another.

I'd once run across Elvin in conversation with a lady of advanced years. They were discussing some sort of colonic ailment her husband was just then enduring, were standing in the post office lobby by a door I had to pass through. So I could hardly avoid them, and Elvin snared me and brought me up-to-date on the nature of that woman's husband's internal complaint.

Then she took her leave, struck out towards the lot, and with advancing disgust I watched Elvin gaze upon her in retreat, looked on as he surveyed her derriere with his incisors on display, and it took him a while as she was a woman of girth and territory. Fortunately for Elvin, she was slow on her pins, was just about old enough to be his mother, so he knew ample leisure for full and deliberate consideration.

Once that woman had gained the door, Elvin visited on me a spot of commentary. "Mmmmm!" he said like a man who'd just enjoyed a fine confection, and I was suffering already a ghastly image of the two of them coupled together when Elvin turned my way to wink and show me the tip of his pebbly tongue.

Elvin was worse with the girls about, both the pubescent adolescents and that variety of sullen hanger-on who'd graduated already from the county high school, had dropped out of community college, lived still at home and worked at the sort of part-time job in town that furnished tattoo and tongue-stud and hair-tint and eyeliner money. That ilk was given to fits of sneering sarcasm, displays of bottomless ennui, tended to dress like tractor mechanics, smoked clove-scented cigarettes, lived on fruit skins and tequila, romanced only parolees and never had a word for a blood relation that wasn't laced with venom.

Living in the country, that sort was usually a good six months behind the various styles and disaffections of authentic urban youth. Our girls were marooned at that spot where the East Village meets up with East Jesus, but what they lacked in timeliness they made up for in ill humor, and they most of them had their parents close at hand to gouge and wound, plain rural folk ordinarily who were shaken to discover that raising a daughter was not a victimless crime.

One of those creatures worked the pharmacy register at the Rexall, and she and Elvin had a pretty notorious history of jousts and set-tos. The girl's given name was Wanda. I happened to know her father a little. He'd sought me out to intervene for him with the IRS once they'd nosed up a decade's worth of questionable Schedule C deductions. The man was an independent plumbing contractor, subbed out on construction about, and he worked alone with lightweight plastic pipe except for those occasions when repairs called for copper or cast iron and his wife would help him out.

He owned a stubby little pickup with the bed awash in fittings, operated out of an "office" in the front room of his house which looked suspiciously like a sofa and a poplar coffee table. He'd laid claim over the years to sundry employees when he'd needed the deductions, had depreciated a regular fleet of wholly nonexistent vans and had written off at twice its cost a prefabricated car shed in the guise of a plumbing-storage facility. The thing actually sheltered his wife's Toyota, his push mower, his propane grill.

By the time I saw him, that gentleman was in the throes of prodigious distress, was convinced he'd go to jail and have his house sold out from under him so as to set right all the chiseling he'd committed through the years. He was fretful and anguished, and as we sat there in discussion on the sofa, the man did everything but beat his breast and wail.

He had, then, problems enough without a daughter to detest him, and once she'd come home from the Rexall she merely ignored us there at first. She was wearing headphones and listening to music with a tinny percussive beat. I could hear the rhythmic whine of it as she plundered through the icebox while I tried to work up estimates of the penalties to be paid. I was just about to devastate her father with a figure when she stepped into the front room with a yogurt tub in hand.

"Hey!" she said in a tone most commonly used on wayward pets. "You eat this?" She tipped up the container to show us the paltry residue left. Her father shook his head and then heard from his child, "Well, somebody fucking did."

What followed was a monologue devoted to the trials she had to suffer, the callous inconsideration she endured from day to day, after which she aired a catalog of her freshest personal hardships which included some sort of hormonal bloat that yogurt seemed to ease. The whole time she talked she never bothered to take her headphones off or lower the volume of her chirpy music, so Wanda ticked off her complaints at pretty much a full-throated shriek.

As her anger swelled and her agitation reached a white-hot pitch, she effectively drowned herself out with the clatter from her tongue stud. The thing knocked against her teeth and, with her mouth for an orchestra shell, sounded to me like a symphony of rim shots.

Wanda either gave out of outrages or yielded to cranial vibration and brought her tirade to a salty close with a string of quite decidedly ungirlish epithets. Then she flung her tub across the room where it bounced off the TV and spilled what yogurt there was in it on the rug. She stalked through the kitchen muttering and left out a back doorway, slammed the screen door hard enough to set the oven timer off.

Her father just let it buzz. He never offered to leave the sofa, tolerated me with a slight flat smile when I told him, "Spirited."

"We used to go fishing, me and her. Up along the river." He said it with no detectable trace of misty paternal nostalgia. Instead

I got the feeling he regretted he'd never shoved her in the water and held her under for maybe an hour or two.

Although I'd never personally witnessed one of the infamous exchanges that Elvin and Wanda were known for there at the pharmacy counter, I had met by then with enough of Elvin's needling palaver and had memories of Wanda's outburst that were quite sufficiently vivid to cause me to want to retire from Elvin once we'd hit the Rexall proper, to induce in me an itch to browse the notions along the far wall. I figured I could hear them well enough from there and remain still safe from shrapnel.

Elvin, however, touched upon that Hooper just as we passed together into the pharmacy proper. He mentioned he'd seen her once at the superstore in the company of her husband, not the superstore out by Lynchburg or the one down Roanoke way but the new superstore at Lexington where he was having a radial mounted. Then Elvin paused for a moment to ruminate, and I got the distinct impression that he was about to embark on a comparative explication of the trio of superstores in our vicinity, felt a need to explain just why he'd chosen one over the others.

That was the trouble. Elvin required some ushering through a conversation, so I couldn't very well just strike out for the notions against the wall, leave Elvin to order up Erlene's ointment and antagonize that girl which was likely to carry Elvin an appreciable distance from Maud Hooper, and I couldn't be sure to succeed at guiding him back her way again.

So I accompanied Elvin across the store and interrupted his rumination, said to him, "Saw them together, did you?" and bore in a little on him.

He nodded, unfolded Erlene's prescription and laid it on the counter. Elvin smiled and said, "Hey, sweetness," to Wanda who snatched up the script and sneered.

"In the superstore?" I said to Elvin. "At Lexington?"

"Yep," Elvin told me, watching Wanda all the while as she

passed Erlene's prescription up to the pharmacist on duty, a woman in a lab coat with a hair-academy flip, and Elvin let himself get caught admiring Wanda's backside which she vented a profanity about. For punctuation her ball bearing rattled sharply against her teeth which, I noticed, served to improve Elvin's leer.

"I ran across him once," I informed Elvin. "Rubbed me wrong," I said. "Seemed kind of a weasel," I added as Elvin stayed fixed still upon Wanda.

He pointed at the tattoo on her neck, a cobra coiled to strike, swabbed his lips with his tongue and made a salacious remark about snake charming.

Wanda was moved to expectorate an uncivil reply which set her stud aclatter, to Elvin's noticeable delight.

"Got in line back of them," Elvin told me, "and he wasn't happy with her." Then Elvin pitched up over the counter to eye Wanda along her length. He frankly contemplated Wanda's rhinestone navel stud, took sneering issue with her sandals on account of they were German.

Wanda responded straightaway with energetic commentary on the topic of ignorant back-hollow hoseheads of Elvin's particular ilk which raised some furious tongue-stud clamor that Elvin savored and soaked in. Then he reached down and adjusted his member in such a way as to cause me to suspect that Wanda's irritation and the racket from her tongue stud were functioning for Elvin as a sexual stimulant.

As I looked on, Elvin rubbed his pants front against the candy rack in a fashion entirely unsuitable for public retail commerce while Wanda fueled him further with corrosive hissed asides between glances towards the pharmacist who was labeling Erlene's ointment.

For my part, I stood there trying still to extract somehow from Elvin further talk of what he'd seen transpire between those Hoopers while Wanda muttered at him with tongue-stud accompaniment as crisp and percussive as hardwood castanets. Pitched against the candy rack, Elvin continued to work his hips, looked hopeful of fathering an Almond Joy. All in all, it was not the seemliest forenoon that I've ever spent.

Wanda finally slapped the ointment sack down on the countertop, rang up the total and demanded payment from Elvin who leered mercilessly at her while he fished his wallet out.

"Grabbed her arm," Elvin said. "Jerked her to him and told her something."

"Those Hoopers?" I asked him, and Elvin nodded while seeking some money out.

Elvin's billfold appeared to have done him service for years. It was crammed full of receipts and coupons and stray tattered bits of paper, was bristling with so much personal archive that Elvin had to mine for cash.

"Struck me as a woman," Elvin told me, "used to being grabbed and jerked." Elvin took care to put his money directly into Wanda's hand so that he could touch her flesh in a way she plainly found repulsive. "Not like you, sugar. Uh-uh."

Wanda flung down his change on the counter and told me, I think, to escort Elvin out. By then, she was so worked up that her stud was raising an infernal ruckus, and I felt like I was taking marching orders from a jarfly. Elvin proved to require but a nudge, was keen to sustain his stimulation and carry it home to his cow barn and his trundle bed. Once back in my Cavalier, he bluntly discouraged talk from me. Elvin showed me his palm as soon as I had touched upon those Hoopers, snorted after I had failed to make on yellow our only traffic light and otherwise held himself and concentrated like a man with a gastric complaint who had rampaging bilious tumult to corral and stopper up.

Elvin turned out to be working through a brand of precoital transference, was occupied (I decided) recalibrating those of Wanda's enticements that had led to Elvin's show of affection for the candy rack. He looked to be seeking a way to affiliate them with Erlene instead.

As we closed on his drive, Elvin seemed to arrive just where he needed to be. He showed me Erlene's ointment, insisted he'd slather it on her feet himself, and then he shared with me news of how he intended to work his way due north. Elvin inventoried the delicates (he called them) Erlene wore beneath her robe. He pantomined for me the way she'd whip that robe open and twitch it off. He announced he'd driven all the way to Roanoke just to buy it.

I was rolling to a stop in back of Elvin's dead Duster when he got to the belt that was whipstitched, he assured me, into place.

2 —⟶ Of course, I knew straightaway just what Elvin meant by the look on the face of a woman who'd met with occasion to grow accustomed to getting grabbed and jerked. There's a brand of domestic cowering that's confined to the eyes alone, a sidelong slightly downcast glance that serves as the equivalent of flinching. It's common to children and yard dogs, but I'd seen it with spouses as well, most particularly once I'd taken up with glorified bookkeeping and had parked my feet under more dinettes than I'd ever feared or hoped.

I generally met with husbands and wives in a state of advancing irritation since, by the time they called me in, they'd faced up to the fact that they likely had taxes to pay. As far as citizenship went, that part of Virginia was in step with the bulk of the country. Everybody, that is to say, wanted the services and the subsidies— the freshly paved roads, the new grade schools, the courthouse renovations, the water projects, the government butter, the Social Security checks, the fees exacted for not growing corn, for not milking cows, for not cutting timber, the food stamps for the slack times, the rebate pittance for the good—but nobody seemed prepared to believe that their tax dollars went for such.

The people I dealt with had usually selected some politician they detested and proved willing to think their levies were financing his lap pool, were keeping him in hair mousse and underwriting Caribbean junkets that he took with lanky buxom women other than his wife. A goodly number of my clients suffered from a strain of Stoney's disease. They nourished their minds exclusively on satellite-dish fare, honed their working sense of civics by tuning in the sorts of shows where guests with dubious qualifications and photogenic features debated by way of assault with nonresponsive propaganda. The prevailing opinion belonged invariably to whoever was least polite.

My clients, then, were frequently irritated on a couple of fronts at once. The natives about were usually tight as a rule and pained to pay out money, and these were honest wages earmarked for a rascally Capital Hill trough. So they were put upon to live with the idea that a chunk of hard-won income would end up with some left-wing (ordinarily) wastrel in a suit. That was just the sort of prospect to make for percolating indignation which oftentimes blossomed into a rant when I'd reveal the payment due.

I had an Avery once who made a sort of living growing bell peppers and cabbage, and I recall we were sitting at his kitchen table where he'd pushed the various condiments and the blood-pressure pills aside to make room for me to antagonize him with his return. He was wearing, I remember, overalls, and he had a pouch of burley tobacco stuck in a pocket at the top of the bib. He kept fishing out pluggets of the stuff to replenish the wad in his mouth which he would, every few minutes, dribble a mucusy scrap of into a bean can.

He was anxious, I could tell, but civil enough until I'd calculated his tax. He didn't owe much, no more than three or four hundred federal dollars, but when I showed him the total, he launched into a rabid diatribe. That Avery was convinced his money would end up with the Congressional Black Caucus. He informed me that he would prefer to simply set fire to the stuff himself which he illustrated and reinforced by taking a match to his 1040. The thing went up for some reason like flash paper and sooted over the ceiling light.

We were both of us a little too shocked to speak. I was authentically stunned anyway while that Avery was occupied tamping out a smoldering nose-hair fire. Along about then his wife came in to ask us what was burning and tell her husband about some Neegra, she called him, she seen on TV. The man was a mayor or an actor or a basketball player—she couldn't remember which—who'd beaten a prostitute half to death over a gold-plated pinky ring.

Her husband massaged his nostrils. He glanced my way and told me, "See."

Occasionally, though, I'd hire out to people who either didn't watch TV or picked up what they could on roof antennas. As a group, they were not so terribly well equipped to rage and vent, lacked the satellite-news-channel models of spitting impropriety.

Those people were poor for the most part, lacked the money for a dish or preferred dipping into the Gospels to watching television, and they ordinarily called me in on the occasion of a letter, one of those charming bits of business favored by the IRS, a bullying appeal to national duty touched with usury. The trouble was generally a neglected filing or some species of underpaid fee, and the news of it would be so mired up in bureaucratic bluster that I'd have to come in and divine exactly what was owed and why.

These were people who customarily coped and managed on their own and were impeccably themselves in front of strangers, so I was exposed in their company to unadulterated family life. The children would romp. The spouses would bicker. The supper dishes would soak in the sink. The dog would sprawl by the kitchen doorsill swabbing its bunghole clean while the cat (there were always cats) dismantled the front-room draperies for sport.

Occasionally, I'd be offered a glass of water from the tap or a slice of picked-over pie from a plate on the stove top, but mostly I was encouraged to tidy the problem up on the quick. Frequently, some family crisis would crop up in the course of my visit, a strain of domestic irritant the wife didn't feel fit to address. So she'd haul it before her husband and serve thereby to call him out as the household's unshaven and slightly rummy embodiment of wrath.

Most of those men would endure the particulars and inflict retribution on whoever within arm's reach appeared in need of a dose of it most. They'd cuff a child or fling a pet, berate sometimes a helpmeet, and the victim would usually look to have rated some medicine to take. But there was a brand of local gentleman I met with from time to time who would wince and seethe and glare at his wife, at his children, in such a way as to cause them to know he had cruelties he was holding in abeyance, abject rage which he was fairly sure, once I'd left, to uncork.

I could usually imbibe a sense of just what those dependents faced since, down to the greasiest eye-rusted lapdog, they had a way of looking condemned.

I remember one fellow in particular, a Settle who goads me still. He'd written off against his income a harrow he'd neglected to buy, and an auditor had found him out and levied an adjustment which that Settle resented in my presence at inordinate length.

Quite naturally, he detested the revenue service but in a cursory and bloodless sort of way. It turned out that Settle reserved his unchecked boiling indignation for the Department of Interior pretty much alone. He'd had dealings with an "operative," that Settle informed me, of the D of I who'd disputed with that Settle over his use of a woodland lot and had, that Settle suspected, alerted the IRS to the unbought harrow.

To hear that Settle tell it, he'd only lopped a few scraggly poplar limbs which he insisted was afforded him as a constitutional privilege couched, he assured me, in the Bill of Rights. Then he cited at me the language that touched on limb-lopping enfranchisement which proved improvisational Federalist hogwash prefaced with "Wherefore."

I heard later that Settle had been caught by a Park Service ranger perched on a deer stand overlooking a meadow that bordered a Blue Ridge Parkway picnic ground. He hadn't owned the woodland lot. The poplar limbs weren't his to cut. And as a practical matter, the Park Service (a branch of the D of I) proved to frown on armed civilians stalking deer where tourists lunched, most especially four months out of season with a Mauser.

Now even at the time, I recognized the man for a prattling ignoramus, and I would have written my usual sniveling letter to the IRS, taken that Settle's money for the service and forgotten all about him but for the fact that his wife dropped a saucer that shattered loudly on the floor just as that Settle was favoring me with a Second Amendment recitation, a spot of talk that came out half boilerplate and half survivalist's prayer.

He only flinched when that dish went to pieces, didn't miss a syllable and declined to glance his wife's way until after he was done. She'd gathered the bulk of the shards and splinters by the time he shifted towards her, and he made a production of fixing the woman with a variety of glare more articulate than anything that had spilled yet from his mouth.

She dropped her head and shrank a little as that Settle turned to me and indulged in a wink and the manner of brief and sour put-upon smile that men of a certain savage stripe are prone to traffic in once they've met with indication that a helpmeet needs correcting. I gleaned enough of a sense of what was coming to have reasonably stepped to the counter, plucked a knife out of the holder there and plunged it in his chest. Instead I shook that Settle's hand and showed myself to the front door.

They were at it already before I could fish out the keys to my Cavalier. I could hear him cataloging his wife's intolerable transgressions, the dull concussion of that woman meeting with the beadboard. From the racket, that Settle might have been tossing a hassock around the house.

I slipped beneath the wheel, and when my engine failed to start, I raised my window and tuned in loudly the qualifying from Martinsville.

3 —⤜ It was entirely Mona's idea that we see Stoney socially. She wouldn't accept my assurances that, in fact, I had no friends to speak of, just assorted nodding acquaintances and the odd trades- man I'd employed, not anyone I was itching to have over for a meal. Mona had read in one of her glossy homemaker magazines an article by some manner of syndicated-TV therapist who'd ad- vised her to honor my buddies and cultivate them as her own in a bid to shore up and reinforce the loving bond between us. So news of my wholesale chum deficiency hit Mona pretty hard.

That homemaker-magazine article had promoted the notion as well that a renovated hairstyle and daring delicates in bed com- bined with bubbly feigned enthusiasm for my leading hobbies would help to fuel and guarantee a spot of heightened passion, but Mona had tried them all at once to no detectable effect. Admit- tedly, Mona's fresh do had been a hair-academy fiasco. She'd dropped by on razor-cut and frosted-highlights day and was fortu- nate to have escaped with her scalp unblistered and her ears intact.

Mona's nightie was one of those items no female has the body to wear, the sort of brief and gauzy negligee that ought to be sold packaged with both an effusive apology and an airbrush. Moreover, she chose to spring the thing on me entirely unawares.

It seems the syndicated TV therapist who'd written the homemaker-magazine article was an advocate of passion gone galvanic through surprise, so Mona had answered my knock on the door screen with a call from the back of the house, a shout from the half bath as if she were grappling with a plumbing complaint. I went in preparing to plunge a toilet, decongest a sink trap, but met instead with Mona in her negligee and do.

I stood there vibrating chiefly while Mona twirled to show herself off, and at length, by way of commentary, I managed to tell her, "Hey."

Mona inflicted upon me a curious scrap of precoital talk. There on the bed as she was nuzzling against me with her bristly head, she delivered a rather learned and rigorously detailed disquisition on the virtues of viscous coupling joints on all-wheel-drive vehicles which she supplemented with a tribute to the Wankel rotary engine before grabbing my organ and rhapsodizing on the magnitude of the thing.

Only later did I recall that I'd been watching Mona's TV the Saturday before with Mona hard beside me on the couch. She'd been rattling on about our future doings as a couple—her usual brand of wishful effervescent filigree—and I'd put a finger to her lips to tempt her to leave off, had indicated I was caught up in a program.

As it happened, the set was tuned to an installment of *Motor-Week*. The host had just climbed out of a sports coupe and was ticking off its features which occasioned a healthy sampling of internal-combustion talk that I let on to comprehend and savor.

I was keenly aware that I didn't rate a radical new hairstyle, gauzy constricting ladies' nightwear, an informed counterfeit zeal for cars, and I'd been in my life in locker rooms sufficiently to know that there was nothing remotely rhapsodic about my member. So I was rigorously unacquainted with cause to think myself a catch, both in the idle abstract and particularly with Mona who I'd been laboring to stave off and frustrate almost from the first. Certainly I'd been guilty of endearments early on. Moral cowardice had wrung from me the odd show of affection those occasions it was easier just to yield ground and agree than take open issue with Mona's plans and Mona's declarations. I hadn't, however, gone out of my way to cultivate her child, had declined most Sundays to join with Mona in evangelical Episcopalian worship, had vented in time my low opinion of Mona's deplorable taste in decor.

I'd even called her Stacy once in what passed for us as the throes of passion—the name of a starlet I'd seen in a translucent tube top in a magazine.

As far as I could tell, I was a regular thicket of unbewitching personal traits and squandered human potential, so I was loath to endure the decisive bother of casting Mona aside when I believed myself an awfully solid candidate for jilting and felt confident any day with Mona might well be my last. Mona, though, proved a little too busy detesting her future ex-husband to pay me proper withering regard. The chances seemed scant she'd get lured away by a local available male unless she weakened against eau de kerosene and incipient emphysema.

In fact, the longer I elected to sit by and wait for Mona to throw me over, the more of a fixture for her I became until we had sufficient history between us to serve as a species of bond. So my insults and rank indifference, callous inconsideration got construed by Mona as trifling bumps in our thoroughfare of love.

After nearly eight months of Mona's tender understanding and unqualified forgiveness, despair drove me into the arms of another woman, or desperation anyway and a dearth of options otherwise prompted me to subject a redhead to what magic I could muster.

She worked as a flag girl for the highway department, waved motorists around paving jobs and bridge-abutment repairs and managed with her willowy frame and her unobstructed midriff to slow them in ways that the threat of a state-police summons never could.

Her given name was Pat, but she'd picked up Suki somewhere along the way. Because she was twenty-two when I met her, she took my word I was thirty-five and probably still considered me a geezer, but that hardly mattered since she was mostly keen on the clients I laid claim to, the glamorous life of high finance I let on to have led.

When I first saw her, she was standing at the magazine rack in the grocery mart, was wearing still her highway-department togs (brogans and short shorts, a halter top under a Day-Glo mesh-weave vest) and flipping through a celebrity monthly. Not the celebrity monthly devoted to the homes of celebrities, or the celebrity monthly given over entirely to celebrity diets and celebrity cooking, or the celebrity monthly that traffics primarily in celebrities' spouses and celebrities' children, or the one concerned with pious displays of celebrity spirituality. No, Suki was riffling through the celebrity periodical that features unflattering photos of blubbery lapsed celebrities, stories about celebrity heartache and celebrity legal misadventure, celebrity stalkers, celebrity tirades, catastrophic celebrity karma reversals.

Suki was hardly the sort of creature I would have ordinarily talked to, provided she'd not asked me for directions or the time. Certainly I would have studied her surreptitiously and indulged in unholy thoughts about her which, as I passed along her aisle, I managed vividly to do. I wouldn't, though, have instigated any actual commerce with her but, I guess, for the reckless state of mind that Mona had driven me to.

The cover of Suki's magazine was dominated by a photo of a frankly enraged megawatt leading man. There were smaller pictures around the edges of news anchors and TV actors captured, a few of them, in the company of wives and husbands not their own or alone in open bibulous emotional distress. Down in a corner was a photo of a ratty porcine blonde who'd once been, her caption insisted, a Solid Gold dancer. That enraged leading man, though, was the star of that magazine cover due to a spot of sensational business he figured prominently in.

By all accounts, he'd become entirely unhinged in a tony Aspen restaurant. I'd read an in-depth treatment of the incident a scant two days before while waiting my turn for Peggy to trim my hair. So I was aware that actor had questioned a charge on his dinner bill, a gratuity for the captain that had been added to the total even though, as it turned out, the captain was off sick that particular night and unavailable for the duties that a surcharge might reward.

When that leading man asked his waiter to point out the captain to him and the waiter confessed the captain wasn't actually about, the manager got called over and could have settled the whole affair with an apology, an adjustment and the offer of a cordial. Instead the manager chose to invoke strict restaurant policy in such matters, failed to offer to cut the captain's gratuity even in half and succeeded at suggesting with his tone and bearing together that he was loath to think well of a movie star who inspected dinner checks.

Now that actor was already at the heart of a spot of notorious ongoing turmoil. The supermodel who'd borne his daughter and had lived with him as a mate had lately undergone a dramatic change of romantic persuasion. She'd taken up with her publicist's sister, and they'd been photographed about in candid displays of Amazonian affection. That leading man had mounted what proved a fruitless effort to win her back, had offered himself anyway for a frolic with the pair of them together which got loosed as an indication of his base perverted nature and evidence of his unfitness to share custody of his child.

To compound his troubles, a movie he'd starred in had opened indifferently just as a videotape he'd made in a motel room with a buxom teen had surfaced for retail purchase on the World Wide Web. Bits of it had shown up on various of the twenty-four-hour news channels, most particularly the part where the young woman chortled once she'd shucked him from his drawers. While it's one thing for a bookkeeper to be indifferently endowed, a leading man ought not to drive a woman to fits of helpless laughter, most particularly on high-definition digital videotape.

So that actor had fled to Colorado for a quasi-religious retreat. His people anyway had let it be known that he intended to pass a week or two in contemplative seclusion, meant to pray and meditate and enjoy daily high colonics, heal and center, ski and diet, relocate his joie de vivre. In truth, though, he spent his afternoons lying around with his entourage—a beefy security consultant, an unemployable middle-school pal, a Miss October from '97, a Filipina shiatsu masseuse, a gastroenterologist with impeccable drug connections and no license to practice in any state or country of the world. They watched pornography, ate snack crackers, drank assorted flavored vodkas, dosed themselves with pharmaceuticals when the pressures of life closed in.

So that actor was not entirely himself in that tony Aspen restaurant. He'd driven his supermodel girlfriend into the arms of another woman, had touched off with his stunted member a bout of national hilarity, had gained about twenty-five pounds on a steady diet of Absolut and Wheat Thins, and he found his grasp of the language (as he vented and he raged) shaky and compromised. That fellow was in no state to call up the words to frame his indignation over the charge of a gratuity for a captain home in bed which left him to spit out the profanities that came instead to hand.

He made, then, the manner of scene the patrons couldn't help but notice. If he'd been, say, a dentist from Boise, they might have taken it all in stride, cut him the odd irritated glance and gone on about their meals since it's grown to be common for adults to pitch public adolescent fits. But that gentleman was a star who'd played the president on the screen. The most of his fellow diners had seen him pilot a deep-space probe, had cheered for him while he and a starlet known for her tresses and her grin fought off an entire legion of swarthy bioterrorists in a race against time and narrative coherence through subway tunnels under Queens. They'd seen him expire piecemeal from exposure high in the Hindu Kush, die from his wounds with his kilt upflung in the Battle of Culloden, succumb histrionically to adder venom in a hovel near Oquitos and just generally perish for four reels in a wretched comedy.

So he was known to those restaurant patrons, beloved even among a few, and they all of them paid strict notice to that leading man's tirade in preparation for their inevitable news-channel interviews.

Broadcast reports of that fellow arguing over a dinner check would have certainly served to further tarnish that actor's troubled image, would have rendered him lovelorn, ill equipped, lascivious and cheap, hardly better than your average civilian. That would have been preferable, though, to the unflattering press he got once he fell to grappling with that restaurant manager in Aspen and managed in the process to jar his hairpiece slightly loose which injected "balding" into the equation.

The thing didn't come off entirely but skewed and rode up in the front, and the backing lifted into view with every lunge he undertook which certainly would have been adequately humiliating without the attendant exposure of a crop of failed plugs underneath. So that actor displayed two layers of tonsorial vanity at once which proved far more photogenic than his niggling parsimony, and a patron or two had cameras handy to capture the moment with.

One of those photos found its way onto the cover of the magazine that Suki was thumbing through in the grocery mart, and I saw fit to pause and tap that picture with my foremost finger, mined the nerve to say to Suki, "Some rug, huh?"

"Real hothead," I told her and tapped for effect that leading man again. "Used to work with him." Then I shook my head and plied her with a wince, let on to be fully stocked with unbecoming revelations which prompted Suki to draw a quick sharp breath and fairly shriek back, "No!"

I had recognized by then that there are essentially two types of Americans. We are a nation comprised in small part of people with monopolizing concerns—faith to practice and observe, activism to pursue, consuming careers or simply blithe impervious self-involvement—while the balance of us are ready candidates for frivolity. On the frothy end were those of us who'd come somehow to hear that the leading man with the unsuccessful plugs and the jostled hairpiece who'd dispatched the lanky supermodel mother of his child into the loving arms of her publicist's sister had done so by dint of a newfound zeal for anal penetration, the brand of fact a civilian would have need to apply himself to know.

That's just the manner of item to get buried and finessed, and I recall that I found it well into the body of the piece I'd read while I was waiting my turn for Peggy to cut my hair, and even then I had to decipher just what that fellow had hoped to put where. Suki, as it turned out, knew everything I knew about that actor, but the difference between us was that Suki cared. She was naturally given to empathetic emotional involvement with anybody she'd ever met occasion to see on her TV as opposed to her neighbors and sundry relations who tended to seem profoundly less real.

Suki's interest in me was immediate and unambiguous. I had been in the personal presence (as far as she knew) of a megawatt leading man who'd known my name and paid for my services, had shaken my hand a time or two, so I was fully equipped to communicate the celebrity experience. Suki proved hungry for the details, lived for firsthand celebrity chat.

I had nerve enough by then to invite her to join me for coffee next door at the torpedo shop where they made, very likely, our nation's worst meatball sandwich which was heavy on ketchup and bread crumbs and suet-laced ground beef. Their java was little better, but we nursed some anyway as I fabricated for Suki a working friendship with that actor—business dinners, Dodger games, personalized Christmas cards—and Suki grabbed me and poked me and smacked me fondly in her unbridled excitement.

Suki confessed she didn't think much of the supermodel girlfriend who'd taken up romantically with her publicist's sister. She revealed that she'd had Sapphic relations with a junior-college classmate, and she spoke of their dalliance with volume enough to attract the gawking notice of the assistant manager in his plastic gloves making a turkey hero along with the telephone repairman who'd ordered the thing.

Suki described in bluff detail encounters she'd had with her junior-college classmate like a biologist might discuss the mating habits of a frog. Suki allowed anymore she far preferred men, and she reached over and gripped my arm as she attempted to acquaint me with the heady female sensation of sexual congress with a male. I felt lucky to be sitting. The assistant manager rained a fistful of shredded lettuce onto the floor while the phone man, for his part, leaned against the condiment sneeze guard and groaned.

Suki was hardly finished as she'd yet to touch upon the matter of anal penetration which she declared she'd had requested of her more times than she could count. She'd given the topic a fair degree of thought and had decided the widespread currency of pornographic movies—in the video store, on the satellite dish, seeping in through the cable modem—had supplied men a false impression of what routinely got stuck where.

The phone man mustered somehow sufficient muscle memory to make his way to the door and motion to his partner out in their van who showed up in time to take in Suki's sphincter disquisition.

In short, her view was that bungholes had been manufactured for egress alone. She allowed that the boys she'd turned down had pouted for a while, but they'd settled at the last, the way men will, for what penetration they could get.

By the time Suki had paused to sip her coffee and dump a bit more sweetener in, I'd known her for probably all of twenty minutes, hadn't even yet bothered to discourage Suki from calling me, like she did, Sean. And yet I felt chummier with her than people I'd known the bulk of my natural life because Suki, I guess, was lacking in editorial inhibitions. She gave voice to nearly everything that popped into her head much in the fashion of my Aunt Ida on my mother's side, but Suki declined to dwell on the value of a nickel in 1934, failed to pine for Truman or blubber over shelties she'd once owned.

Suki was randy and flirtatious and deliciously underdressed, struck me as just the sort of creature I might discourage Mona with. So I labored to make myself riveting with lies about other celebrities, clients of mine whose enormous wealth and lavish deductible expenses were only outstripped by their pecadilloes and deviant indulgences.

I learned that Suki stopped by the grocery mart every Tuesday and Thursday evenings to shop for the icebox dinners that she and her roommate were partial to. That's when she'd loiter at the magazine rack to catch up on her culture, so I began to orchestrate outings with Mona to pick up the odd food item those occasions Suki might well be about.

It took a few weeks for me to run up on her with Mona in close tow, but we came wheeling one night from the baking-goods aisle and nearly collided with her. Suki squealed at the sight of me and and caught me up in a full-body hug that I hoped might convey upon me standing as a Lothario. I had been for a pretty good while by then attempting to acquaint Mona with the notion that I required a slew of women in my life, that I was the sort of man who liked to shift among his females, preferred a populated stable to one filly at a time.

I had long entertained intentions, that is, of saying as much to Mona, had even worked up and practiced a few occasions in my bathroom glass a presentation designed to sound like a spontaneous bit of talk on the topic of women I'd enjoyed Old Testament knowledge of, creatures I kept up with carnally, dallied with from time to time which, I reasoned, would make me seem a man no one female could snare.

The problem was, however, I'd yet to spit my presentation out.

My plan was for Suki to serve as an edifying visual aid. I'd noticed that she was given to helpless displays of affection, and after my hug she stood there nattering with my fingers twined in hers. I figured that once she'd taken leave and wandered out of sight, Mona would press me to tell her where exactly I knew Suki from and so present me occasion to prevaricate.

Unfortunately, Suki turned out to be shopping that evening with her roommate who, by the looks of him, worked for the highway department as well. He was gritty and sunburned and smelled of asphalt, had some manner of serpent tattooed onto his ropy forearm.

"Ronnie," Suki told me as she jabbed a thumb in his direction. "Sean," she said to him and added, "Remember?" before naming the leading man with the rug and the plugs and the tasteless spate of cruel publicity.

"Oh," Ronnie said and jerked his head by way of a hello. "Come on," he told Suki and laid a veiny hand upon her backside, steered her away from me and Mona by way of a lobe of derriere.

Consequently, Mona failed to ask me the question I had hoped for, didn't trouble herself to pay any heed to Suki in retreat. Instead she jotted a note on her list and said, "What about my chicken marsala?"

I was allowed a quarter minute of blank uncomprehending silence before she added, "For dinner. That friend of yours." She labored to name him. "Rocky," she said.

So I eventually had to invite him since Mona wouldn't let it die, and I spied Stoney one evening out by his van drop-kicking cats in the yard. I walked over, and we indulged in the usual laconic formalities made up of two parts viscous expectorants to every scrap of actual talk, and I finally got around to asking Stoney if he thought he might like to come to dinner one night at my house.

Of course, I made mention of Mona and laid the blame entirely on her and then looked on as Stoney gazed across the meadow towards my rental, watched him weigh the bother of an evening out against potential virtues, endured him to spit and shake his head and tell me simply, "No."

4—⟶ Mona was not remotely the sort congenial to "No." I had hardly informed her that Stoney had declined our invitation before she charged out of my rental house and stalked across the yard, gained the drive and made for Stoney's prune-infested ditch. She cleared the road without a glance, fairly yodeled out, "Yoohoo!" and raised, I guess, a shout from Stoney that I missed from where I was since he proved to be inserted partway through his pumphouse door, was stanching a leak with a turn on a band clamp when Mona arrived to call him out.

I chose to watch from behind my door screen, elected to linger out of view and thereby avoid the searching glance that Stoney was bound to cast my way. As far as I knew, he'd never met Mona, so she started in on him with (as best I could tell) orienting niceties. She pointed in the general direction of my rental property and acquainted Stoney, I have to think, with her romantic attachment to me, probably gave it out as something on the order of betrothed.

Stoney, for his part, tapped his chin with the slotted end of his screwdriver and looked in time to be actively cowering as Mona peppered him with talk. I withdrew behind the jamb once he had turned to peer my way and seek me out with a spot of perusal that was tainted with betrayal. I saw Stoney nod, watched Mona insist on reaching out to shake his hand before she left him vanquished and deflated in his weedy yard.

There was not, of course, authentic marsala wine available about, so Mona usually substituted cooking sherry mixed with merlot. She had come to consider chicken marsala her signature entrée, had convinced herself the people about she'd fed the concoction to—both at home and as her contribution to countless potluck affairs—had been charmed by the stuff and won to its earthy quasi-Italianate flavors which, in fact, was a wholesale culinary delusion on Mona's part.

By that time, I'd eaten Mona's chicken marsala more occasions than I cared to count, or had shoved helpings anyway around my plate to make them look devoured. The recipe that Mona had clipped from one of her homemaker magazines called for figs and pinenuts, shallots and fresh thyme, a bread-crumb coating for the chicken, butter and a touch of cream. Local necessity, however, along with Mona's inflated sense of her improvisational skills, had conspired to work an unfortunate renovation on the dish. Mona used prunes and cashews, spring onions and dried sage, pulverized saltines, margarine, evaporated milk. The result was greasy and sweet like something you'd get at the state fair on a stick.

Stoney showed up in clean twill trousers and a freshly laundered poplin shirt, looked to have wet and combed what hair was left to him and smelled like he'd bobbed for wintergreen mints in his side yard fuel-oil tank. Once he'd entered the house, however, his scent got routed and overcome by the stink from the panful of creamed corn Mona was scorching on the stovetop. She left it to bubble and burn while she greeted Stoney and showed him to the couch. Mona offered what cashews she'd not had need of in her chicken marsala, encouraged me to spread cheese for Stoney on the rye toasts that she'd bought.

Ever so eventually, Mona turned her notice once more to her corn which was burned on the bottom and stuck to the pan and, by all rights, beyond salvage. Mona, though, scraped the crusty bits up, added a pinch of cayenne to the stuff, an overambitious dash of onion salt and then pronounced that creamed corn blackened in the Cajun way. That was typical Mona. Her culinary gifts tended towards the semantic.

Stoney lacked the social skills to disguise the fact he'd rather have stayed home. He drank the bourbon I gave him, ate a few nuts, smelled some cheese but declined to ingest it. He even mounted a bid to hold up his end of a chat I instigated on the topic of the skeletal leavings of a creature plowed up in Ecuador. The bones indicated that the thing had been reptilian and two-headed which I had to think Stoney had watched a few pseudoscience specials about.

I was attempting to force cheese on Stoney when I saw him swivel around and peek out my front window towards his house across the road. He had a yellow bulb for a porch light that he'd left to burn while he was away, and I watched Stoney linger over the glow for a moment. He seemed almost moved to grief by the evening he'd agreed to squander on us, appeared to miss his frozen breaded cutlet, his cat dander, his house shoes, his usual television shows, his heaps of periodicals, his freedom to go quite audibly vaporish each occasion he met with the urge.

From us, Stoney was getting just Dickel and nuts, cheese he couldn't be troubled to eat, and I was worrying him with bursts of conversational excelsior, a manner of talk I'd never inflicted on Stoney when we were out by the street. He had to suspect, like I did, that the evening would only deteriorate once we'd sat at the table and Mona had favored us with her full attention.

She was mercifully occupied in the kitchen but still chirped at us now and then, would come to the doorway with her slotted spoon and warble out, "Isn't this fun?" or "I think it's so nice when neighbors get together," and then she would shoot us a toothy grin in a display of dogged effervescence.

Once she'd called us to the table, me and Stoney struggled upright and trudged across the room to a meal that turned out, somehow, oddly savory. The char on the corn seemed to temper somehow the inordinate treacle of Mona's marsala sauce, and the cheese-and-bread-crumb topping on Mona's broccoli-and-scallion gratin would, once it had cooled a little, detach entirely from the roughage, so a fellow could get his dairy unencumbered by florets.

Unfortunately, the conversation was appreciably less winning. Mona was the sort who insisted on orchestrating her table chat. She would formally introduce a topic and invite commentary, would shift her notice primly from guest to guest to guest as she extracted dull involuntary freshets of opinion which Mona was equipped to take for sparkling dinner conversation. Stoney foiled her, though, since he preferred to feed before a plate and remained for a solid quarter hour in no fit shape to speak.

He invariably had a mouthful of chicken or cheese, even shoveled in the corn with some fervor, and once he'd scarfed up all the actual helpings he could tolerate, Stoney applied himself to sopping with Mona's store-bought garlic bread. She preferred the split-top loaf with the herbs and the saturating lubrication, so Stoney was obliged to wring out the slices to make absorbing room for sauce. He went at his dinner seepage with a conscientiousness that left him as closed to chat with a bread-crust in hand as he had been with a fork.

So Mona was obliged to turn her full regard my way instead, and she laid serial siege to me with her inquiries. What did I think of the national economic forecast in the short term? Had I heard about the dogwood blight? Did I have affected trees? Were I the

ruling judge, what sentence would I pass on the Wichita woman
who'd gone off on a date and left her infant in a bureau drawer?
Was I familiar with the cause of the violent tribal unrest in Sri
Lanka? Acquainted with the asteroid threatening Mercury? The
health benefits of kale? Did I have an opinion on woven sisal as a
flooring product? A position on federal anti-ballistic-missile policy? Favorites among the Oscar contenders? Any use for herbal
cures?

I tend not to be, I'll have to confess, expansive on demand. My
involved deliberately reasoned views and even my transient passions never quite seemed to meet with Mona's rotating concerns.
And since I wasn't company, Mona never permitted me to stray
however I saw fit from the topic at hand. Guests were allowed to
wander a little but never got encouraged at it because, by nature,
Mona wanted to know just what she wanted to know and wasn't
looking to come by the manner of piffle you might want to tell her.

Not that Mona was a listener with an appetite for lively honest
debate. She would lord over a social gathering with a reliably half-
cocked sense of what sophisticated people in the wide world were
discussing, was keen to inflict their manner of sparkling conversation on us. She was guilty, at bottom, of a brand of chauvinistic
provincialism and had allies about among some locals who, like
Mona, were determined to prove that they didn't reside in the ignorant backwater where they, in fact, resided.

Mona was just the sort to declare that the Wednesday-night
trout amandine entrée served at the clubby interstate junction
restaurant—a place called The Downs with fake chestnut paneling
and a home office in Cincinnati—was the equal of any dish a person might go clean to Paris to get. She proved evermore prepared,
when outlanders came calling, to haul them up to see a mountain
rift, a well-known local rocky gully, that Mona insisted on refer-
ring to as "the Yosemite of the East."

She visited extravagant gobbets of entirely unmerited praise on
what Mona insisted was our splendid colony of artisans. We had a

blacksmith who made fireplace tools, a fellow who gouged out poplar dough bowls, a woman who cobbled up wind chimes from fishing line and tarnished flatware and a painter who worked, Mona told it, in the style of Whistler and of Sargent. He preferred to canvas, however, slabs of cedar and squares of mirror glass.

We, in fact, compared poorly to the capitals of Europe, not even to mention the eastern-seaboard megalopoli. By meager backwater standards, we hardly constituted a shining example, had no enduring local traditions of craft or cuisine that we worked to uphold. We had barely preserved any architectural heritage to speak of, were manufactured-home enthusiasts, strip-mall habitués. Our local drama guild had disbanded. The garden club met biannually and only then in order to play canasta and recriminate. A fellow south of town who'd earned a name for himself with his homemade salt-cured hams turned out to have been buying the things all along from a packing plant in Georgia.

We had some decent fishing here and there, predominantly crappie, and pockets (thanks to timbering) of spectacular erosion, but we didn't have much of anything Mona liked to think we had, particularly a native disposition for stimulating table talk. The trend, once the dishes were cleared, was for groaning and rollicking eructations.

Once Stoney had swabbed his plate clean and had flopped against his chair back, he behaved like common fauna for a time, did about everything short of gargling and evacuating. He loosed the occasional phlegmy necknoise by way of conversation, proved to harbor instead of opinions a limitless methane supply.

He wore Mona down. She'd visit on Stoney an ornate considered inquiry, permit him an untroubled quarter minute to cobble up a response and then reformulate her question and put it to him once again which would invariably incite Stoney to a strain of commentary. He'd either snort and tell her, "Uh-huh," or shake his head and tell her, "Naw."

He gave the impression of being a fellow with no elaboration in him. I knew it to be a masterful bit of business on Stoney's part since I'd stood at my mailbox and suffered the man to hose me off with talk more occasions than I could possibly recall. I could see he'd grown comfortable, that the bourbon and the wine he'd thrown back throughout the meal like so much water had put him at ease enough so that he might have mustered chat. But he just sat and let Mona's overtures rebound off him and expire, turned out to be devoted to his manner of palaver as faithfully as Mona was to hers.

Mona preferred sowing tidy rows of cultivated seed while Stoney could only stomach volunteers.

So Mona plagued Stoney with all the ordnance at her disposal, and Stoney hunkered down and loosed the occasional stingy neck-noise back until Mona had altogether despaired of extracting his opinions on the congressional omnibus-budget bill, on the conflict in Ramallah, on the raging Texas refinery fire some fool had set with a cigarette which led, naturally, to the topic of alternative fuel sources—wind generation, solar collection, hybrid automobiles—that Stoney successfully resisted comment on as well.

He refused to be drawn out on the local influx of coyotes, had next to nothing to say about our legislative delegate who a trooper had discovered at an interstate rest stop shut up in the trunk of his sedan. That fellow was bound with tape and largely naked from his shirttails down, proved keen to portray himself the victim of a simple misunderstanding which the young man who got caught with his Visa card endorsed as his view as well.

Even when Mona touched upon the celebrity scandal of the day—a spot of litigation between a starlet and her cosmetic surgeon who had either made something bigger than that starlet had intended or had left some item smaller than she'd hoped—Stoney couldn't be bothered to weigh in on our decadent frothy culture and take occasion to congratulate Mona for persevering unimproved.

Instead, Stoney nodded as a sign he was aware that she had spoken and loudly oversaw the circulation of a gob of spit.

Mona gave up on Stoney after that and exiled us to the front porch where we roamed for a time and discharged vapors, settled on the glider at length. Stoney was the sort who carried toothpicks in his front shirt pocket, the mint-flavored cellophane-wrapped variety filched from the luncheonette, and he fished out a couple and offered me one, so we mined tooth gaps for a time to the rhythmic metallic complaint of my corroded glider works.

We listened to the cry of a woodcock from across the meadow by the ditch, the snort and crash of a deer punching through my ironwood hedgerow. We could see the lights of Dulles-bound jets overhead and barely hear the hum of their engines along with the chopping bark of our neighbor's mutt from up at the end of the road. He was some sort of unfortunate collie mix with the tail of a terrier and the ears of a hound, and he passed his life chained to a stake atop a patch of rooty hardpan, tended to bark with the diligence most dogs reserve for nosing their nether parts.

In time, we heard the voice of his master—a Cobb from local sorry stock—shouting out from his house to suggest that his mongrel shut for fuck's sake the hell up. The creature paused, I suppose, to mull the proposal and consider his canine options. He elected after a minute or so to set about barking again. That's pretty much when Stoney saw fit to ask me, "Where'd your dog get off to?"

Now I have in my repertoire a facial expression that serves me at such times. It's a squinty look of bewilderment, the stripe of face I'd instinctively pull if I got asked on the street for directions to Murmansk in colloquial Farsi. I'd learned to conjure that look for inquiries I hoped to shunt aside, and I inflicted the thing on Stoney who, maybe because the light was low, chose to come back at me as if I hadn't made his question out and wasn't so much confounded as simply a little hard of hearing.

"You know," he said and described with his hands my canine from New York. He said he'd seen me playing with Lincoln out in my front yard, had joined anyway with that dog in watching me throw a ball and fetch it. Then Stoney sniffed to bring to my notice the dog-urine stink of my glider works.

"Oh," I said. "Him." And I plied Stoney with a scrap of my consoling fabrication, described Lincoln as a stray who'd just fetched up one night from somewhere and had lingered for a while in passing through. "I gave him some scraps, a little water, but he wasn't ever mine."

"Really?" Stoney said.

Now in that part of the world, there were essentially two ways to take a "Really?" You'd occasionally get a "Really?" instead of a nod and an "I see," but more commonly a "Really?" served as handy local shorthand for "Yeah, right, you lying sack of shit."

Stoney's "Really?" struck me as a hybrid of the two. He was a guest, after all, at my house and had been raised to be polite, but quite clearly he'd watched me with Lincoln and knew what to make of what he'd seen. Consequently, we observed a passing moratorium on chat, a brief silence during which Stoney failed to impeach me with his view that I'd actually owned the dog I had assured him was a stray while, for my part, I held in check the fabrication I'd concocted on the allergies that stole from me the joy of keeping pets.

As a manly compromise, we rode the glider and said nothing in a way that probably didn't look strategic. Mona, had she come outside, would not have seen we were communing, would have encumbered us with topics and resolves fit for debate when Stoney and I were having a gender-specific exchange already. We were failing to quarrel, electing to let discrepancies go ignored, doubts remain unexercised, contradictions unexamined. Stoney was effectively saying to me, "I forgive you, brother," without signs or words or any sort of palpable display beyond the odd squeak and warble of intermittent gastric distress.

For my part I shifted and groaned in such a way as to inform Stoney, "I know you know I'm lying to you. I'm glad you're willing not to care."

Shortly thereafter, Stoney felt need to relocate some spit which he performed with sudsy clamor enough to attract my full regard and so lured me to look on as he nodded and told me finally, "Yep." Stoney added beyond it, "Kept a dog once for some people."

He confessed to only ever having owned yard cats himself. Stoney told me he'd grown up on a tobacco farmstead in Tidewater where they'd needed cats to rid the place of moles. They'd tried terriers early on, but the dogs had killed their chickens while the cats proved satisfied with a steady regimen of vermin—moles and mice and wood rats with the odd tree squirrel for sport. So Stoney had known meager occasion to learn anything of dogs and had kept cats out of habit once he'd moved west to the valley where he grew the sorts of leggy weeds and prickly creeping brambles that no self-respecting rodent would even gnaw on for a snack.

But then some people (that's all he called them at first) had asked him to tend their dog once the woman they'd usually relied upon, a quasi-professional sitter, had begged off her obligations due to a gallbladder inflammation which served to shunt Stoney onto medical matters for a time. As it turned out, he descended from people given to gall- and kidney stones and so was equipped with anecdote enough to drive me to distraction. I recall talk of the urinary torments of a cousin twice removed before I lost the thread of Stoney's disquisition for a while.

I suspect I looked attentive hard beside him on the glider, stayed upright anyway and grunted enough to make me seem engaged, but I drifted in truth among my own stray percolating worries before Stoney ensnared me at last with talk of the actual dog he'd kept—a Welsh corgi afflicted with a crusty skin complaint and an appetite for table legs and shoes.

Stoney raised a leg to put on display the tooth-scarred welt of his brogan. "Amos, they called him," Stoney told me. Then pointed with his nose out across the woodlands in a vaguely northerly direction. "Those Hoopers," he said. "You know. The ones up the pike."

I nodded, I believe, told Stoney, "Right. Those Hoopers up the pike," though I was busy primarily admiring Stoney's deft way with a tactic, recognized at the time that Amos the corgi was simply Stoney's way in. Somehow I sensed straightaway that Stoney had come by word I was sniffing around, had gotten wind I was asking about him in a pointed and resolute fashion, something closer to prying than local custom tended to embrace.

Talk in those parts was often incidentally indiscreet. It was perfectly acceptable for people to meet, say, in a grocery-mart aisle and catch up with each other in a casual scattershot way—ask after spouses and relations, the circumstances of mutual friends, glory in the weather or actively fret over treacherous world events. Now in the course of such exchanges, scraps of imprudent information (the sorts of asides and enlargements surely better left unsaid) were prone to figure into the weft and weave of the conversation.

A citizen couldn't, for instance, distinguish among our local crop of McGuires, indicate anyway the particular clan he was meaning to touch upon without signifying mention of some current family scandal that set the McGuires he intended to speak of apart from all the rest. So if a fellow about was hoping to tell how he'd hunted with a McGuire and they'd between them enjoyed no measurable luck to speak of, he would usually have to establish that the specific McGuire he meant was the uncle of the girl who'd run with a boy the law was after in Blacksburg, a boy who'd tried to force his ardor on the drive-thru teller at the bank, the loose bottle blonde with the baby she'd had by a Mauritanian, and not a decent hardworking Mauritanian but a Third World layabout.

In local circles it was considered wholly proper to linger briefly over such peripheral details, discuss the niece, the boy, the bottle blonde, vilify the Mauritanian, wonder what kind of ungodly

Sodom Blacksburg had become and only then get back to the matter of the actual McGuire in question who rated mention merely for the deer he hadn't shot.

My transgression was that I'd solicited talk directly, hadn't waited for information on Stoney to reach me roundabout in the context of some wholly unrelated conversation which called for news of Stoney's dealings with those Hoopers up the pike as passing means of clarifying family pedigree. Instead I'd made blunt queries of Elvin who'd passed them, doubtless, to Erlene who'd met occasion to trot them out for some friend of hers or three, and word of my indelicate interest had circulated locally until Stoney had entered probably into some exchange in town during the course of which I qualified for mention. There on my porch, Stoney seized the opportunity to answer what I'd asked some weeks before and elsewhere to someone otherwise.

"I worked for those Hoopers," Stoney declared. "Got to know them both a little." He said it in a way that impressed me as wistful and forlorn.

I nodded and made a noise I hoped would serve as lubricational, a kind of throaty inarticulate "and then?" Stoney responded shortly with mention of the sink valve he'd replaced, the double dead bolt he'd installed, the bathroom gooseneck he'd unclotted.

"That dog of theirs, Amos," Stoney told me. He smiled. "Went everywhere I went."

I could sense he was ripe to apprise me of what precisely had transpired between him and those Hoopers to leave him touched with nagging melancholy. Moreover, it struck me that there on my reeky glider in the moonless dark Stoney was likely to be more singular, less wayward in his chatter than was the case those days when I'd check my mail and we'd jaw across his ditch.

Out in the open afternoon, Stoney proved frequently helpless against distractions. He'd interrupt himself to point out a buzzard, examine ear reamings, correct a cat. In the lull, he'd invariably mislay the general thrust of the conversation which Stoney was rarely nostalgic enough about to try to seek out again. He'd christen instead a new topic and flog it until something else had caught his eye. Out on the porch, though, there was little that might put him off those Hoopers, and I got the feeling Stoney was settling into the matter at hand.

By way of preamble, he told me how those Hoopers had come to hire him, mentioned the tradesman who'd recommended him, a bricklayer from a neighboring town, and Stoney failed like he normally would to get shunted off onto masonry matters. He didn't touch on his taste in patio patterns or his preference in portland cement but hewed to those Hoopers in a way that, for Stoney, approached unprecedented.

I had reason, then, to anticipate a valuable spot of talk, something pertinent from Stoney and maybe genuinely revealing, and I recall I was marshaling questions for Stoney, organizing them in my head—nothing probing, just modest directional queries to help keep him on the rails—when I noticed an ebb in the clatter Mona had been raising at the sink.

She'd been busy with the creamed corn pot, had been pecking at the char, gouging and scouring and scraping by turns at the adamantine corn scab that covered the saucepan bottom to a quarter inch in depth. Mona had given up on the thing and had left it to steep in the sink which, unfortunately for me, had freed her up, so the sound that I was hearing instead of tinny Revere Ware racket was her footfall on the floor. I allowed myself to hope that she was meaning to crumb the table, that she had flatware still to gather, leftovers to pack away, but Mona failed to pause at my dining niche and continued to the door where she fetched up at the screen and uncorked a frisky "Well now."

Stoney fell silent. I turned with him towards her, and we watched as Mona reminded us how awfully nice she thought it was when neighbors got together. Then she opened the door screen and bid us to come to the table for dessert as it was Mona's way to be one part bubbly hostess and three parts tireless guest wrangler. She wasn't happy unless she kept her dinner victims on the move, would size them up for comfort and, once they were fully at their ease, drive them out of the room they were in to someplace else altogether and then watch and wait for a fresh occasion to shift them yet again.

I wanted to tell her that Stoney and I, in fact, were comfortable on the glider, inform Mona that we were just at that moment engaged in conversation on a rather delicate matter that was of interest to us both. I entertained the idea of asking her to retire please to the crawl space, draw closed the plywood door behind her and sit for an hour or two in the dark.

Just then, however, Stoney stood up out of courtesy perhaps or due to a helplessness against confections. He spat over the porch rail into the shrubbery and asked Mona, "You got pie?"

Mona served grapefruit sections in sponge-cake cups with dairy-case whipped topping, and Stoney toyed with his like a man who would have far preferred some pie. She had plainly spent a productive quarter hour at the sink because Mona came at dessert and coffee with a bevy of fresh topics, and when we'd grunt and shrug to dispatch one, she'd sling another our way.

We worked through free-market economics, deer deterrents in the garden, were made (me and Stoney) to pass judgment on social standards anymore that allowed for people to wear their gym clothes virtually everywhere they went. We signed on to Mona's poor opinion of a popular girl singer, a lithe redhead who seemed in performance a hooker with choreography.

Unfortunately for us, Mona had lately seen on public television a documentary devoted to the bloody history of Maori tribesmen in New Zealand, and once Mona had exhausted her full supply of topics otherwise, she set about regurgitating for us what she could call up from that show—corrupted facts mostly and half-remembered tribal episodes. Mona demonstrated that the only thing worse than sitting through an arid public-TV documentary was hearing about one piecemeal over dessert.

Stoney looked at his watch a couple of times, no small reflexive matter for him since he kept it in his pocket. Stoney used for a timepiece an old brass wristwatch with the straps and the strap dowels gone. He carried it in with his loose change and had to dig through his coins to find it, so for Stoney checking the time was a bit of a production, required contortions and came with jangling that Mona paid no notice to since she had Maori traditions to misrepresent and history to remanufacture.

It got left to me then to imbibe Stoney's tedium and make for him the excuses that he was a little too timid to make.

"I think Stoney's got to go," I informed Mona once I'd found a chink to insert it, somewhere between word of the Auckland diaspora and talk of Maori preferences in indigenous vegetable dyes.

Being the sort of hostess who could never quite see why a guest might want to go home, Mona shifted to favor Stoney with her full consideration. "He's got cats," I told to Mona, and I believe I said it in such a way as to suggest that while Mona owned a cat herself, the fluffy indoor sort, Stoney had a regular herd of the outdoor open-air variety which, unlike house cats, had to be watered and grazed and shifted maybe into the barn. I insinuated with my tone that a man who owned a pack of outdoor felines was involved not in simple pet keeping but animal husbandry instead.

Mona considered what I'd told her and took in my manly nod before sagging a little and saying simply, "Oh."

So Stoney got away clean, didn't stay around to get shifted to the living room for spirits and a fresh interval of raking conversation. He took leave of me and Mona on the front porch and forged off into the dark, was soon lost to us but for his faint footfall and the rip of his gastritis. The postmortem began before we'd made it back into the house.

Under the guise of an objective pursuit of untempered information, Mona fairly interviewed me about the evening, about the meal. She framed her questions as if she were hoping for constructive criticism, but when I ventured a joke about the creamed corn's Cajun pedigree, Mona snapped at me and grew quarrelsome, so I abandoned honesty and suggested to her she'd both engineered a culinary triumph and orchestrated somehow a scintillating night of table talk. I managed to sell it with enough residual phony authority to satisfy Mona and prompt her to leave me uninterrogated, alone with my own case of volcanic reflux and my batch of recriminations.

Stoney, after all, had gone off with Hooper secrets I'd have plumbed but for Mona's untimely interference, and I might even have wrung from Stoney pertinent talk over dessert but for Mona's breathless half-cocked history of New Zealand's Maori tribesmen. Furthermore, I couldn't imagine that grapefruit sections in spongecake cups was much of anybody's notion of a sweet, and I was well on my way to making myself abrasive and unpleasant when I stepped into the kitchen to find the dishes all misplaced.

Mona had put the tumblers where the saucers went, the plates where I kept the bowls, and she'd mixed spoons in with the salad forks in the divided flatware drawer which I was primed to take as proof of our unfitness for each other. If I'd had any pluck, I'd have sat Mona down and revealed to her my thinking, informed her I'd become persuaded we were not a proper match which was itself a sort of consoling lie since I'd known we were ill suited even the night we met as Mona swabbed my eardrum with her tongue.

I occasionally meet with moments of abject clarity of purpose, instances when I'm certain of just what I think and what I ought to do. My trouble invariably lies in the constipated execution, and on this occasion I started out by showing Mona a mislaid spoon. I intended to employ that spoon as a telling symbol and a point of departure, had been working for weeks on a crock of pseudopsychological prattle designed to establish that Mona rated a finer specimen than me, somebody who wouldn't care where his spoons got put or where his plates got stacked.

I figured I could touch on traits of Mona's that irritated me and let on I was far too doctrinaire and insensitive a fellow to rate Mona's allegiance when there were more appropriate mates about. I was even prepared to name a few, had picked out men for Mona. I'd conducted a sort of survey among various of my clients and had come up with a quartet of local gentlemen who were widowed or unwed and not by any ordinary standard clods.

I was intending to push most particularly a bachelor beer distributor who I knew to be wealthy and, just at that moment, unaffiliated. He leased himself a brand-new Cadillac every other year, owned a share of a Lynchburg supper club and had Gobbler season tickets. He'd built a hideous oversized mansion with a view of the Blue Ridge, with a koi pond in the foyer and topiary in the yard.

I couldn't, however, recall his name as I stood there with my spoon or figure out how best to persuade Mona I wasn't worth her time. So instead I told her, "Look," and had her join me at the counter to watch me sort and segregate my flatware.

I tried to pout and be sullen for the rest of the night, but Mona failed to notice. She never invited me, like I'd hoped, to tell her what was on my mind but just rattled on about whatever popped into her head while I sat in glum silence and conveyed, I guess, the general impression of listening.

Later in bed, when Mona reached an arm across my shoulder and stroked my chest in her customary call to congress, I was ill enough still to very nearly fail to roll her way, to almost bring myself to tell her, "No."

5 ⟶ I should have had a hobby, a leisure interest to engage me. Most of the men I know have cultivated passions over time. They garden. They golf. They hunt. They read. They follow college athletics. They day-trade. They fish. They attend stock-car races. They restore antiques, collect gewgaws, wallow in Internet porn. They cook, some of them. They make birdhouses. They rebuild automobiles. They go on bus tours with their spouses, the occasional ocean cruise. They bowl. They play competitive bridge. They frequent breakfast klatches where they eat thirty-weight sausage biscuits and debate politics. Not, though, in any useful and enlightened sort of way since the lower a man's hair part migrates and the higher he wears his pants, the more his world philosophy tends to verge on paleolithic.

I once attended for diversion a softball game between the Baptists and Moravians which eroded into an unchristian melee in the bottom of the fourth when a deacon spoiled a double play with a violent rolling tackle that both dislodged the ball and sprained the shortstop's wrist. The brawl that ensued proved enormously entertaining, complete with scandalous imprecations and bloody tussling on the infield. The next game I attended, however, had but pop-ups and poor fielding, an overabundance of pasty legs in shorts. Soon enough I was staying home evenings instead and getting about half drunk.

Swilling liquor, after all, is a bit of a hobby since one man can love his bourbon the way another one adores his niblick collection or the thrill of monster-truck shows. Drinking in those parts, though, was customarily conducted on the sly, wasn't thought a worthy upstanding pursuit and fit cause for invested attention. Hard liquor most particularly was widely believed a source of shiftlessness, and it didn't help that the closest state store was a full two towns removed, leaving parched citizens to make an outright pilgrimage for spirits.

Now a man who can only get his alcohol by hopping into his car and driving each way three-quarters of an hour knows ample leisure to contemplate his urges and his habits. He rides the roads in the heavy company of the burning itch of shame, is pestered by temptation to reform. That's my theory anyway. In personal practice, I bought the limit the law allowed to save myself undue road wear and needless rumination.

When the weather permitted, I'd take my evening cocktail on the porch, and I never just swilled but confined myself to a regular measured ration. I had a favorite jelly glass. It was sturdy and squat and held easily over ice three fingers and a splash which I'd freshen (I called it) with invariably four fingers more once I'd reached the watery dregs and the frosty slivers.

I'd just sit and smoke and sip and gaze out across the meadow, over towards Stoney's place which was about the only thing to see. There were usually cats or yard fowl to watch and Stoney often on the lawn where he was frequently occupied tidying up, shifting anyway refuse about without noticeable effect on the general air of squalid dilapidation.

These days I'll allow that my persistent personal interest in Stoney was very likely a variety of glancing self-inspection as well. We were both of us bachelor gentlemen leading the carefree single life well past the age when we could be unwed without explanation, and I can see now that Stoney functioned as a primitive version of me. His hygiene was considerably worse than mine. His hair loss more unsightly. His social skills a bit less cultivated. His physique was closing a little harder than mine on full collapse, and Stoney's preference in clothes, unlike my own, ran towards grease-monkey wear.

So while no sensible soul would have mistaken one of us for the other, I'd detected a troubling residual resemblance between Stoney and me. I suspected he'd been like I was once, half feared I'd be what he'd become—a solitary figure, that is to say, on society's frontier, too far out in the untamed boondocks to get properly reeled in.

Accordingly, as I'd watch Stoney stalking about his yard or listen to him from across his pruny ditch, I was evermore gauging myself against him, cataloging his liabilities and checking to see that they were more potent still than frailties of my own. I'd consider the whiskers his razor had missed, the hair sprouting from his ears, the flecks and splotches of encrusted foodstuff ornamenting his shirtfront, take note of the way his trouser fly was usually at half mast. I'd digest whatever inanity Stoney had picked up on TV and observe him as he'd ream his nostrils clotless with his pinky.

Upon returning home, I'd loiter for a while in front of the bathroom mirror. I'd study my facial trouble spots, stand in profile for paunch assessment, grin to ensure I lacked the sheath of tartar Stoney had built up. Since to my way of thinking Stoney was effectively me degenerated, I stayed hungry for reassurance that he was too far ahead to catch.

Given, then, the complicated nature of my relationship with Stoney—the selfish uses I employed him for, the trifling roadside chats we had—it was no simple matter for me to strike up an incisive spot of talk since he proved naturally resistant to specific inquiries, meaningful give-and-take, and far preferred brief interludes of haphazard disquisition.

Consequently, I couldn't resuscitate the chat that we'd been having in between Mona's chicken marsala and grapefruit in a sponge-cake cup. I certainly tried to, made noises out there as I sifted through my bulk mail to suggest I'd welcome revival of that particular line of talk. I introduced anyway that Hooper, her husband, made mention of their corgi, while Stoney nodded to have me know he was aware that I was speaking, but he never quite seized the topic and proceeded on his own. Instead he'd wince in a fashion that impressed me as fueled by melancholy, seemed engineered to suggest that his Hooper candor belonged to our dead past.

There out at the road with me at my postbox and Stoney beyond his ditch, he would reliably forge ahead to some fresh matter that had gripped him. A spot of cosmic pseudoscience half remembered from TV. A drive-time-tinged regurgitation of the world event du jour. Or just some wayward snatch of troublesome philosophical inquiry, an item Stoney had been chewing on that simply bubbled up.

He'd wonder aloud about the logistics, let's say, of unholy transsexual congress, convey to me the proper medical name of a useless flap of skin that he'd picked up on the surgical channel while watching a cosmetic procedure. He'd frequently speak at length of some dish he'd seen a TV chef prepare and speculate as to who might trouble himself to make such a thing for supper. Every now and again he'd even hew to wholly untelevised matter, mention the weather if it were dry or wet, unduly hot or cold, and touch often upon the latest exploits of our clan of Dabneys, a larcenous pack of halfwits who lived en masse in a glorified gully that was one part landfill and two parts trailer park.

As a partner in conversation, Stoney's gift was for mulishness. He went where he wanted. He wouldn't be led or guided or nudged or steered, so I was obliged to wait for Stoney to work his way back around to those Hoopers. I tried, like I said, to help things along with artless mention of them, but he relied so by way of rejoinder on his melancholy wince that I determined I needed a visual aid to properly draw him out, required particularly an audience with Stoney in the presence of his Saint George which I had grown to suspect was bound up somehow in his mind with all things Hooper.

So I set my sights on a chat with Stoney in his front room proper where I'd be free to refer to the various versions and fragments of his Saint George, but it proved no simple matter to get myself invited inside. Stoney's custom was to exit his house and cross his yard to meet his callers much the way our presidents intercept heads of state in the White House drive. So Stoney would evermore see you coming and stanch your progress on his lawn.

It didn't matter that Stoney knew me, that I'd been in his house before. He was helpless against his impulse to head me off in his yard. I tried returning to him a vise grip that wasn't in fact his, made it halfway up the porch steps before Stoney caught sight of me and came out to herd me back to his van where he showed me the grip he owned. I brought him over a chunk of pound cake a client of mine had given to me. She wasn't a baker by instinct or nature and had shown me the recipe she'd followed. It was printed on the back of an artificial-sweetener box, and though that cake looked a confection, it smelled a bit of chemistry.

I got as far as the doorway on that occasion, put the chunk in Stoney's hand and was hoping to ease my way in for a slice maybe and coffee when I made the mistake of telling Stoney who exactly had baked that cake which prompted him to eye the chunk and cut loose with, "Lord Jesus!" and not in a tone remotely close to beatific praise.

Stoney, as it turned out, had worked for the woman, had repaired a sag for her in her half-bath floor, and she'd plagued him (he told me) with cookies throughout the term of his employment.

"Little flat things." He described one for me with his finger and thumb. "Tough as jerky. Tasted like cream rinse."

Then he threw that pound cake past my head and out into the yard where it rebounded off a tree trunk and dispersed a quorum of cats.

So I needed a better overture to put me in his house, and not just clear of Stoney's threshold but full across to Stoney's sideboard where I could soak in Stoney's souvenir reproduction of Saint George and revive as a topic the spooky resemblance between Stoney and him.

I mulled, consequently, for a month or three and awaited inspiration which finally came to me, oddly enough, in the form of a lovelorn guinea hen. Stoney kept guineas. Not in a scrupulous animal husbandry sort of way but much in the fashion that he kept mice in his insulation, chipmunks under his front lawn, cats all over the place. He had eight or ten birds that pecked and roamed, living loose on ticks and ants, and they raised an infernal clamor whenever anyone stopped by—the mailman, the meter reader, the odd intrepid Jehovah's Witness.

Guineas are hopeless alarmists by nature, specialize in hue and cry, and they make quite enough of a racket to rouse the deepest sleeping human whenever a thief is afoot in the area or a tree squirrel happens past.

Stoney's cats tolerated them, tormented those birds a little, but they didn't kill and devour them like they killed and devoured most everything else. They seemed to have made their peace with the notion of a flock of fowl touring the yard, though a feline would sometimes wade in and swat a bird or two when the squawking became more than even a reasonable cat could bear.

Every now and again, that flock of guineas would stray from

Stoney's yard. They'd haunt for a while the scrubby thicket at the bottom of Stoney's lot or cross the road and take up business in the meadow before my house until I'd tired of the hubbub enough to run them off. Like guineas will, they stuck together and traveled in a fretful clutch, so I remarked the lone guinea I saw one evening approaching down my drive since the only lone guineas I'd previously seen were flattened in the roadway.

This guinea was meandering and consulting with herself, waddling along and clucking. She'd stop every now and again to survey the bordering fields and see, I guess, if there was anything handy worth raising a furor about. Then she'd forge again down the driveway making her throaty guinea noises.

I watched her from the porch, was fairly deep by then into my freshened cocktail and had heaped with Chesterfield butts the bulk of eastern Tennessee. So I was about as relaxed as I could get and still be fully conscious which turned out a proper state for watching a guinea walk the drive. She was slow and haphazard, a victim of guinea nerves and paranoia. She would stop and wheel to see who was closing on her from behind, pause to inspect the bordering grass for assassins slipping through it.

At length, she reached my front yard and pecked at the fescue for a while, long enough anyway for my interest in her to falter and to wane or get supplanted at least by one of my store of goading antagonisms. I curate with care a couple of dozen episodes from my past, the sort that bourbon helps me seize upon and tempts me to revisit. They are given over largely to slights I've suffered, choice humiliations I've endured, stinging bons mots I've lacked the wit to cobble up and air.

So I didn't notice at first that Stoney's guinea had mounted the roof of my car, and I looked up to find her admiring herself upside down in the front-window glass. Now while I've never taken scrupulous care of any vehicles I've owned, I'm hardly so far gone in sloth and general shiftlessness to tolerate yard fowl perched upon the roof of my sedan. Their claws are sharp enough to scratch and gouge clean to the primer coat, and the droppings they leave can bore in time entirely through sheet steel.

So I immediately attempted to put to rout Stoney's errant guinea hen, lowered anyway my freshened cocktail and told the creature, "Hey!" which prompted it to lift its head and contemplate me for a moment, but it returned soon enough to savoring its reflection in the glass.

I had enough bourbon in me to take that sort of thing personally, was in a state to believe that I could be snubbed by domesticated fowl. Consequently, I got irritated and at least a touch indignant and responded like a garden-variety mental deficient might. I picked up, that is, a scrap of flowerpot off of the porch floor and threw it.

Together that bird and I watched as that chunk of terra-cotta hit the windshield and made initially just a tiny ding, a grainy pit in the glass that stayed for several minutes minuscule before it sent out cracks and actively began to creep and spread. I left the porch and crossed the yard and meant to exorcise my rage by sweeping Stoney's guinea off the roof of my sedan, but once I'd arrived within reach of the thing, I'd decided I didn't want to touch it. I feared it would peck me or brush against my exposed flesh with its leathery feet. So together me and that yard fowl watched those spidery cracks expand—her upside down from the Cavalier roof, me by the fender well.

She shortly got bored and took her leave of my sedan, threw herself off the roof with all of the aerodynamic grace of a saucepan. For my part, I stayed where I was and passed a productive quarter hour updating my personal catalog of humiliations and regrets which I met with cause to further revise the following afternoon when rain seeped in through my windshield cracks, pooled up on the dash and sloshed at length through the perforations of my speaker cover to short out both the dashboard lights and the radio.

Due to assorted deficiencies in my insurance coverage, I was obliged to pay the replacement cost of a new windshield myself. So I drove out to the shabby unfranchised garage on the rise behind the Sinclair where Kenny the rescue-squad boy was listening to his scanner while his colleagues debated the cup size of a lawyer on TV. An actual lawyer, as it turned out, some news-channel commentator with a flyaway mane of highlighted hair, an acid disposition, a taste for mohair sweaters and maddening decolletage.

They were all of them delighted for occasion to work on something other than mufflers, and two of the brawniest of the garage hands climbed straightaway into my sedan. They reared back on the seats and raised their legs and kicked the windshield out. It collapsed in rubbery segments onto the wipers and the hood, and their colleagues commiserated with me over the resulting dents and scratches before they set about casting around for a window glass to put in its place.

They finally found one to fit at an auto-supply house an hour up the highway though it was slightly mauve tinted and had leaned against a wall long enough to go out of true. But they made it work as they were, after all, muffler men and tailpipe benders and had yet to meet a problem that a hard rubber mallet and a wire welder couldn't cure. The new window leaked a little at the edges, dripped harmlessly into the defroster vents, and I managed over time to convince myself that the pinkish hue was soothing.

Of course, I was prepared from the beginning to blame the whole mess on Stoney's guinea hen who proved to be, as yard birds go, a curious specimen. She chose to linger around my property once I'd swept her off my car, retreated for the balance of the evening into the high grass of the meadow, but I could hear her out there warbling and rustling in the stalks. And I awoke with a start the following morning to find her peering in through my bedroom window.

I could only make her out from her beak holes up, saw her eyes and the top of her head. She was perched on the sill and leering in over the sash. I yelled at her, made her to understand I wished she would go home as I chased her away from the house with the stubby broom from my fireplace set.

Come evening, she'd returned, though I wasn't aware of it until I'd killed the television and switched off the parlor lamps when I saw her looking at me through the front bay-window glass. I could make out her chunky silhouette against the ambient vapor light, and I went at her this time with, instead of the broom, my bright-brass fireplace shovel as I was fully prepared to manufacture a helping of guinea paillard. She'd slipped under the fence and into the meadow before I could land a blow.

The next morning she was at the kitchen window peeking in over the sash, and I detected that night the outline of her through the frosted bathroom pane. No matter what I chased her with or the pitch of my abuse, she always returned to the house and sought a perch upon a sill due to a fondness, I decided, for her reflection in the glass. She would coo and nuzzle and seem enchanted by the guinea gazing back which she tended to express through a combination of burbling and defecation.

I was determined to shift her back to Stoney's yard somehow, but I'm the sort who happens to find all birds revolting. So I didn't have the stomach to snatch that guinea up and hardly felt I could call on Stoney to come and take his yard fowl home without ex-plaining why I hadn't simply dropped her off myself. There ex-isted the genuine risk that I would come off in his eyes as girlish, and my relationship with Stoney was based on the fiction that we were both regular guys which permitted Stoney the freedom to speak to me of sports and internal combustion, show me his bass lures and his socket set and confess to infatuations with the ginger-haired girl on The Weather Channel and the brunette on the cold sore ad.

I eventually managed to trap that guinea in an upended packing box but couldn't work out the engineering that would allow me to transport her. Worse still, that box was small enough that she could carry it around the yard, and the packaging somehow made her seem to me a touch more creepy. I finally caught her by sheer accident in my faux-wicker laundry hamper. The thing had sat for a couple of weeks packed full of clothes and damp bath towels and was releasing in ever-intensified doses a CDC bouquet.

I packed my clothes into pillowcases, sprayed my hamper with disinfectant and laid it open to air itself out on the porch. While I was at the Laundromat, that guinea—attracted, I guess, by the ungodly musk of the thing—pecked for a while at the exterior of my rank faux-wicker hamper. She scarred up the plastic and half removed a band of epoxied trim before she discovered, I have to imagine, the clear plastic hamper bottom from where a bewitching creature watched her back.

I came home to find her inside that hamper doting on herself, and I captured that guinea by shutting the lid and standing the thing upright.

I skirted the meadow up by the tree line and avoided my driveway altogether in hopes I could frustrate Stoney from intercepting me on his porch. I struggled through a stand of clammy locusts, crossed the road and gained his lawn there at the greasy fuel-oil tank that supplied Stoney's front-room heater. I passed through the bushes to reach the steps and charged onto the porch, had tapped on the door and stuck my head inside before Stoney could stir from his chair.

"Damnedest thing," I told Stoney as I bulled in with my hamper. "This guinea of yours . . ." And with that I lifted the faux-wicker lid of the thing just, I guess, as Stoney's bird was fluttering up in agitation because she popped out and cleared the hamper lid and dropped onto the floor.

I only noticed the cats about once they had taken heed of that guinea. There were four that I saw, and together they went from slinky lethargy to utterly undivided feral devotion. They rose where they were into crouches—the sideboard, the hutch, the settee back— and watched that guinea in a fashion that I took for culinary.

A lumpy piebald creature with an abbreviated tail was closest to me on the hutch, and me and that guinea together contemplated him as he wriggled in rhythm his haunches and tensed up in preparation for a leap. Stoney saw him too and yelled to stop him. His name, I believe, was Claude, and Stoney addressed him personally with provisos and instructions, had managed even to list potential baleful consequences before Claude hit the floor precisely where that guinea had recently been.

That guinea had the advantage of a variety of flight. Though she was plump and sluggish, she managed to gain the bonnet of a highboy. Those four cats together tried to follow her up, but there was little for them to hold to beyond the maple veneer their back claws separated along the grain.

Stoney maneuvered towards that highboy along a back periodical trail, informed his cats as he approached them, "Hey, goddamn it!" He tossed their way for emphatic effect a *Cosmopolitan* that rebounded off the highboy with force enough to spook that guinea as well. She leaped off the bonnet and soared (I'll call it) directly into the kitchen with those cats and, just behind them, Stoney himself in pursuit. So I was suddenly left alone in Stoney's rubbish heap of a front room, and straightaway I knew exactly what to do.

Stoney didn't trouble himself to maintain a proper seat for guests. He was hardly the sort to encourage callers, was wholly bereft of hospitable urges, had in his front room just his favorite chair and his camelback settee which was loaded from bolster to bolster with grocery flyers and drugstore circulars, mail-order catalogs, newspaper inserts, unopened solicitations.

The stuff was heavy too, I discovered as I set about shoveling a cushion clean, and it became a wonder to me Stoney's couch hadn't yielded at the joints and collapsed, in a cloud of dander, into a heap of horsehair and springs. I shifted bulk-rate ballast off onto a hassock, raked enough of it onto the floor to clear a slot for myself on the end of Stoney's camelback settee that was separated by just a floor lamp from Stoney's favorite chair.

That lamp had a little wire-mesh tabletop riveted to the stalk, and it was junked up with antacid jars and dime-store reading glasses, littered with grocery coupons and rotted rubber bands. Stoney had paper-clipped to the shade, I noticed, a detail of his painting, one of those blowups I'd seen previously taped to Stoney's drywall, obscured by intervening clutter and hidden well away. Stoney had fished it out and brought it over and had fixed it to his lampshade where all he had to do was glance up to see it from his favorite chair. The thing featured primarily Saint George himself with his head of frizzy blond hair and his look of actuarial determination—Stoney in pigment handy for Stoney in mortal flesh to see.

I could hear him in the kitchen driving that guinea and herding those cats out the door with a blend, it sounded, of applied shoe leather and blistering imprecations, and I conspired to look well settled as Stoney crossed the kitchen floor. I lounged, that is to say, on that sofa and draped an arm along the back to give the impression of a man at loose ends with no appetite for hurry, a fellow steeped and saturated in wholly shiftless lethargy.

To his credit, Stoney proved gracious and hospitable in defeat. He ducked back into the kitchen to spill some saltines on a plate and fetch us each a can of beer, the discounted twelve-pack brand that tastes a bit like carbonated saliva.

Stoney raked clear a portion of coffee table to accommodate the crackers and then dropped into his chair and, with a minimum of prodding, proceeded to tell me everything I'd hoped to come to know.

6 —•» The way Stoney told it, he'd been for a while in the market for someone to save and had already, ahead of that Hooper, squandered a fair bit of his valor on a couple of local females in apparent difficulty, women Stoney had hardly driven to unfettered gratitude.

"I can't for the life of me understand," Stoney told me from his chair, pausing to burp and pluck a stray saltine crumb from his shirt and eat it, "why people are anymore happy enough to stay just like they are."

Stoney, you see, had been rendered by that painted saint and painted dragon a strident emissary of assisted self-actualization which was chiefly due to the paucity of large reptiles about with appetites for meaty American youth. There was nothing in the vicinity with scaly flesh and teeth that had need of a crusader to dispatch it. Most any fool with motor skills and a garden hoe would do, so Stoney found himself constrained to redefine salvation.

Stoney recalled for me the evening he'd first met with his Saint George. He'd been watching a documentary on the topic of forensic science, one of those shows devoted to the strain of savage homicide that lab technicians tend to solve by visiting chemistry on effluvia due to how there's usually precious little of the victim left—a bit of gristle, a flap of crusty skin, a few hair tufts, some seepage. That show, doubtless, aspired to the usual tone of somber considered inquiry that's employed anymore to hoist the standing of lurid TV titillation and suggest, say, that an installment about a transient in Houston who (due chiefly to the fact that he took acetone medicinally) vivisected a pal of his for sport with a sharpened length of rebar is somehow educational and probing.

So Stoney had been induced to think himself inquisitive at worst by the time, he told it, a manner of homicidal reenactment which featured a trio of spirited youths flaying a retiree alive set him scrabbling in revulsion for his remote control. He succeeded at tuning in queasy disgust to a neighboring satellite channel, a network that divided its fare between conventional travelogues and far-flung paranormal investigations.

"'Haunted Yurts of the High Mongolian Plain,'" Stoney told me and shook his head. "Windiest place I ever hope to see."

It seems Stoney would check in from time to time to gauge the forensic progress on the grisly retiree litter those spirited youths had made, but that state police lab had too much of the slaughterhouse about it to tempt Stoney to linger on that show for long, most particularly when—one click away—he could watch two Ph.D.'s with scruffy academic beards and canary-yellow parkas measure ectoplasmic pulses (they called them) on the banks of the Orhon Gol with a metal detector they'd souped up and refitted.

Stoney told me Mongolia turned out to be ectoplasm-rich.

Once Stoney had switched back to the forensic channel in time to see an organ weighed—he couldn't say which organ precisely, but something viscous and unbecoming—Stoney decided that ectoplasmic pulses were probably more his thing and so stuck with the travelogue and far-flung restless-spirits channel in hopes of finally seeing an actual haunted yurt.

It turned out what yurts he saw were not so grand as he'd expected and were haunted in ways that hardly impressed Stoney as unnerving. Cups would tip over, and lantern light would dim. Stools would get mysteriously upended, but no diaphanous specters wandered about with their heads in the crooks of their arms.

"Spooks just aren't what they used to be," Stoney told me. "Not anywhere, I guess."

And he was musing on the dreary nature of ectoplasmic afterlife when that Mongolian-haunted-yurt show yielded to a travelogue devoted to the scenic and artistic riches of the Veneto. Stoney sat through a Palladian-villa tour, a discussion of Giotto frescoes in Padua, a geologic history of the eastern Dolomites which, taken together, were rendering Mongolian ectoplasm scintillating, so Stoney was reaching for his remote control when George came on the screen.

"Like looking in a mirror," Stoney told me and nodded. He added, "Damnedest thing."

Stoney was hardly impulsive by nature, was instead sluggish and sedentary, and, like people who sit around and do next to nothing for years on end, Stoney was hardly a stranger to regret and self-recrimination. Over time, he'd accumulated inexhaustible opportunity to wish he'd traveled somewhere or another or done, like he'd meant to, some one thing or three. He'd never learned conversational French or jigs on the clawhammer banjo, had neglected to pursue leathercraft beyond the purchase of gouges and taps, had only ever meant to tour Luray Caverns, see Monticello in the spring.

He'd collected coins for a year or two but had ultimately spent them well before he'd come by the expertise to know what a wastrel he'd been. Stoney had purchased a shortwave-radio kit that he'd left piecemeal in the box, had taken delivery of materials for a prefabricated sunroof that were heaped still where the building-supply truck had dumped them in his yard. He'd known an interest in lepidoptera that had gone uncultivated beyond a Northern Metalmark Stoney kept flattened in an atlas of the stars, and he'd succeeded for years at intending to restore a roadster in his shed so that he might drive the thing one summer west to the Pacific.

These were all, of course, in addition to Stoney's basic expectations that he'd take a bride and have a family, enjoy a fruitful fulfilling career. He'd never, I discovered, much coveted the company of cats or hoped to generate a livelihood by dint of being handy but had come by both as a residue of all he'd left undone. That anyway appeared to serve as Stoney's prevailing theory. He felt he was what he'd ended up because of what he'd not become, lived like he lived as a consequence of passions gone unstoked and fever-pitch enthusiasms allowed to wane untended.

He regretted, as a rule, his stagnancy. I'd noticed early on from the slouch he assumed those occasions when he'd plunder through his van, from the weary put-upon breath he would reliably expel as prelude to every chance he knew to boot or toss a cat.

So I'm guessing along about when Stoney saw that Venetian painting on the travelogue and far-flung paranormal investigation channel, he was mired in a bit of a psychic trough and more sensitive than normal to his history of anemic follow-through. According to Stoney, once he'd recognized the remarkable resemblance between himself and that Carpaccio Saint George, he decided he would welcome the chance to see the thing in person, guessed aloud he could stand to fly on over and have himself a look. Naturally Stoney enjoyed an ensuing spot of uncompromised resolve, his customary placid quarter hour of unassailable conviction that he was doomed to perforate at length with doubts and qualifiers, erode with reservations and drab practicalities.

Stoney could only ever mean to build a bark-sheathed Navajo

sweat lodge for a while or briefly hope to send for bees so he might bottle his own honey before he'd find himself immobilized, mired up in his misgivings, paralyzed by swarming obligations he had conjured up.

The way I figure it, he'd reached his upper limit of personal disgust by the time he'd noted the resemblance between himself and that Saint George, so Stoney had need to thwart and overcome the usual progression that kept him staying where he was and kept him doing nothing much. I have to think that's why he called a travel agent straightaway, out of fear the zeal would dissipate and the passion would waver and flag. He dialed the woman at home and told her precisely where he meant to go, let it be known he'd pay whatever it took to get there, and then Stoney unplugged the telephone and set it in the yard as a hedge, he confessed, against backsliding and reconsideration.

The travel agent he used was, in fact, a ladies' hairdresser by training. Her name was Polly or Meg, depending on the pitch of your acquaintance. As for myself, I only knew her as Lanny the well-driller's brother's wife and had spied her in person but once at the scene of a throttling Lanny was taking from a fellow Lanny had bored two arid holes for in his yard. As a practical matter, a well-drilling job is ordinarily a blend of dynamic engineering and improvisational graft. Lanny was the sort to let on he knew just where the water was. He'd dowse occasionally with willow branches, study topographical plats and talk up his gift for finding rifts and fissures in the bedrock until his customers had agreed to pay him eight and a half dollars a foot.

Then he'd bring in his rig and drill for maybe the bulk of an afternoon, and more often than not he'd tap into a vein of the aquifer which would occasion talk from Lanny of his savvy and expertise, his professional talents that bordered in Lanny's opinion on mystical. Occasionally, though, he'd bring up little more than pulverized shale and slurry which called, on Lanny's part, for an alternative response, required from him talk of the sly elusive nature of groundwater and the suggestion he'd only been hired, after all, to sink a hole in the yard.

He never made an overt guarantee or an actionable promise and gave a paltry class of discount on unproductive wells which was intended as solace for people worse off than when work had begun, folks who'd bought a pile or two of gravel for several thousand dollars. Occasionally, however, that discount failed to function as consolation enough, like with the gentleman I saw bouncing Lanny off a paper box. He turned out to be a Buncombe from the reaches of the county, a man of few words and what looked (from where I stood) about size-fifteen boots that he was applying to portions of Lanny meant in this life to go unkicked.

Now in that part of the world, fights between men weren't at all uncommon. Fights between grown women weren't even very rare. The bulk of the local rhetorical eloquence seemed to have gone to Thomas Jefferson, leaving the rest of the population to descend from the sorts of people given to phlegm manipulation and bouts of inarticulate rage. In my time in that territory, I saw a regular host of fights, two men usually rolling around on the ground to no discernible advantage while a wife or a girlfriend stood by screaming and unallied onlookers floated speculative theories as to what the row was about.

The quarters usually were far too close for any effective punching. There was biting and kicking, all manner of grappling, forehead battery, but hardly ever anything in the way of a punishing blow. So usually neither combatant suffered ignominious defeat, but they'd both end up just spent and winded and comprehensively mussed instead. Onlookers with sound civic impulses would invariably stop those fights only after the participants were too whipped to continue.

There'd usually be a searching glance or two from the tussling principals, desperate looks with lots of eye white intended to convey "for the love of sweet holy Jesus, separate us!" but local audiences preferred to let a good fracas play out.

In that part of the world, there was precious little live secular entertainment. The only racetrack of any size was clear over in Martinsville, and the local high-school teams were all so hapless and deplorable that even actual parents of student participants were loath to watch them compete. There were theatrical productions every now and again of middling quality, but how many times can a self-respecting adult sit through *Barefoot in the Park*? They had a kind of fair in October—half livestock, half kiddie rides—and a bluegrass festival in summer notorious for its biting flies.

Churchgoing sorts had their potlucks and their revivals, their gospel-quartet concerts in their linoleumed fellowship halls, but the heathens only met with the occasional crime of passion, the odd gruesome highway fatality, the biannual super flea, so a fight between two grown men (and especially grown women) qualified as a sort of improvisational godless social event.

Accordingly, people were caught up in the jaunty festival air of the proceedings by the time I stepped from the office-supply store with a fresh gross of rollerball pens and saw that Buncombe applying a brogan toe to Lanny's solar plexus.

Walking up, I could see that Lanny's features were pretty well fixed and frozen in the customary sweet-holy-Jesus-separate-us! expression, but nobody watching the spectacle looked tempted to intervene which I'm inclined to believe anymore was probably aquifer-related. There were parts of that county where the water table often proved deep and evasive, where a usable flow was devilish to come by, and more than a few of the residents had purchased dry holes from the likes of Lanny. So there were people who knew people who were acquainted with people themselves who'd paid good money to Lanny's ilk for gravel and disappointment, and I had to think more than a few of that sort were probably standing about delighted to take that Buncombe for their proxy.

Lanny, then, was enduring worse than local combatants usually endured because he seemed, by virtue of his profession, to rate a comprehensive beating a trifle more than your average lowlife with a taste for wayward wives. So the onlookers were pleased to allow that Buncombe to exhaust himself on Lanny. They stood by in silence and permitted that fellow to get both winded and spent, allowed him to pull up a little lame after an awkward thrust and pivot, and only then did anybody bother to say, "All right. That's enough."

Lanny went unaided as the onlookers dispersed. He propped himself against the paper box and dabbed at his contusions which served as occupation enough to keep him from spying his brother's wife who slipped up on him, leaned down close and informed Lanny, "SEE!"

She favored him with a kick herself by way of emphasis, a glancing blow with her open-toed mule to Lanny's kidney region, and then she resituated her Rexall sack and marched off up the street while I watched her go and settled in my mind on what she'd meant. I decided she'd previously acquainted Lanny with the scoundrel she thought he was, had availed herself of the opportunity at holiday family gatherings to suggest the way Lanny held himself out as some manner of groundwater mystic would likely return in the form of a thrashing to plague and haunt him in the end.

The way I imagined it, she'd been forceful and frank and casually insulting in that fashion in-laws the world over enjoy collective license to be, and once she'd come across Lanny paying for his avocational sins, that Meg or Polly (depending) had merely waited out that Buncombe for occasion to tell her husband's sorry shiftless brother, "SEE!"

She didn't so much as glance back. I remember watching her leave, most particularly because she was hardly a creature who open-toed mules flattered. She was big-boned and strapping and looked from the rear like a steelworker or a Guernsey, a pile of female any sane man would take strict care not to cross. Accordingly, I felt armed with special insight into Stoney's thinking, decided Stoney had known a moment of stark and crystalline resolve, had been rendered decisive by his uncanny resemblance to Saint George and had purposefully dialed up that woman before he could lapse back into inertia, knew her somehow for a female who'd take cancellations hard.

Now I never quite succeeded at actually picturing Stoney in Venice, notwithstanding his descriptions of the buildings he'd been into, the *calli* and *fondamente* he'd explored and roamed along, the millefiori glassware that he fractured in his luggage, the deep-fried cuttlefish he'd eaten, the dram of grappa he'd thrown up.

Stoney had even made time on his short weekend trip to bathe in the Adriatic. "Didn't take any trunks," he confessed and hooked out his underpants' band with his thumb, but even still I couldn't envision Stoney sitting in his briefs in the scummy anemic surf under the dull mist-softened sun. I conjured instead the woman I'd seen years before in the bathing cap, the skirt.

Only in that gloomy guildhall did I get a sense of Stoney stumbling in blind from the *campo*, jostling tourists like I'd done. It was essentially as if I were Stoney myself seeing what Stoney had seen, sharing with Stoney the rattling jolt of spying my own uncanny likeness not at home on the television but out in the world in varnished oil. I could readily conjure the smell of the place—septic estuarial seepage leavened with the drowsy guard's cologne and four centuries of must. I could hear the whispered polyglot exchanges in the murk, the scuff of footfall on the stone floor, the flutter of guidebook pages and, when the visitors rose or sat, the shrill complaint of joinery.

"Hell of a sight," Stoney told me, and I knew just what he meant, could recall the impression that painting had made on me looming out of the half-light which, of course, was partly due to the gaping bloody transfixed dragon and the look of officious purpose on Saint George's pallid face but was a product as well of the rich unearthly amber hue of the thing, a consequence of fissured resin and rank antiquity.

At any rate, I could certainly imagine that if Saint George had looked like me, I might well have seen clear to take the coincidence of it for a calling. Stoney glanced up at the detail he'd attached to his lampshade, reached and pecked at Saint George's cheek with the callused tip of his foremost finger. He shrugged, and his smile impressed me as gastrointestinally involved.

"I didn't guess a man could look like him and go on doing nothing."

Now Stoney took a while to settle on which something he'd best do. He made of himself a cheerful all-purpose Samaritan at first. He passed, he confessed, a month or two chiefly squiring geriatrics. He'd walk them the breadth of the main street where the crosswalk used to be before the new water line went in and the roadway was resurfaced. He'd carry sacks for them in the superstore lot, help them up the courthouse steps, parallel-park their oversized sedans when they knew difficulties and distinguish, when need be, nickels from dimes for the meters along the street.

Consequently, Stoney was handy for chat in a way he'd not previously been, and he discovered the elders about were not congenial to his brand of parley, harbored no patience for Stoney's usual scattershot sensational talk but preferred instead to visit upon him news of their thankless children who themselves were neglecting to properly bring up children of their own. So Stoney got to tour through various portions of our slight bedraggled town at nearly a sixteenth of a mile an hour while enduring unremittingly uncharitable revelations about offspring who, with rare exception, Stoney didn't know.

Once he'd made of himself a thoughtful guide and a conscientious Sherpa, Stoney met with special favor from a few of the local ladies who'd have him over for coffee and stale store-bought cookies as prelude usually to an interval of recreational furniture shifting. He was often invited to mount a roof and clean the gutters out. He changed lightbulbs in ceiling fixtures, plucked items from high closet shelves and got conscripted into a fair amount of third-party refuse hauling once the geriatric grapevine had broadcast word he drove a van.

"They damn near worked me to death," Stoney told me and then revealed he'd been fixed up with a couple of the available ingrate daughters.

One of those girls had borrowed money from him that she'd neglected to repay and had taken out a revolving charge at a jewelry store in Stoney's name. The other had made it with Stoney only so far as the Super Shell by the highway where he'd stopped to gas up for the drive to dinner and she'd seen someone she knew.

"Black-headed boy in a ragtop. She went off somewhere with him."

Stoney allowed he'd never imagined that part-time relative saintliness of the variety he'd decided to observe would turn out to be so troublesome and trying a pursuit.

"Most people, as soon as you give them a hand, they make you wish you hadn't." Here Stoney paused to sweep a cat off of the back of the settee and contemplate, I suppose, the dilapidated state of humankind since the thing he said next when he opened his mouth was "Fallen, don't you know."

I got the distinct impression that Stoney had lapsed from saintliness for a time, that the grind of living an operationally beatific life had turned out a little more than he could bear. So he'd gone back to being undemonstratively decent, made himself helpful when help appeared needed but left off seeking candidates out. He told how he went for three full months carrying his own grocery sacks and carting exclusively personal rubbish out to the county landfill before he met one afternoon with a couple at the Dairy-O who served to identify for Stoney his saintly specialty.

They were quarreling at a table on the margin of the lot, bickering, as it turned out, over an infidelity. The boy—and Stoney knew him for a Simms from up the valley, the youngest of a clan of drywall roughnecks—had given a former girlfriend a lift into town in his truck, and somebody his present girlfriend knew had seen them and had told her.

She'd been assured they were sitting femur to femur and had looked inordinately jolly, like maybe that former girlfriend was holding an item other than that Simms's hand. So there at the table on the margin of the Dairy-O lot, that Simms's current girlfriend set about enumerating his indiscretions. She did it tearfully at full volume and with adequate detail to suggest that Simms, by nature, was a stripe of free-range goat.

To hear it from Stoney, that Simms grew provoked by the airing of his betrayals, and he responded straightaway with a catalog of counterdeclarations that served as unflattering commentary on the shape of his girlfriend's heels. Then they passed a few minutes engaged in shrill competing litanies while Stoney ordered his chili dogs up at the window, his slaw and his dirty fries, and pretty thoroughly misapprehended the situation across the lot.

"I thought he was going to have a go at her," Stoney told me, and he raised a fist and shook my way the knuckles. "I had to figure a right-thinking fellow would step in and try to keep him from it." Here Stoney paused. He shrugged and said, "Wasn't nobody else around."

So Stoney stopped by with his greasy sack and sweaty soda cup at the edge of the lot where that Simms and his girlfriend were snarling at each other, and as he approached that Simms was reminding the bitch (he called her as an endearment) of the Sheetrocking tools and the wall-compound troughs he kept on his passenger floorboard which required any rider to rest his feet upon the driveshaft hump, and not exclusively former girlfriends with balky alternators but just about anybody with lower extremities.

Stoney, then, turned out to be a little unfortunate in his timing, since he'd fetched up to say, "Let's go easy now, bud," just as that Simms and his current girlfriend had achieved the pitch of aggravation that usually set them off. The girlfriend, that is, was primed to forgive him for driving a past flame in his truck, no matter where her hand had lain and her feet had come to rest, because that Simms had ranted quite enough to ignite her hunger for him while she'd displayed sufficient vinegar to engorge his vital parts.

Consequently, as Stoney was speaking, they flew together in an embrace, a lively but upright mutual esophageal exploration that went horizontal once that Simms had hoisted his current girlfriend onto their Dairy-O redwood picnic table to render her handy for pelvic thrusts. Somehow that was along about when the two of them noticed Stoney, and that Simms and his girlfriend paused to contemplate him tableside.

"They wondered together what exactly I might want." Stoney chose to omit, for propriety's sake, their salty corrosive enlargements and failed to recite the vile profanities they'd pelted him with as he retired to his van.

"You know that table," he said, "with the busted plank, the one hard by the hawthorn tree?" I nodded, and Stoney favored me with a sour revolted wince. "I don't believe I'd eat at it again."

He was chastened and freely admitted those two had put him off saintliness, well-intended interference anyway between aggravated men and infuriated women, so it was only eventually that he interceded with a couple in the homewares store, the big one down by Roanoke at the interstate exchange.

"They were fighting over a basin wrench." Stoney described the thing with his hands. "They were speaking pretty poorly of each other."

Those two were brother and sister as it turned out, the sort that rarely find cause to leave home, and fair chunks of their days were devoted to lively sibling recrimination. They chafed and bickered at home, argued in the car, quarreled without inhibition in public, and Stoney just happened upon them while the topic at hand was the use of that basin wrench.

"I thought they were married," Stoney told me. "Probably decent sorts at bottom, but once I'd grabbed his arms and she got the wrench, she hit us both in the head."

Stoney laid aside a hair tuft to show me a scar, a discolored dent in his scalp, and then he stood to let gravity scour his shirtfront clean of cracker crumbs.

"People," Stoney said as he flopped back onto the couch. "Hard to figure sometimes."

7 —⟶ I knew precisely what he meant due to how I was being hard to figure just then myself. I was deeper than I had any right to be in the throes of a Mona crisis, a spot of torture I'd gone to extravagant trouble to orchestrate firsthand. I had succeeded, you see, at putting Mona together in a social setting with our bachelor beer distributor of execrable taste and inordinate wealth.

I'd been hired to untangle a back-taxes problem one of that gentleman's beer-truck drivers had managed to get himself mired up in. He'd been caught selling headcheese and air-cured sausage from the cab of his delivery truck. As it turned out, that beer-truck driver kept pigs that he slaughtered and butchered himself, and his wife—as a gainful sideline—turned them into savory bar snacks which her husband was pleased to make whispered offers of while delivering beer.

It seems a certified licensed manufacturer of pork-byproduct treats found out that beer-truck driver was undercutting him on the sly and turned him in to every pertinent government agency he could think of. That driver had the FDA on his back, the health department and the state police, along, of course, with revenue offices both federal and local which was the particular wing of his troubles I'd been hired to oversee. And I went to his beer-distributor boss in the vain hope, as it turned out, that he'd front his driver a chunk of back-tax money to be paid off in time.

That gentleman's name was Murry. He was a Blankenship from down in what's called the Mountain Kingdom—an especially rugged run of the Alleghenies in the southwestern tip of the state. It's a territory known for timber rattlers and widespread toothlessness. Young natives with ambition and a proper sense of hygiene are obliged either to learn to love cousins unduly or strike out as refugees.

Murry had escaped first to Bristol where he'd caught on at a die-casting plant and then had migrated east to Danville and on to Roanoke after that, working all along at any sort of job that he could land. He'd married a girl from Lexington who'd proven to be faithless, and he'd apprenticed to a soda bottler out in Richmond for a time, a man of impeccable business instincts and unimpeachable ethics who'd set up Murry, he had me call him, in his first distributorship.

I learned all of this in Murry's foyer, barely over Murry's doorsill, due to Murry's feverish appetite for autobiography. His own life served as a source of deep infatuation for him, a topic of inexhaustible intrigue, and Murry was blessed with the capacity gaseous prattlers seem to share for believing everybody else was just as keen on him as he was.

I immediately sensed he was hardly the sort to help my client out since by the time we'd arrived at his koi pond in the lee of his master stairwell, Murry had acquainted me already with several passages in his life when he'd been down on his luck and besieged and had hoisted himself into solvency. Like a fair number of other men I'd met who'd enjoyed benefactors—a burger franchisee in

Georgia, a legislator in Kentucky, a college chum up D.C. way who ran his dad's shoe-insert empire—Murry was ready to allow that he'd been helped along in his success while embracing the conviction he had earned it all himself.

So I got the glorified Murry Blankenship story as we strolled into the parlor which featured chiefly the bits about Murry's conquests and Murry's accolades with passing mention of the little people Murry had run across in his life and had, quite naturally, bested and surpassed. Murry met with occasion to be expansive between the foyer and the great room because his house had been constructed on a fairly gargantuan scale. In fact, it was known in those parts for being monstrously oversized, probably a full twelve thousand square feet for just Murry to rattle around in. Or rather Murry and his housekeeper and his woman friend of the moment, usually a platinum blonde or a new-penny redhead with several thirty-ninth birthdays behind her, along with at least one former husband and a stint or two in exotic dance—the sort of woman helpless against a man with a monstrously oversized house.

The digs and the money, truth be told, were about all Murry had to recommend him. He was far too ready a moralizer to be much worth talking to, and once he'd told me he planned to fire the beer-truck driver I'd come to plead for as a favor to the man, he insisted, whose enterprising nature Murry claimed to admire, I should have thanked him for his time, retreated to my Cavalier and negotiated Murry's stately elliptical faux-antique-paver drive.

There was something almost bewitching, however, in the magnitude of Murry's offenses—against patience and taste and interior decor, against local standards in seemly yard care, against county building codes. Murry was so very deeply invested in his abominations that they rendered him more intriguing than he'd any right to be.

For starters, Murry had an absurdly architectural coiffure that I felt drawn to examine in hopes of comprehending its engineering.

Murry had lost his topknot hair, and in a bid to conceal his scalp, he appeared to have grown a cover crop of spindly strands at the nape of his neck that reached, when he combed them up and over, all the way to his forehead. So Murry had bangs that were rooted, essentially, on his upper back, and he'd lacquered them together, it looked to me, with some sort of high-tensile-strength mousse. When Murry met with a headwind, even the meager sort he made by walking, the crusty hair on the top of his head all fluttered together of a piece.

I couldn't help but wonder just how Murry greeted the morning, if he awoke with a head of hair or if he had instead a mane. While following the man into his great room, though, I strayed into the wake of his scent and got put off of Murry's coiffure by the tang of his cologne. The stuff was citrusy and minty with a slight dash of gardenia, and I carried a bit of it home as a chemical burn in the back of my throat.

That was the way with Murry. You had to shift among his enormities, couldn't hope to dwell on one to the exclusion of the others since they all demanded an equal measure of ghastly disbelief. I was, for instance, enduring respiratory cologne distress by the time we'd finally entered Murry's great room proper, and I dropped into an armchair in a bid to recover my breath, a massive roll-armed item upholstered in saddle leather with an ottoman before it about the size of my dinette.

Murry was a third of an acre away before he'd recognized he'd lost me. He'd been rattling on about the ravishing splendor of being him which allowed me opportunity to survey Murry's furnishings and imbibe the full effect of Murry's curious decor, a cross between early Raj and Cattleman's Association. Given its size, that great room felt inordinately cluttered. There were separate groupings of chairs and settees and tables all over the place, urns and lamps and brass gimcrackery on every surface that would bear them, rugs strewn about in lively profusion, fully grown date palms in pots. The head of a bison hung over the mantelpiece. A massive canvas on one wall served essentially as a larger-than-life-size study of a Hereford. Opposite hung a tapestry, worn in spots and faded with age, which depicted swarthy turbaned men of Arabic extraction doing something culinary, I decided, to a goat.

From that oversized Chesterfield chair, the full effect of Murry's decor overtook me rather like a wave of nausea. First I was weak and unsettled and sweaty, and then I was pleased I'd not gagged and thrown up. I felt a passing debt to tastefulness to set fire to the place.

Eventually, Murry missed me and circled back to see just where I was. He found me in his massive chair, and he perched upon his ottoman from where Murry shared with me news of his own robust constitution and declared he'd never required a rest while walking through his house. Then he shouted out, "Sheila!" a few times to no perceivable effect before rising and stepping my way so I might feel his biceps.

Murry was one of those fellows who claimed to be in tip-top shape even though he was conspicuously pudgy, and as he stood there detailing for me his wellness regimen—whole grains, antioxidants and the Rolls-Royce of abdominal contraptions—I had the chance to study him baldly like I'd not enjoyed before. I merely nodded every now and again so as to seem attentive.

Murry's shirt was tailored and daisy yellow. His cardigan was green, and he had clearly broken with local tradition in his choice of trousers since Murry's were neither poplin nor denim but something sheer with an elegant drape. His slippers were maroon with a nappy velourish finish, and Murry's initials (MJB) were monogrammed on the uppers in gold. Even by then I knew already that Murry, in part, was named for the man who was named for the man who was named for the man who was named for Jubal Early.

In a quarter of the world where some civilians thought a wristwatch a fey adornment, Murry was courageous enough to wear a bracelet and a signet ring both. The bracelet was bright gold and faceted in such a way as to heighten its offensiveness while the ring was modest in size and of a considerably lower luster which would have left it to go unnoticed if Murry had not fingered it constantly. He wore some sort of choker around his neck that featured polished turquoise.

I heard Sheila before I saw her, a weary voice from the cavernous reaches. "What?" she said, and even then she was a while heaving into view. Sheila was a large woman, a Caribbean import who moved at a leisurely island pace, and she kept pausing to shift and straighten Murry's unending bric-a-brac.

Sheila was wearing what I had to imagine was Murry's idea of a proper domestic's uniform. The thing was gray and severely waisted in a French-parlormaid sort of way with doily trim and a matching doily tiara. That dress looked a couple of sizes too small for Sheila who was actively distressing the seams and who would likely have been cheerier and more agreeable in a muumuu.

She stopped beside an occasional table a mere love seat or two away. The thing had a slice of varnished tree trunk for a top and what looked steer horns for legs. Sheila snatched up an item from in among the clutter and examined it on her palm. Like most everything else in that great room, it was some little etched-brass piece of junk, but it belonged on another table in a different portion of the house. That anyway is what I managed to gather from the ensuing exchange. Sheila held the item up for Murry to see and then glared at him sourly which prompted from Murry a rather vague bout of jabbing with his thumb that he enlarged upon by telling Sheila, "I brought it in to show it to . . ." Here Murry trailed off and fell silent in shame and in defeat while Sheila, for her part, carried that trinket with her as she closed.

"What?" she said once she'd reached us, unfreighting the word with stark charmlessness.

"I think Mr. Tatum here," Murry told her, "could use a glass of water," which had the effect of deflecting Sheila's stony regard from Murry to me.

I shook my head and made the only noise that I could muster, a throaty squeak by which I hoped I might cause Sheila to understand that I had not, in fact, made overtures to Murry about water, that I didn't swill the stuff in any regular sort of way and would far prefer to imposing on Sheila the chance to dehydrate.

Sheila responded by studying me scathingly up and down. Then she snorted once with the strain of disgust that's common to deer in the wild before turning and moving off at a veritable crawl across Murry's great room. I didn't suppose there were hours of light enough left for me to see Sheila again.

Murry informed me Sheila had been in his employ for untold years and professed he had no clue what he would ever do without her. Go around with his sphincter unclenched, I suspected, his neck extended to full height.

Murry escorted me with painful deliberation throughout the rest of his house. I had to visit every bedroom, peek in all five of the half baths, inspect Murry's boiler works in the basement, the vintage Bentley in his garage, the home office where Murry's beer-distributor genius enjoyed full rein. Then it was out to the grounds, Murry called the yard, for a tour of Murry's plantings. He had patios and pools and all manner of leafy exotica in the back. Out front, where they could be seen from the road, Murry had his topiary which he was locally infamous for because it was widely thought obscene.

Now that part of the world is hardly known for its accomplished topiarists, and up close to those boxwoods in Murry's front yard I could see that the scandalous tableaux were the result of a wholesale failure of hedge-trimming craftsmanship. As far as Murry was concerned, he had a menagerie in his yard—an oversized rabbit, an elephant, a walrus, a giraffe, a couple of cows and what looked to me a mackerel or a salmon—but from a slow-rolling Nova sport coupe, for instance, on the road before Murry's house, a car with the sort of people in it who disapproved by nature of almost everyone who wasn't them, I could see most particularly how the elephant with its trunk upflung and the walrus with its tusks that had gone bushy and misshapen could get taken for clutches of drunken heathens entangled in mid-debauch.

I might even have shared with Murry popular opinion of his shrubbery, might have warned him anyway of the scandal he was causing in some quarters and put him in touch with the scrupulous fellow who trimmed my shrubs and mowed my yard and demonstrated an artful touch with electric clippers, but once I'd sought help for my client and Murry had told me firmly, "No," I decided I'd rather Murry simply proceed unenlightened.

As we were taking leave of each other at my Cavalier, Murry inflicted on me one last fillip of philosophy, something about the priceless educational value of personal hardship, and he paused on his porch to actively envy my client for the trials he'd soon know. Then Murry disappeared into his monstrously oversized house, and I had my car door open and my right foot on the floorboard when I spotted Sheila in the side yard creeping towards me with a tray.

She was probably seventy-five yards or more away, and I'd seen her slyly sidelong. So by all rights I could have climbed in my car and driven cleanly away, but my nagging misplaced sense of human decency kicked in, and I decided I owed the woman an audience if she ever reached me.

Accordingly, I stayed where I was and waited for Sheila to come which was precisely the sort of accommodation I'd make for perfect strangers though I would rarely exert myself for people I authentically knew. Like my cousin in Tucson whose calls I only grudgingly returned, my father's sister in Knoxville who I kept promising to visit, the school-aged godchild I'd not seen since back when he was christened. I was routinely prepared to treat that class of people callously, but Murry's maid I felt a personal duty to stand by and wait out.

There was a tumbler on her tray and a sort of carafe that water appeared to slosh from whenever Sheila lurched on uneven ground or accelerated beyond a crawl. So I had to imagine that she was moving even more slowly than normal since it took her almost a quarter hour to reach my Cavalier. She did stop once outright on the grounds by the elephant topiary and looked up at the thing in such a way as to cause me to understand that she hardly thought it an innocent pachyderm.

I thanked her extravagantly for her trouble once she'd ventured within range, and Sheila glared at me and made what sounded a disapproving necknoise. Then she shoved the tray my way and watched as I poured a glass of water. She continued to contemplate me while I drained the tumbler dry and favored me once I'd finished with the manner of perusal that suggested she didn't intend to retire with a half-emptied carafe. Consequently, I refilled my glass and poured down a second pint, and then I took up the carafe and dumped the leavings on the fescue because even my misplaced sense of decency tends to evaporate over time.

I came away nursing a rather exhaustively poor opinion of Murry. I didn't care for his taste in furnishings, resented his palaver, thought the EPA should probably hear about the man's cologne. As I drove towards home, I sifted through assorted crisp rejoinders with which I would have peppered Murry had I known the nerve and pluck. Had I not been serving, I told myself, my moonlighting client's interests. Had I not, in point of fact, been who I was.

I proved far too irrigated to make it home without relief, and I stopped at the no-name gas mart a couple of miles shy of my turnoff, a homely little place that sold off-brand fuel with no appreciable octane to it, tallboys and generic cigarettes, scratch-and-win lottery cards. The toilet there was probably last cleaned to celebrate Nixon's resignation, so I pulled up by the kerosene pump and stepped around to the back of the building where I slipped into the woods that customers used for facilities.

I say woods, but it was a patch really of spindly poplar saplings intermingled with the odd locust and slash pine, cluttered with rotting leaf mulch and trash. I remember quite vividly that I was doing my business, had zeroed in on a Baby Ruth wrapper after making adjustments for windage and the pitch of the terrain, and I was mulling over how very disagreeable I'd found Murry to be, was composing an extemporaneous tabulation of his offenses from the vain foolishness of his hair hat to his gold-leafed bamboo bedroom suite, when I was seized by the galvanizing suspicion that, with the proper guidance, Mona could probably be steered to a view of Murry different from my own, led to a weakness for Murry's ever-so-marginal allure, tempted possibly to an appetite for Murry's companionship.

I don't quite know if I thought too highly of my powers of persuasion or too poorly of Mona's judgments of the heart, but I remember standing distracted—trickling onto nothing much—while contemplating the variety of conniving it would take to bring Mona and Murry together in romance. As I shook and tucked and zipped and picked my way out of that thicket, I did endure an uneasy moment of acrid disgust with myself, but it lifted and passed and left me free to forge ahead unchastened.

Now I'd previously entertained idle whimsies about pawning Mona off and had considered Murry a candidate chiefly because he was flush and single. At the time, I'd only seen his monstrously oversized house from the road and Murry himself at the far end of grocery-mart aisles or at stoplights in his car. So it was easy back then to imagine Murry a source of contentment for Mona, picture her happily sprawled on a divan in Murry's gargantuan digs, no more difficult anyway than picturing Mona carrying the phone man's baby or caught up in a torrid dalliance with the county agent's wife since it was all at first just bourbon-tainted sporting wishfulness.

But there by my Cavalier fender well opposite the kerosene pump at that no-name gas mart a few miles shy of my turnoff, I settled on a brand of actual deceit to employ as a substitute for spine.

I had no reason, of course, to expect a scheme I'd hatched to bear much fruit since I was already by then the engineer of countless unproductive ventures. I'd pursued more ruinous investment strategies than any human should be allowed, had systematically failed at every attempt I'd made to improve my physique or expand my French and Italian skills beyond requests for the check.

I'd once bought a few acres of woodland in the Allegheny piedmont, but the cabin I'd meant to build there with my sweat and indifferent skill never got terribly much past stakes and string. I'd made brief forays into cartooning and art photography, had withdrawn from a Lynchburg cooking school because of cutlery injuries. I'd taken in lieu of payment once a Thunderbird I'd hoped to restore, but I'd only ever scoured a spot of rust off a sideview-mirror housing, and the sprocket receptacle I'd invented for pocket change and keys (which I'd intended to live a swell and decadent life on the proceeds from) got busted up one night for kindling when there was nothing else at hand.

I had fit reason, then, to doubt my schemes and designs would amount to much, could look back on a damning history of truncated prosecution which gave me cause to believe that Mona would know the sense to recognize Murry for a gardenia-soaked coiffurially challenged dud.

The man, however, crossed me up with his unqualified fondness for children which even included Mona's daughter who was, by nature, an ill-tempered trial. I'd been reluctant to work Dinky into the Murry-and-Mona equation since, in my experience, she specialized in piercing wails and stomping fits, but I turned out to have need of her for my scheme once I'd secured Murry's permission to carry Dinky out to see his topiaries.

Nobody much came to see Murry's bushes in the spirit of joy and wonder. Most of his visitors were full of brimstone and recriminations instead. They usually stood at the ditch with hand-lettered placards threatening Murry with perdition, so maybe it was the novelty as much as anything that made Murry eager for us to come.

Dinky, for her part, didn't prove keen to see Murry's topiaries notwithstanding my fanciful descriptions of them and the sparkling fun I promised we'd have. Dinky just stood, I remember, and chewed on the fluke of her slug while she listened to me. I'd knelt down and put on my frothy gay voice and my fraudulent toothy grin, was burbling at the child about the jolly time before us as she slobbered and watched me, crusty and morose, peering in as if she could see straight through to my arid bookkeeper's soul. Once I'd checked to make sure we were unobserved, I gave Dinky a tug (I'll call it) and acquainted her in a treacherous whisper with her plans for the afternoon.

Murry came out to meet us before we were well out of my Cavalier. He fairly jigged down the massive front steps of his absurdly oversized house, was wearing a cardigan in a shade of alarming electric green that did such ferocious battle with Murry's powder-blue trousers that I was tempted in ocular self-defense to turn my back and run.

He seemed barely even to notice Mona at first. That's how fixed Murry was on her daughter who he gathered in his arms, snatched up off the ground and kissed flush upon the cheek which, experience had taught me, was just the sort of thing to touch off calamity. I was expecting Dinky to flail and looking for her to caterwaul. I noticed her feet were hanging effectively at testicle level, so it seemed to me likely she'd punt Murry's scrotum and thereby put him down. Instead, though, Dinky tolerated Murry almost graciously which I'm inclined to attribute to the soporific effect of Murry's cologne.

By that time, Mona had known near-limitless opportunity to see the stiff and flinty sort of dealings I had with her child, so I have to think she was gratified by Murry's easy show of affection and was warming towards him even before he'd raised her knuckles to his lips. Murry then stepped back to admire Mona along her length and congratulate her on her classic beauty, not really the sort of enterprise I'd ever bothered with.

Mona responded by intentionally sniffing the man and fairly mooning over his scent. "Nice," she said and with a sincerity that spurred me to recognize the kinship between Murry's florid aroma and Mona's candle reek. Moreover, with Murry's appallingly mismatched clothes and the stubble he'd missed in shaving, he looked a bit like Mona's deplorable tenor who'd lately regained his hearing.

I got a sensation along about then in my gut, an effervescent twinge which suggested to me that Mona and Murry were taken with each other, fond instinctively to a pitch I'd hardly expected and didn't entirely like. That was the queer thing about it. There I'd gone to no little trouble to bring them together. Yet once I'd met with cause to suspect that they were actually hitting it off, I suffered a spot of reflexive regret, a molten tremor of jealousy which I ascribed to some sort of testosterone-addled territorial impulse and persuaded myself it was probably as irresistible as a sneeze.

Murry called out to summon Sheila from the bowels of his house and charged her to "whip up" a pitcher of lemonade which was a little like asking Mahler to dash off a symphony. Sheila snorted by way of response and slogged back into Murry's foyer. I figured it would take a quarter hour for her to reach the kitchen alone and couldn't guess what chunk of afternoon the whipping up might eat, but I felt sure that Mona and Murry would know appreciable leisure to bond, most particularly if I took charge of Dinky and left them undistracted.

So I grabbed Dinky's hand and drew her along the drive to see Murry's shrubs. I lifted her up to have a closer peek at Murry's walrus while I kept discreet lookout on Murry and Mona by my car where they were engaged in sprightly conversation. I could tell, even back from where I stood, that Murry had some charm, that he wasn't anyway obliged to get by on abominable taste in decor and unsavory Old Testament rectitude alone but was perfectly capable of surprising laughter from a woman and could tilt his head in a way to make him seem sympathetic to what she said.

I don't suppose it hurt for Murry to have his oversized house behind him, to have trotted out already his uniformed domestic, to be standing in the airless afternoon flanked by his manicured grounds where he could give the alluring impression of a grandee with rooted hair. He might as well have been wearing a mantle, holding a scepter, sporting a crown. It seemed wholly inconceivable to me that Mona might resist him as I found him a little beguiling myself even back from where I stood.

Holding Dinky there in the driveway where she examined Murry's walrus while I listened to the lilting chatter of a woman I knew I didn't love, I was visited by a sour adolescent brand of upset, proved capable of fearing the loss of a creature I didn't remotely want back and could, at the same time, recognize the stark foolishness of it. I was fully equipped, that is, to know I was in the grips of tumult a better man would long since have outgrown. "Hey," Dinky said. It was my name with her, was all she ever troubled herself to call me. She was perched on this occasion in the vicinity of my hair tufts and tugged on one to painful emphatic effect.

"What?"

She pointed towards Murry's topiary walrus with its bushy tusks. "What are those people doing?" she wanted to know.

III

1 —◦◈ "That gooseneck," Stoney told me. "It had a bracelet in it. Those Hoopers," he added. "You know. Up the pike."

And that's how Stoney chose to broach what we neither one could know was, in fact, the beginning of the end. He took up a fractured saltine from the saucer on the table, examined it for a moment, sniffed it once and tossed it back onto the plate.

"The sink was running slow. I was expecting grease and hair."

Stoney told me that Hooper's husband had fallen out with their previous plumber. They'd quarreled, he seemed to recall, over the state of a bead of grout that plumber had run around a shower stall. Apparently, it wavered in girth in a fashion that Hooper's husband found displeasing, even strayed here and there up onto the actual tiles.

"He's a funny one," Stoney told me, speaking of that Hooper's husband. "Douglas," he said with a curl of his lips and an expecto-rational tinge.

To hear it from Stoney, Douglas ran towards rigorously particular and, like most of his sort, hardly hewed to those things worth being particular about. He liked his house tidy in the way the bulk of decent people would, but he also liked his driveway gravel raked to an even depth and had engaged a Honduran whose chief job was to rake it. In slack times the man raised a sheen on the Hooper copper downspouts and touched up the porch-plank edges where they extended past the rails. A different gentleman gathered and carted the rubbish the Hoopers' magnolia dropped and collected needles from under their white pines to carpet a boggy portion of paddock. He and the driveway raker together scoured the bushes of snared oak leaves.

Now that all might have passed for little more than solid stewardship if that Hooper had shown much sense of restraint or appetite for discretion. Instead he seemed driven to lord his will over every unruly condition he met and proved prepared to inflict manpower on a thing until it was harnessed and docile.

He employed a man whose job it was to travel the edges of that estate and brush fresh coats of paint onto the white-plank fencing. By the time he'd finished a circuit, his oldest work was invariably dingy again. Douglas kept on retainer a turf specialist from the agricultural school in Blacksburg who was charged with maintaining the Hoopers' zoysia at an uninterrupted green. He had a regular window-cleaning crew, a gentleman and his two daughters, who squeegeed his panes and tended his glazing, sprayed rust inhibitor on his screens, and he employed a trio of barn hands who pounced so on the horse droppings, were such meticulous paddock muckers and pasture-grass custodians that, when the horses were out of sight, it was hard to believe there was livestock about.

"Yea high," Stoney told me and described that Hooper with a hand across his sternum. "Loafers and pleated trousers. You know the sort."

I puckered and nodded and joined with Stoney in a moment of sour disdain before acquainting him with the lone encounter I'd had with that Hooper. I told how he'd rolled up on me at the Citgo. I informed Stoney he'd called me "sport," and then we shared a moment further of corrosive disapproval before confessing ourselves unable to locate that Hooper's residual charms and entirely helpless against the suspicion he'd won his wife through the black arts.

Stoney favored me with a description of the inside of their house which sounded so orderly and antiseptic as to be curated. That first visit, Stoney spent the bulk of his time on a powder-room floor, half on the cleft quarry slate and half under the lavatory with Douglas hovering so close by that each occasion Stoney twitched, he barked up against a tapered loafer or brushed a trouser cuff.

"That dog came in to sniff me, and Douglas kicked him out the door." Stoney said this with an air of tenderhearted indignation, as if he'd never passed an evening booting cats around his yard. Then he described for me the way he'd had to heat that gooseneck up, play a hot blue propane jet upon it to loosen up the joints which Douglas, apparently, tolerated poorly. It seems he'd as soon have kept sheep in his front hall as suffer an open flame in his half bath.

"He just about came crawling in on me. Afraid I'd burn the place clean down."

We indulged together, Stoney and I, in fresh contempt for the man who was plainly wanting in the brand of brawny nerve we had which, when taken with the pleated trousers and the tapered tassel loafers, served to render Douglas all the riper for revulsion, and I was fully prepared to detest him as soon as occasion presented itself.

Shortly thereafter it did, once Stoney had set about describing how he'd finally worked that gooseneck free and reamed it with a length of wire. He'd spilled the contents into a bucket and had discovered, mixed in with the sludge, a woman's ornate silver bracelet crusted over with gemstones. Douglas wouldn't touch the thing until Stoney had wiped it clean, and even then he'd only handle it with an intervening tissue. Stoney watched as Douglas examined it, and Stoney volunteered the theory that some woman was probably washing her hands when that bracelet dropped off her wrist. Douglas failed, for his part, to trouble himself to so much as grunt in reply.

It seems Douglas was busy cultivating a theory of his own that Stoney, in a fashion, watched coalesce and accrue. He looked on, that is, as Douglas lavished notice on that bracelet and tried to decide (it turned out) how the thing had happened to slip from his wife's wrist, how it had worked its way past the stopper posts and vanished down the drain which Douglas looked to believe had called for a spot of intentional assistance.

Stoney described to me how Douglas closed that bracelet in his fist with soggy bits of tissue end protruding either side, and Stoney imitated the way the man spoke chiefly to his knuckles. There in his magazine-choked front room in his ratty favorite chair, Stoney raised an arm and told his closed hand, "Maud!"

"She stirred somewhere. I could hear her," Stoney said. "Rustled, you know, like a mouse in the wall."

"MAUD!"

It seems the second one was the brand of shriek that demanded a reply, and she called back (Stoney told me) as she closed along the hall. Stoney could hear the floor planks creaking. "Where are you, Doug?" she said.

"He grinned at me, the rascal did. Like I was in it with him." Stoney said the man whispered, "Where are you?" in a poisonous hiss and with uncovered teeth.

"She walked right into it," Stoney said. "Got called like that, and still she came. Fetched up in the doorway." And here Stoney paused to savor his first sight of her. I took occasion to conjure her fingering percale in the remnant shop.

"Don't see much of that out here," Stoney told me. He shook his head and added at length, "No sir," for decisive effect.

And that's essentially why I'd stuck with Stoney in spite of his frothy talk, why I'd battled through his inexhaustible interest in TV and his appetite for wishful unsubstantiated scandal, why I'd engaged across his prune-fouled ditch in uninvolving chats. It was because I had sensed somehow he'd know exotica when he saw it, was equipped with a knack for distinguishing the mundane from the rare and was hardly the sort to mine his solace in the commonplace.

That Hooper woman was fragile there where females were prized for being sturdy. She was unguardedly troubled in a region of bluff and hardy veneers. She had something of tragedy hanging about her and unmendable regret which seemed agreeably free of scattershot New Testament scholarship. She went about unadorned—unlacquered, unpowdered, mercifully underperfumed—in dungarees and paddock boots and what appeared cast-off menswear with her hair gathered and clipped on top of her head, carelessly as if for a bath. And yet she still had more of elegance and casual unchecked allure than any befrocked and barber-school-coiffured female about.

That Stoney proved fit to detect as much confirmed him as my sort. Now, granted, I've never been a man of profuse alliances, and I could claim few even marginal friends to speak of at the time, so there was no one really for Stoney to shoulder by and to displace, but still and all there we were talking together sensibly of a woman without having first acknowledged her a candidate for intercourse. In my experience, that was rare between men, possibly even unheard of. Stoney and I were feeling authentic protective urges towards that Hooper which had nothing to do with separating her from her delicates and turning the creature, for recreational purposes, entirely upside down. So we were guilty together of a strain of gender blasphemy.

"He opened his hand and showed it to her," Stoney told me while opening a hand of his own and assuming the expression that Hooper's husband had treated his wife to. It was tight-lipped and curdled in Stoney's rendition, touched with the manner of primal pity that's ordinarily expended upon doomed undomesticated beasts.

"She just shrank a little," Stoney said, and he added a "you know" as he dropped his chin and contracted ever so slightly at the shoulders in what looked both a show of disappointment and preparation for a blow.

"I don't recall that so much as a word passed between them." Stoney shook his head. "Not a peep."

Then Stoney took occasion to touch upon the species of byplay he was customarily exposed to when he worked in people's homes. He described a regular stew of resentments and antagonisms, of matrimonial shorthand and forced jocularity, of articulate grunts and snorts and purely damning exhalations, bursts of laughter as sharp and catastrophic as artillery fire. And it was all usually frosted over with a confectionary glaze, a blend of hollow courtesy and insincere endearments thrown up in the face of company to serve as a candy crust.

He'd be painting or plumbing or pulling wire, measuring for trim while his customers oversaw the work and sniped hotly at each other but always with the odd "now, honey," the occasional "now, dear."

Stoney assured me it was different with those Hoopers out the pike. Rawer, he said, with not even a dash of chirpy domestic theater. Once that bracelet from the sink trap had been offered on display and Douglas had supplied his sneering wordless commentary, Stoney knew he'd shown up with his channel locks and his propane torch and manufactured inadvertently dire peril for a woman. And not a sturdy local sort who'd probably earned it over time but that delicate Hooper instead who couldn't have had much of anything coming.

"It looked to me like he'd go at her as soon as I walked out the door, so I did everything I could to try to stay."

Stoney took so long to change the sink valve on the kitchen tap that Douglas worked up a freshet of ire to spend exclusively upon him. He stayed ill while Stoney fiddled with the balky double dead bolt that Douglas didn't want repaired but meant instead to have replaced. Stoney tried to make an ordeal from a sagging closet door which turned out to only need three of its upper hinge screws snugged, and then Stoney dropped onto the floor to play with Amos the dog for a time and wax nostalgic about canines he'd owned when he was a boy in Wheeling.

Stoney romped with the Hoopers' dog in a bid to malinger in their house and present Douglas the opportunity to settle and cool off. That was before Stoney realized that Douglas wasn't exactly the hair-trigger sort, hardly your garden-variety manner of hot-head. He just stood and watched Stoney play with his dog, his wife hard beside him in the foyer, and Stoney noticed he clung to her wrist in what looked a preamble to torque.

"She was sure to get hers," Stoney told me, "even if I'd stayed the night." And here Stoney volunteered his impression of a man who was rigorous and thorough and obliged to correct his wife because it simply had to be done.

Stoney packed up the five-gallon bucket that did him duty as a toolbox. He recalled that he paused on the doorsill and troubled himself to catch Maud Hooper's eye, took occasion to tell her, "Ma'am," in case she gave sign of an impulse to abandon her executive estate and her appreciable lout of a husband and escape with a local jackleg in his battered Econoline van.

"I didn't leave out right away," Stoney told me. "Just sat there for a minute."

Stoney paused to bite the corner of a saltine, worked it over pensively. "The place looked so nice," he said, and I knew just what Stoney meant. I could readily picture that tidy Hooper executive estate with its pristine lawn, its manicured shrubs, its furrowed driveway gravel, the Provençal garden shaggy in its orchestrated way.

I was reminded of my similar interlude out at the Settle place where I'd listened to a gentleman bodily pitch his wife about the house before I'd drowned them out with AM radio. Sadly I told Stoney what I'd heard and gravely I told him from whom which provoked from Stoney a snort out of all keeping with my mood.

"That old bat," he said and shifted phlegm in a recreational way. "Don't know but that I'd kick her around myself."

2 —⟶ Fundamentally, the trouble was that Hooper struck us as defenseless. It hardly hurt that she was willowy and agreeable to see, but it probably mattered most that she impressed us both as helpless and constitutionally at the mercy of Douglas's every vengeful whim. Since Stoney and I were both of us men, we had no authentic choice between us but to contemplate saving that Hooper whenever we had a free moment to think.

I've no personal sense of the inner workings of the female mind, can't even guess at the brand of musing, at the school of speculative thought a woman might indulge in once she's happened on a man who has impressed her as beguiling and worthwhile. I have reason to know, however, that when men fix on a woman, we go juvenile and bombastically heroic.

So I feel confident in saying that Stoney and I were rescuing Maud Hooper, that we passed more time between us than was seemly and becoming imagining the woman in dire situations from which we'd pluck her out. Not that Stoney and I ever spoke to each other about what we were thinking. We met with occasion to chat across the ditch, and those Hoopers sometimes came up but invariably so we could throw in together and heap contempt on Douglas, affirm our mutual view that he hardly deserved much of anything he had. We meant chiefly, of course, the devoted company of a willowy woman, but we were probably between us prepared to begrudge him the rest of his spoils as well.

For my part, I saved Maud Hooper from a raging barn fire or three, and I'd always venture selflessly back into the inferno—deaf to the woman's protests that I, for the love of sweet Jesus, not go— to lead that Hooper's priceless warmbloods out to safety as well. The injuries I sustained were usually in the survivable blunt-force family, cuts and gashes ordinarily from falling timbers and the occasional fractured bone that Maud Hooper would clean and dress herself before carrying me to the doctor who'd suture me shut or set me in plaster, pronounce me lucky to be alive.

Occasionally, I would stumble out to smolder and expire in the paddock with Amos the corgi singed but otherwise healthy in my arms. Maud Hooper would sob and wail and keen over my lifeless carcass, regret that she had come to love me only once I was deceased.

Sometimes I'd pull her from various bodies of water she'd steered her car into, happen by her house to throttle thieving marauders who'd set upon her. I'd save her from rampaging bears in the national forest. Packs of wolves and rabid bobcats. The odd congregation of venomous snakes. In an actual dream one night, I strayed across her in the grocery mart, or in a store anyway remarkably similar to the grocery mart but for its pneumatic auto lift and its women's shoe department. She was backed into a corner hard beside the dairy case—flanked by deli Swiss, egg substitutes and herring—and she was being actively stalked and menaced by a guinea hen.

I'd come for bacon apparently. I was pushing a cart loaded clear to the child seat with it. Organic apple-smoked bacon wanting en- tirely in sulfites. I sized up Maud's predicament, abandoned my cart and confronted that guinea. When the bird refused to hear reason, I fell upon it and snatched it up.

Maud Hooper, for her part, failed to exhibit a freshening pas- sion for me. She looked on me in the fashion a man with a guinea in hand deserves. Without quivering emotion, that is to say. With wan and clinical interest. I only made things worse by gloating, subjecting that guinea to jeers and taunts.

By the time she told me, "It's only a bird," Maud had become Mona instead. She was wearing but a yachting cap and a pair of dime-store flip-flops. Mona squirted a shot of whipped cream into her mouth straight out of the can. The sharp pressurized hiss of the stuff jolted me awake. I'd kicked off the bedclothes in my sleep and cast my pillow onto the floor. The room was bright with moonlight, and some insect in the shrubbery was making some- thing close to the sound canned whipped cream makes.

To his credit, Stoney had acted as best he could on Maud Hooper's behalf. He might have passed assorted evenings in my brand of reverie, but after the bracelet in the sink trap and the ten- sion it had prompted, Stoney made a point of hurrying back with a new kitchen sink trap valve. He showed up, in fact, the follow- ing morning to find Maud Hooper in one piece if a little wary of Douglas once he'd joined them in the foyer. Douglas made a pre- cipitous reach for his tie knot, and Stoney claimed to see Maud shy and twitch.

It turned out they had numerous items throughout their place in need of attention. The sorts of problems their gravel raker, their stable muckers, their board-fence painter, their lawn tenders and window cleaners weren't well suited to see to and mend. Be- fore Stoney, those Hoopers had enjoyed no luck much with our local tradesmen. As is generally the case anymore, they could find somebody to roof their house, dig them a pond, build an addition, resurface their drive, but if they needed some sort of trifling wholly unmonumental repair—a light switch swapped out for a dimmer, a vent pipe flashed, a door screen replaced—nobody would bother with them until Stoney.

All-purpose fix-it men are hard to come by anymore since, as a people, we're taught not to set our sights on modest goals and trifles. Better to aim, thinking goes, for the stars and incinerate in the atmosphere. But as long as there are widows and lawyers and tenured professors, this world will be afflicted with mechanical haplessness.

Consequently, even if Douglas Hooper had wanted to shift from Stoney, had hoped to hire a man more subtle with his disapproving glances, more veiled in his distaste for Douglas's treatment of his wife, he likely wouldn't have found anybody within a hundred miles, certainly no one as competent and even remotely as capable as Stoney whose sole offense lay in a certain frankness of expression, an inability not to look like he was thinking what he thought.

And the way Stoney told it, he met with ample reason to bristle and huff, couldn't approve of the tone that Douglas took routinely with his wife when she would ask an innocent question or volunteer a trifling comment, stand inadvertently in her husband's light as that Hooper led Stoney about the house to show him the trouble spots—the leaks, the stains, the tears, the puckers he meant for Stoney to see to. Stoney told me the man came up with a fresh batch almost every day.

Consequently, Stoney worked out at the Hoopers' steadily for a time. He went for several weeks straight addressing the afflictions of an ancient settling house. He planed doors so they would fit in jambs. He reattached weights to sashes. He patched failing plaster and replaced suspect floorboards, lifted sags with screw jacks in the cellar, rebricked the frost-blasted stoop. He installed new outlets and ran fresh circuits, changed out washers in all of the taps, reanchored curtain rods that had pulled free of the chalky walls, replaced furnace filters and lamp works, dumped bugs out of the ceiling light globes.

Stoney performed, in short, each task that Douglas charged him to see after, and he witnessed as well the domestic Hooper byplay every morning when Maud, back from the barn, would set before Douglas the breakfast he'd not hoped for, when she'd select for him the wrong tie and root out his misplaced socks, advise him what precisely she'd done with his goddamn keys and tell him to be careful as he headed out the door which invariably only earned from Douglas, "Yeah."

To hear it from Stoney, Douglas habitually treated Maud Hooper poorly. He was sharp and churlish with her as a matter of course, ridiculed the bulk of what she told him and ignored with baleful snorts the rest, never vented so much as the faintest whisper of husbandly affection, volunteered no endearments, indulged no temptations to buss her on the cheek. And according to Stoney, he looked at the woman like most men eye their mechanics, with a decided touch—that is to say—of dyspeptic exasperation.

He shook her once in Stoney's presence. He grabbed her by her upper arm and wrenched her around to help train her attention exclusively upon him so that Douglas might acquaint her with some transgression face-to-face. Stoney told me he was nailing up shoe mold at the time, and he rose from his knees with his punch in hand, with his sixteen-ounce clawhammer, so as to take but half a stride in the direction of Douglas across the room. Douglas noticed, Stoney told me. Douglas apparently understood because he loosed his grip from Maud Hooper's arm and abandoned his corrective. He shot Stoney a sour grin and went on about something else.

But they had for a moment there, Stoney felt sure, come to understand each other. There is a species of common language that is particular to men. It's comprised of a blend of dumbshow and guttural necknoises, ornamented usually with head tilts and semi-articulate glares. As forms of expression go, this one is blunt and starkly economical. Stoney effectively told that Hooper, "I'm half ready to put you down," and in loosing his hold on his wife, that Hooper informed him back, "I hear you."

So the lines of allegiance and sympathy were plotted early on. Stoney tolerated Douglas and saw fit to take his money as a means of passing time in the vicinity of his wife. And it wasn't like Stoney mooned over the woman the way I probably would have or ached for her after the fashion I'd personally ached for women before. As best I could tell, Stoney's intentions were chaste and admirably selfless. He could see well enough that Maud Hooper was getting squandered in this life, and Stoney just wanted to remedy and curb the situation.

They ate lunch together most days, Stoney with his deviled ham and that Hooper with her yogurts, with her microwaved soup cups. They'd talk chiefly, he told me, of horses since Stoney knew enough of mules to pass himself off as barn wise and conversant on the topic. And Stoney told me that Hooper had up and departed one day from paddock chat to indulge in something franker and far closer to the bone, to visit on Stoney a line of talk perfumed with wistfulness. She said that thanks to Douglas's "business" (and she'd hunted for the word, had expelled it like it truly didn't fit and hardly served) she could afford the sorts of horses that were rarely ever well, occupied their time with being halt and fragile. With a snort, Stoney told me, with a manner of wan smile, the woman had cast back to her girlhood out along the Eastern Shore when she'd had sturdy plugs for mounts and no inkling yet of Douglas.

Stoney told me he sat and nibbled his crackers dabbed with potted meat and contributed but the occasional nod, the odd empathetic grunt. For a man with satellite reception and a headful of dubious facts, Stoney could readily distinguish the worthwhile significant chatter from the piffle, and he allowed he'd recognized

Maud Hooper was sharing something with him beyond the plea-sures of riding the Chesapeake dunes, the rank joys of girlishness.

Of course, I came along in time to explicate the business for him, lay out what he'd been told by the woman and explain what it had meant. That was, after all, my specialty and the foundation of my career. I collected information—chits and check stubs and invoices—and transformed them from clutter into semifictional fiscal sense. I distilled by profession, deciphered, extrapolated on the fly, so once I'd heard what Maud had shared with Stoney, I was just the guy to tell him what she'd said. Even at the time, though, sitting across the kitchen table from her, Stoney had imbibed enough of a sense of Maud Hooper's profound unhappiness and had witnessed quite sufficient of Douglas's crude manhandling ways to feel called, in his capacity as the look-alike Saint George, to insert himself into the situation.

Now it's no easy matter to function as a savior on the ground. Stoney had been suitably chastened by his experience at the Dairy-O, and he had a basin-wrench scar on his scalp if he needed reminding of those siblings who'd not been, it turned out, ripe for matrimonial advice. So Stoney was hardly apt to be rash where it came to an intervention, and he explained to me one evening as we spoke over his prune-fouled ditch how he'd cobbled up with care and honed a piece of talk for Douglas, had tried to give it the form of a spot of advice from a well-meaning interested friend.

He'd held it close and rehearsed it until he'd finished most all of the work that Douglas had requested him to do, and Stoney had packed up one evening, was hauling his hand tools out in his joint-compound bucket, when Douglas rolled in and sought out Stoney to consult him on gravel options. It turned out Douglas was satis-fied with the size and lay of his driveway stone, with the way the rock stayed out of tire treads, with the way it responded to raking, but he'd come to harbor reservations about the color of it. He'd grown to prefer the dark gray of his driveway stone wet to the flat dusty gray of it dry and figured Stoney for a man sufficiently familiar with the local quarry to have some knowledge of the shades of rock available about.

At the heart of that assumption lay a stark indication of the difference between Douglas and Stoney. Like most men in those parts, Stoney gauged quarry gravel pretty much by size alone. The color of the rock you got was whatever the color of the rock you got was. Stoney had likely never contemplated the decorative qualities of gravel while the look of the stuff was plainly a prime consideration for Douglas.

So you had the pair of them standing there in the drive by Douglas's shiny Range Rover with Douglas in his tailored khakis and his pointed tassel loafers and Stoney in his shabby greasy forest-green twill trousers holding a compound bucket tumbled rudely full of tools. Douglas was actually floating the notion of replacing his driveway gravel with precisely the same size stone in a slightly darker shade of gray which Stoney was trying to embrace as a sensible proposition, or stifle anyway the impulse to declare it lunacy.

These were hardly the sort of men to share together an understanding about, truth be told, much of anything at all. Most particularly the welfare of an item as complex as a female, a woman Douglas was acquainted with clear down to her bones while Stoney had come to know her chiefly from the jodhpurs out.

The way I heard it from Stoney, though, he felt he had an obligation which was due in but slight part to his resemblance to Saint George and could largely be ascribed to Stoney's innate sense of people. He couldn't help but feel he'd plumbed Maud Hooper, had come to know her better than he ought just by watching her about the house and listening to her at the table which had rendered him conversant in her pitch of melancholy—the persistent desolate sting of it, the primal causes at its core.

Stoney merely meant to suggest Douglas be gentle with his wife, revive in him a sense of Maud's grace, of her considerable native savor. He hoped to encourage Douglas to comport himself like the fortunate man he was, but it turned out he might have known better luck persuading Douglas Hooper to surrender to the chaos of unpainted fencing, a shaggy lawn, disheveled driveway stone.

Apparently, Stoney delivered his practiced sentiment capably enough and included with it a wish that Douglas's wife might go unhanded which Douglas seemed, at length, to take as a warning and construe as a threat. At the time, he kept his peace and ground enamel off his molars, let Stoney bumble through his monologue and climb into his van, and only later and by proxy did Douglas air his indignation in the form of a regular heap of a man who showed up on Stoney's porch.

Douglas, you see, was the sort of attorney with favors to call in. He had an office up in Gaithersburg and clients in Baltimore proper with funds, most of them, they needed to shelter, to shift offshore, to hide. Douglas never set foot in a courtroom but attended to contracts and titles, was particularly deft in the manufacture of that strain of enterprise that's prone to exist on notarized paper alone, and he naturally attracted the species of client in need of his expertise.

They were men, almost invariably, blessed with uncivic moxie and pluck, no regular employment, no domestic bank accounts, wives and girlfriends at the same time, sundry Social Security numbers. They were by nature decisive and by necessity wholly unsentimental. Every now and again they'd get indicted for some trifle or another, but they only ever went to the local lockup Sunday afternoons to visit cousins and retainers, loyal steadfast underlings.

By law, they were free to say whatever they wished in front of Douglas without the worry of Douglas whispering to upright citizens what he'd heard. And I have to believe routine exposure to the exploits of his clients, privileged knowledge of enormities

218 • T. R. PEARSON

they'd gone undiscovered at, spots of vengeance that they'd over-
seen, correctives they'd inflicted, competitors they'd dispatched,
colleagues they'd rendered scant, had served over time to throw
out of true the compass of Douglas's life. Not that he'd become a
renegade, an outlaw by standard measure, but he was privy almost
daily to a strain of problem solving that was bound to work upon
the man to poisonous effect.

Since Douglas wasn't big and tough and especially bloodthirsty
and lacked, by dint of profession, his clients' healthy contempt for
the law, he was largely bereft of antisocial opportunities with the
exception of private evenings at home in the company of his wife
who was weaker than Douglas and quite conveniently exasperat-
ing. Most everything he couldn't bring himself to do to other
people, Douglas found he could muster the nerve to do to her.

That anyway became my theory, particularly once I'd heard
from Stoney about the gentleman Douglas had sent to call on
Stoney at his home. He was a meaty fellow. I saw his car—a massive maroon sedan—and figured him for the siding salesman I'd
heard was in the area. He was struggling out of his driver's seat
when I spied him through the screen, looked to have reached the
blubbery far frontier of portly.

Stoney told me he'd heard the fellow long before he'd knocked.
He made him out over the TV laboring up the front-porch steps
and moving heavily across the planking. And Stoney, who had no
use for siding, yelled at him to go away and had neglected to answer the door until that man had dispensed with his knuckles and
had set about knocking instead with the toe of his shoe.

Accordingly, Stoney answered the door in a less-than-cordial
mood and discovered, instead of a siding salesman, a Baltimore
ne'er-do-well of appreciable girth and labored respiration. He was
leaning against the porch rail cleaning his nails with the tip of a
knife that looked to Stoney stout enough to butcher livestock
with. The trip up the steps from the car along with the shoe toe on

Stoney's door had left that fellow inordinately spent and unduly winded, so he wasn't in any shape to air his business straightaway which meant Stoney was free for a time to eye that gentleman undistracted.

Stoney allowed he couldn't help but notice the state of the nails that fellow was tending, and he'd never seen any in less need of the taper of a knife. That fellow found the breath to speak at length, but only after Stoney had informed him that he wouldn't install vinyl siding on a bet and then offered, as a courtesy, his disparaging opinion of the integrity of the porch rail that gentleman was leaning against.

"Hate to see you in the bushes," Stoney told him which served to bring that Baltimore ne'er-do-well unsupported to his feet. He turned and gave that rail a couple of shoves by way of testing Stoney's assessment, kept at it until he'd knocked it—pickets and all—into the boxwood. Then he nodded and told Stoney by way of commentary, "Hmm."

Then he looked Stoney up and down and inquired of him, "Stoney, right?"

Stoney nodded and watched as he touched his knife blade to his own lapel by way of prelude to an introduction.

"Friend of Doug's," he informed Stoney and then permitted him a moment to come to grips as best he might with the dire gravity afoot.

"Got business of your own, I'm guessing," that gentleman presently said to Stoney who confessed to me he'd hardly settled on just what the man had meant when the prick of the knife upon his shirtfront captured his attention, and that fellow (to hear it from Stoney) heightened the pressure as he spoke. "Why don't you keep your nose in that," he offered up as a suggestion, and he punctuated the sentiment by breaking Stoney's skin.

That pile of a man wasn't in any condition to depart with appropriate flair. He took the front steps slowly, a tread at a time, while holding to the rail, and he was obliged to maneuver backwards into his sedan with all of the deft alacrity of an Apollo astronaut. Stoney stood on the porch and watched him, stanched his slight knife wound with spit. He told me he'd felt called to reconsider everything Saint Georgian.

As that fellow whipped around in the yard and scattered guineas and cats, went lurching across Stoney's culvert and out into the roadway proper, Stoney consoled himself with the recollection of a buddy from the army, a McKenzie from Indiana who'd been the image of Tab Hunter. He'd had the shock of wavy hair, the azure eyes, the cleft chin, the chiseled boot-camp physique of an Adonis, and yet Stoney had met with news at length that he had come to nothing, had yielded to liver complications in a residential motel.

Stoney stepped back inside determined to keep his nose where it belonged.

3

—❧ So he would have been fine most likely, would have carried on the way he'd been with his Banquet chicken diet and his satellite reception, his monumental clutter and his feline infestation, his scattershot employment, his ratty Ford Econoline van, the mangled facts that he regurgitated by way of conversation, the hygiene he failed to trouble with, his skimpy deplorable head of hair. Stoney could, that is, have long survived his washout as a savior if I'd only known at the time engaging business of my own.

But assorted of my affairs were simultaneously curdling on me. Mona, for one, had taken to Murry with a velocity I found goading. Yes, I'd brought them together in a bid to put her off of me, but I'd expected a show of reluctance and some residual nostalgia for the fond months we had passed in each other's company. I'd meant for Mona to be torn, had calculated on misgivings and had thought I could count on Mona for a display of tender regrets. I guess instead she'd measured me and Murry, one against the other, and had found me so grievously wanting that she had endured but a twinge.

Murry turned out to be thoughtful in a way I'd never bothered with. He proved the sort to commemorate meaningless occasions with toys for Dinky and trinkets and sprays of flowers for Mona herself. They got swag on the solstice. Dinky was given a Bible embossed with her name on the day she turned precisely five and a half. Murry presented Mona with earrings to mark a favorable stock transaction, gave the girls together identical bracelets in honor of the waning moon, and he was attentive enough to Mona's clothes and Mona's taste in decor to fairly rain upon her the sorts of items she was geared to adore.

I'd once purchased Mona a plastic ladle at the grocery mart. She'd sent me there after dish soap and ultra-maxi feminine cork-age, and I'd bought her the thing because she'd melted hers on a burner eye. As I recall, she was touched by my thoughtfulness and immoderately aroused, so I never could really see much need to graduate to gemstones.

Now it's painful enough to get cast aside with callous clinical dispatch, even for a man entirely aware he's set his own downfall in motion. But by the time that Mona had summoned me over for our heart-to-heart, she was so deeply in Murry's thrall as to have embraced his personal customs of hopelessly shopworn advice and ungilded honesty. Murry was quite sufficiently lacking in basic hu-man warmth to do service as a Republican officeholder, and I dis-covered that he had altered and contaminated Mona once I had joined her on her couch and she began to speak from notes.

Even before I'd arrived, I'd known that I was due to be dis-missed, that Mona had called me in for a ceremonial brush-off. She'd been dropping hints for weeks by then and keeping steadier company with Murry. I'd even made a sort of peace with myself about driving her away. I had pilfered one evening from a shelf in Mona's front room a particularly hideous figurine. It featured a frolicking porcelain spring lamb and a basket of gerbera daisies on a hummock of meadow in the company of a towheaded wide-eyed child. A boy, as it turned out, with a slingshot in the pocket of his smock.

I placed the thing on the sill of the window over my kitchen sink where I could contemplate it evenings while I washed my dinner dishes, and I would occasionally carry it outside to rest on the rail of the porch as I sopped up my bourbon and informed myself I was no fit match for Mona. I knew at bottom that Mona and Murry were better suited for each other. I harbored the firm conviction that Maud Hooper was more my type, and I tried to employ Mona's figurine as gimcrack confirmation, even once she had missed it and punished her daughter for spiriting it away.

So I'd laid what groundwork a fellow can lay for getting dispatched by a woman, and the night I got summoned, I showed up intending to put appreciable grace on display. But the urge dissipated once Mona had produced her speaking points, a list of my failings and accumulated infelicities very much like the list I imagined Saint Peter would consult one day.

Initially, Mona held me to account for my sundry insensitivities. She informed me I was incapable of a sound rapport with children, was testy with geriatrics and showed no aptitude for pets. She hardly approved of the contempt I lavished on organized religion, revealed she'd observed me on several occasions studying women's derrieres, and she confessed she didn't care for the men I'd struck up friendships with. She even troubled herself to mention Elvin by name.

I tried to interrupt her and mount some manner of defense, but Mona cut me off with the promise she'd endure rebuttal later and moved on to speak at length of my professional fecklessness. In Mona's view I wasn't nearly earning up to my potential because I lacked ambition and even rudimentary people skills which presented Mona occasion to tell me damning things she'd heard from sundry locals I'd been gruff with or, even worse, had underbilled. Mona laid out the wretched professional future she envisioned for me, a bookkeeper sour on clients and charging them far less than he might.

Then still without allowing me opportunity to respond, Mona proceeded to our sexual incompatibility which hit me, I'll confess, as a fairly mortifying revelation. I'm the sort of guy who prides himself on knowing what goes where, and I'd entertained enough compliments through the years on my technique that I'd come to think myself a solid capable performer. I was put in mind immediately of emphatic orgasmic shrieks that I had tempted and prodded Mona to yield up in the course of relations, and I would have made mention of them if Mona hadn't volunteered that she had seen clear to favor me now and again with spots of theatrical wailing.

Extemporaneously—choosing to stray from her prepared text for a moment—Mona laid a hand to my forearm and confessed she had playacted because it had seemed the kindest thing to do.

Apparently, my professional insignificance was compounded in Mona's mind by my dearth of native romance, my sexual ineptitude and—she told me grimly—the skimpiness of my member. Now I had no reason to expect a fundamentalist Episcopalian who was lumpy and sagging and hardly much of a specimen herself would complain to me that I was wanting in the magnitude to suit her, and I got a little hotter than probably was strictly helpful at the time.

I belittled various of Mona's parts and demeaned a few of her features which, but for the fact that I'd been wounded, I would have surely kept to myself. So soon enough, we were both of us stung, and we traded barbs on Mona's sofa which culminated with the revelation that Mona had lain (she called it) with Murry. So she had reason to know he was large enough for her. Skilled, she informed me, and tender. In unbecoming triumph, Mona declared she'd yelped in earnest.

I don't remember just what I responded with, but it wasn't benign and gracious, was instead some salty corrosive insult that had popped to mind. Mona proved pleased to react in kind, and since I was ripe for provocation, we descended pretty shortly into vitriol and bile and were soon enough dredging up affronts, no matter how niggling and petty, and flinging them at each other in place of stones and boiling lye.

The whole business was oddly volcanic given the nature of our attachment which had always been a little bit tepid on my end at least. There I'd pushed Mona and Murry together and should have welcomed their affection, but instead I was pitching the manner of self-righteous unholy tantrum that I wouldn't even need to bolt awake in the morning to regret. I was sick about it even as I made myself a jackass, knew that Mona's brush-off should have been just hollow ritual, no more meaningful than a sitting governor signing a decree. I should have looked on in appreciative silence and maybe been presented a pen.

But I chose to become irate and abusive and stormed around the room in such a dudgeon that Mona felt compelled to summon Murry in. As it turned out, they had agreed on a sign if Mona was in distress, a manipulation of a window shade that brought Murry from his car where he'd been parked just up the road before a neighbor's house.

The sight of him in the doorway rendered me exponentially more irate. I was upset to learn they'd feared that I would act like I was acting which I knew for a stark departure from my customary habit of emotional moderation and Zen-like serenity. So I stalked towards the door in order to shriek most particularly at Murry and acquaint the man with what a placid gentleman I routinely was which impressed him as quite enough of a threat to earn me a look at his weapon. It appeared to be half of an ash ax handle with tape on the stout head end.

Murry brought it out from behind his thigh as I approached him in the doorway. He didn't raise it and threaten to club me, but I took his intentions well enough, understood that if I persevered with what I was about, Murry would treat me to a debilitating cranial fracture. The mere sight of that item, in fact, made sufficient of an impression on me that I drew up short so as to weigh and contemplate my options. There I was raging about the house of a woman I didn't love, a creature I didn't (in truth) much like in any way that mattered and wouldn't have fallen in with but for my constitutional lack of pluck and inability not to follow my unfurled member where it led me.

I found her child a reliable irritant. I disapproved of Mona's faith, didn't much care for her taste in clothing, in movies and books, in household decor. As a conversationalist, Mona impressed me as reliably stultifying. Her cooking was an abomination. Her politics put her just right of the pope. I couldn't recall that we'd ever enjoyed between us a meaningful exchange, and friends of hers she'd thrown me in with I'd instinctively detested.

So there was nothing between us to salvage, no alliance worth preserving which was why I'd carried Mona and Dinky out to Murry's house. And standing there in Mona's foyer with an ax handle to focus my mind, I weighed the scant elusive virtues of my and Mona's romantic attachment against the overwhelming liabilities, and I was prompted to wonder about the genuine source of my agitation, even sensed in the moment that Mona alone wasn't worth getting worked up about.

I paused there on the rug between Mona and her beer-distributor boyfriend to indulge in a brand of searching personal assessment which, from the outside, probably looked like respiratory distress touched with grief, improvement enough anyway on my emotional incontinence to tempt Mona and Murry to leave me in peace for as long as I might need.

I was afforded, then, the leisure for a spot of contemplation, the half minute or so I needed for freeform analysis which presented me the chance to realize that acute professional problems had likely served to heighten my volatility and had forestalled me from being as gracious with Mona as I otherwise might have been.

Elvin, you see, had received a letter of inquiry from the IRS. They were interested in the nature of a few of his deductions and the overall financial lassitude of his cattle-keeping business, the sort of thing I could have probably settled with a letter back. Elvin, though, only told me about that letter once he'd spoken to a revenue agent or had screamed anyway at the gentleman for the best part of a half hour. As near as Elvin could reconstruct the conversation for me later, he'd lambasted that agent with a blend of populist indignation and constitutional pseudoscholarship.

It turned out the suspicious deductions that had been questioned in Elvin's return were not, Elvin confessed once duly prodded, strictly livestock-related. Elvin had purchased over the Internet assorted organic treatments which were more in the loved-up-on-his-trundle-bed realm of pursuit and had essentially nothing at all to do with creatures on the hoof. Elvin had bought a fair number of the leading penis-enlargement potions which, at the time he'd told me about them, I'd not realized I might need.

A couple were brewed up as teas, one was an ointment, another an aerosol, and I permitted Elvin's claim that he had added a full three inches to go unchallenged and allowed it to stand wholly unconfirmed by me.

Instead I tried to anticipate the revenue service's likely objections to honoring Elvin's member, with its newfound quarter foot, as a legitimate business implement. Elvin, of course, fell back on the ponderous stress of cattle keeping and tried to build a case for the fiduciary necessity of release. And while I was prepared to accept the odd whimsical entertainment expense and even allow a man like Elvin his unorthodox pursuits, I was not at the time equipped to fully appreciate the need for an extra three inches of Schedule C deductible real estate.

Now you have to remember I'd not yet known the pleasure of hearing from Mona and so considered myself adequate if not regally endowed which, as personal convictions go, is fairly widespread among men since, as a gender, we're reluctant to size up the competition and even naked in a locker room look each other in the eye. So the pursuit of an extra inch or three impressed me as frivolity, and my sole intrigue lay with the curious science of the thing. I couldn't for the life of me figure what, once sprayed or dabbed upon a member or ingested instead in the form of tea, could produced enough of a growth spurt to lay a ruler to. Unless, of course, those penis treatments were all hallucinogenic and Elvin still had what God gave him but was sure he'd added more.

Elvin, however, elected not to wait for me to quiz him. Once I'd called on him in his cow-stall office, examined the letter he'd received and had endured from Elvin a dramatic recitation of his phone call, Elvin supplied me with a penis-enlargement testimonial. He enlisted, that is, Erlene to comment on his fresh addition. She was out in the lot beyond Elvin's window tossing corn to her hens, and Elvin yelled at her through the crack between the stuck sash and the sill.

"Tell him," he said which induced Erlene, in her housecoat and nasty slippers and with a battered hot-dipped bucket in the crook of one of her arms, to raise her free hand and show me a gap between her thumb and forefinger which I was fully prepared to stipulate as three inches more or less. Elvin wouldn't, however, be satisfied until Erlene had indicated the pitch of newfound pleasure his extra inches had bestowed. So he bent again to call out between the sash and the stuck sill, "And . . . ?" which prompted Erlene to as girlish a grin as a creature like her could probably manage, and the fistful of corn she flung playfully our way clattered off the panes.

Now I imagine I could have made some stripe of quasi-legitimate case for the bearing of Elvin's extra inches on his cattle keeping. Or at the very least I could have responded to the inquiring agent with the news that Elvin's ointment, his spray, his organic steeping potion, had constituted a last-ditch effort to treat a grievous bovine condition which no revenue service employee would seek an elaboration about. But Elvin had gone and antagonized them with his telephone call, and (worse for me) he'd spread word locally of the letter he'd received, had shown it about as a token of contemptuous federal intrusion.

Knowing Elvin, I can't imagine that he meant me any harm. He'd merely spent the bulk of his adult life detesting bureaucrats and deploring for no particular reason civic institutions, and there he'd fished out of his postbox unassailable confirmation that he'd not for decades manufactured vitriol in vain. The trouble was that people as a rule tend to be leery of tax preparers who submit a return to the revenue service and get an inquiry back. The general preference is for rebate checks or, at the very least, blessed silence, and an official query is commonly taken as proof the preparer is cursed.

Better to be a surgeon with a bothersome negligent-homicide indictment than a bookkeeper who earns for a client a pen pal at the IRS.

So the additional inches Elvin had managed to add somehow to his member had served, at length, to drive the balance of my customers away. None of them would come right out and tell me that my karma had gone south, but it was plain to me they all had gotten wind of Elvin's letter and chose to view it as a special sign of my degraded luck. Consequently, they trickled away with squirrelly evasive justifications until I had just Elvin left, a couple of back-hollow Christmas-tree farmers who I figured would throw me over as soon as they'd come by the news and Cora and Miss Addie at the remnant shop who didn't put much stock in luck and were old enough to be effectively unintimidatable.

I could imagine Miss Addie taking the fireplace shovel she used on vermin to the skull of a revenue-service agent if given half a chance.

But the rest of them had abandoned me by the time I'd been summoned to Mona's, so I was fit to imbibe everything she told me as a stinging variation on what I knew by then for a purely wretched theme. I'd passed already a solid two weeks mired up in self-pity. I had virtually nothing to do most days and little to occupy my nights beyond nursing bourbons and cultivating virulent resentments.

The thing about life in a modest rental house in the wilds of a rural county is that the bills are not so pressing and the obligations so acute as to keep a man from bottoming out at his deliberate leisure. A fellow can live on next to nothing in the country for a while, can meet with ample occasion to fester and opportunity to ferment. So I was very probably souring already from the inside out by the time that Mona summoned me over for a sanctified dismissal which made our breakup just one damn thing else happening to me. It supplied fresh evidence I was put upon, further proof I was aggrieved.

So all of that storming around I'd done was merely wallowing on the hoof and was more the result of my own pitiable personal circumstances than any injury Mona had inflicted with boasts of Murry's sexual prowess, news of his intrinsic tenderness. Accordingly, once I'd mounted an adequate victimized display, I went in for a spot of nobility and a show of selfless charm. I allowed, that is, that Mona might be better off with Murry, bestowed upon her both my blessing and a chaste kiss on the cheek before approaching Murry parked there in the doorway with his ax helve.

I like to think anymore I offered him heartfelt congratulations, but I seem to recall I told him instead, "Move!"

4 —⟶ Over time, I've grown to understand and openly acknowledge that I was never authentically captivated by Maud Hooper herself but was more in the way of intrigued with her colossal lout of a husband. That's provided, of course, you take "captivated" to mean gaily bewitched and charmed and "intrigued" to mean repelled to the point of clinical distraction.

I'd like to blame it all on bourbon, but the Dickel merely made me bolder, made me louder and more insistent and a little less worth listening to. So while the stuff did serve to loosen me up and functioned, doubtless, to fuel me, its only practical effect was to let my raging indignation out. I can see now that I've always been angry but stoppered up, for the most part, and governed, and those first few weeks post-Mona when I was acutely underemployed, the cocktails I fairly survived on served me as license to fulminate.

One of the leading virtues of country living is the insulating distance it provides. There's room enough out in the rural landscape for everyone to go uncrowded. So a man can perch nights upon his urine-corroded glider and look to be doing little more from the road than taking the evening air when, in fact, he's percolating with venom and deep in the throes of galvanic fury which, given the buffer of meadow and cow lot, can come off as harmless flouncing around.

In the daytime, for a while at least, I kept up persuasive appearances. I'd iron the front of my cleanest dress shirt and wear it underneath my blazer with whichever I'd established as my least encrusted tie, and I'd venture out to call on clients and try to make them understand that Elvin's letter from the IRS was inconsequential to them, was hardly much of a thorny matter even, in truth, for Elvin himself.

Elvin, of course, was making the rounds just then and contradicting me. He'd quite apparently gotten his Duster started and was frequenting town in the thing due to how he was armed anymore with a splendid hardship to convey. In that part of the world, the customary course of social conversation tended to take the form of an ever-escalating litany. Parties to idle chat were given, in turn, to anteing up their complaints. They'd make mention of current infirmities and personal disappointments until one of the participants had trotted out a trial of such devastating pitch and moment that everyone else was obliged to acknowledge they were not, just then, worse off.

At the time, there was a MacAvoy lurking about with a congestive heart condition, a touch both of emphysema and rheumatoid arthritis in addition to a wife in a vegetative state in a Raphine care facility and an ingrate of a daughter who'd been arrested in Lynchburg for stealing that MacAvoy's Century Sedan. Even still, that fellow would have needed a brother (very possibly a twin) on deathwatch at the penitentiary for mayhem he'd not committed to have even a chance of besting Elvin's revenue-service letter, not because of what it said but what the mere fact of it meant.

People like Elvin—and that county was brimming over with

people like him—tend to make a kind of religion out of anonymity. Elvin's phone number was unlisted. Elvin was deeply suspicious of strangers. If he'd had any money to speak of, he wouldn't have kept it in a bank. Elvin never filled out warranty cards or subscribed to magazines. He'd signed Erlene up for a Visa only once he'd proven helpless against the pull of Internet pornography. When the census taker had come around a couple of years back and was known to be lurking in the vicinity, Elvin and Erlene had actually moved for two weeks into the barn so as to ensure they'd go unfound and stay uncounted.

Elvin liked to believe the government had no clear sense who he was. He made a point of signing official documents, particularly his tax returns, with the full and proper Christian name nobody knew him by. He collected his mail at a postbox downtown, had always declined to apply for subsistence. He'd permitted his driver's license to lapse some ten or twelve years before, and though Elvin railed with bottomless venom against politicians, he'd never cast a ballot to put one into office or herd one out.

Elvin had taken, in his view, scrupulous care to remain a nonentity which he considered to be entirely necessary because, to Elvin's way of thinking, the federal government chiefly existed to menace him in two distinct and contradictory fashions. Depending on Elvin's mood and his seditious influences du jour, Elvin either believed our federal agencies were staffed by sullen wastrels who made damn certain nothing of civic merit ever got done or the government instead functioned as a seamless intelligence network tracking its citizens with both satellites and bar-code-scanner data. So Elvin's federal bureaucracy either didn't care that you existed or was armed with sufficient fruits of surveillance to anticipate your thoughts.

Elvin lurched rather barometrically between the two positions. Either way, it was Elvin's persistent personal goal to remain obscure, and he would far rather have been caught driving with his decade-expired license in the Plymouth he'd not had inspected for probably seven or eight years than receive even an actual refund check from the IRS who'd have to know just what he'd been about to pay him.

A letter, then, requesting explanation and enlargement from Elvin qualified as a regular philosophical tragedy for the man, and he couldn't seem to help but share his misfortune with most everyone he strayed across in town. Because Elvin knew no shame, he'd even whip his letter out and give an accounting of the nature of the revenue-service inquiry, explain the purpose of the treatments they were asking him about, which generated, as a rule, a reliable brace of responses. People tended to be irate over the government's intrusion in the matter of a citizen and his manly deficiency while at the same time marveling over the economy of three additional penile inches. You likely couldn't have made your big toe longer at even twice the price.

Furthermore, there was never disagreement as to where the fault should lie. By local acclamation, the trouble Elvin faced was just the sort of thing he'd employed me to keep him from. It didn't matter that I could've straightened the whole business out by return mail. Elvin had been essentially trapped and tagged and could never entirely disappear into the wilderness again.

So for a few weeks there I called on clients and tolerated their demurs, suffered through the excuses they visited on me to account for my dismissal until those back-hollow Christmas-tree farmers had heard enough to let me go and Elvin had set about agitating to have me give back all the money he'd ever paid me for reconciling his books and enduring his palaver. I fired him and thereby seasoned his story with fresh insult and irony.

I had left to me, then, just Cora and Miss Addie at the remnant shop, and for a couple of weeks I lavished the pair of them with undue attention. I'd pop in with my shirt front ironed and my tie decrusted for the moment and attempt to allay their misgivings without actually addressing them as such. Instead I'd make out, as best I could, to exude professional competence which is hardly the sort of thing a fellow is likely to know success at, most particularly in a place like the remnant shop where there was so very much tension afoot—what with the infesting vermin and the customer caste conflicts.

Cora and Miss Addie, it turned out, kept me on primarily out of inertia. They were as likely to switch bookkeepers as they were to rotate their stock.

Aside from them, however, everything was different for me. Even midday meals at the luncheonette lost their allure in time, most particularly as soon as strangers and vague passing acquaintances began to greet me by inquiring, "Aren't you Elvin's guy?"

I even once heard the fry cook belting out the saga of Elvin's three inches to the tune of "Must Jesus Bear the Cross Alone?"

At length, it got to where I only went out for liquor and for groceries, and the balance of my days I chose to spend in idle despair. At first, I was democratic with my regrets and recriminations and wished I'd never left my salaried actuarial job in Roanoke. But soon enough I had shaped and tapered my ire and had seen fit to home in on what I chose to think of as "the likes of Douglas Hooper," by which I came to understand I meant the man himself.

Now he'd never done a thing to me by any conventional standard beyond rolling up behind my Cavalier at a service-station pump and directing me to clear a spot out for him. I'd not cared for his shirt, his slacks, his alligator tasseled loafers, his haughty dismissive manner, his two-ton British landing craft. But if it were my personal habit to take special lingering interest in everybody on this planet I instinctively disliked, I'd hardly know the leisure to feed myself or draw sustaining breath, would spend virtually all my waking hours manufacturing bile.

That Hooper, however, proved to be a rather special case, most particularly after Stoney had supplied me with an insight on domestic life out at the man's executive estate. I chose to think his wife a lanky antiquated damsel, the sort of creature Douglas had corralled and ground down over time, while Douglas had visited on Stoney at least a display of spinelessness in the form of a massive Baltimore lowlife in a maroon sedan. I told myself I couldn't respect a man who refused to fight his fights.

With enough bourbon in me, I could think it noble and enriching for a man to keep his ire corked up and simply ulcerate.

At bottom, I believe I resented that Hooper because he was successful, and it hardly mattered to me I'd scant clue just what he did. Or, more to the point, I probably despised him because I was such a failure and so resembled Elvin with his curious take on Stoney's luck. That Hooper, in my view, had enjoyed more than his share of plunder. He had lavishly paying clients, a willowy wife, a handsome estate, while I'd been professionally undone by a revenue-service letter and not even, on close examination, undone from awfully much.

I lived in a homely rental house that I'd taken deplorably furnished. Even in my heyday of paying clients, my labor had brought me but modest return. My car was rust-eaten and third-hand and required a bribe to clear inspection. My shoes looked orthopedic. My trousers all were from the mall. My dog had preferred, to my care and affection, the rude life of an urban stray, and my lady friend had thrown me over for just the sort of tiresome fellow I'd calculated she'd throw me over for. So my gifts were apparently for low-five-figure incomes and orchestrating betrayal which, once saturated with bourbon, I found I could blame on Douglas. Bonded alcohol, after all, serves well as liquid victimhood.

So I sat on my porch for just evenings at first but, in time, throughout afternoons too and indulged in bouts of aimless and altogether besotted self-pity until I'd managed to fix on Douglas as the source of my distress. Back then it made crystalline sense for me to believe that Douglas Hooper had somehow pilfered my rightful blessings and, in rising up, had kept me down. He had the wealth I should have known, the mate I felt equipped to cherish, the arrogance I would have brought to bear on life as gratitude. It proved pleasant to despise him and wish for Douglas's destruction until the uselessness of wishing turned out more than I could bear.

I worked on Stoney right along for maybe a month or two. I'd watch for him and essentially intercept him at his mailbox, steer our prattle to those Hoopers most every chance I got. I talked up the human disgrace of Douglas's treatment of his wife, the historically hollow nature of threats of violence from Baltimore hoodlums, the obligation a man who looked just like Saint George was saddled with, the righteous duty the resemblance conveyed. Then I waited for proper occasion to put Stoney into play.

Mona delivered it to me, oddly enough. She turned out to be one of those people with a need to turn her former romantic attachments into friends which explains why she took such a dim view of her former husband, Larry, who'd stayed sharp and spiteful with her, had no itch to be a pal.

I had bought a county paper, my first one in many months, because I was contemplating selling off my entertainment center which seemed a bit of an extravagance given my lack of paying work along with the fact that I'd sold my TV to an Atwell down the road to pay up the arrears on my outstanding fuel-oil bill. They ran ads in the paper for items that people were selling or looking to buy, and I'd hoped I might see what the likes of entertainment centers were bringing, but I happened to hit the classifieds on a particularly arid week.

A man was shopping a pig. A woman was offering a case of unused dress shields along with a 1958 Willys Jeep which she identified both as "Like New!!" and, without enlargement, "upside down in a creek." There was seasoned firewood on offer at inflated rates for quarter cords. One man was looking to rent a smokehouse. Another hoped to place a hound in a loving home. The only furniture available was a mahogany hall tree ("$62 as is") from which I couldn't hope to extrapolate entertainment-center values.

I even nearly folded that paper and pitched it into the trash, but it was such a dreadful thing as to hold inherent fascination, and I decided at the very least I should read the local wedding announcements which led to the obituaries and the Rotary Club proceedings and the column about which citizens had traveled and to where. They were mostly off to see blood relations up and down the rust belt. The Utleys, Hal and Reba, had gone to Halifax on a bus tour. The Giddings were keeping their grandkids whose parents were snorkeling in Belize, and then I read how Mona and Murry and little Alice Marie, Mona's child, had taken a Disney cruise together so that Mona and Murry might know occasion to "celebrate their love."

Because it was our county paper and deplorable by nature, news of a microbe Murry had picked up at a buffet lunch in Freeport was included along with word from Mona that their trip might have been more festive if Murry could have kept much of anything down. I phoned up Mona (I'll confess) with uncharitable intentions, planned to be snide and caustic as I asked after the happiest gastrointestinal tract on earth. But I guess I compromised my tone the way I usually do and came off sounding, simultaneously, vinegary and cheerful.

Mona loosed one of her thespianic bubbly laughs in reply and proceeded to engage me in a spot of benign chat that ended with our agreeing to meet for lunch the following day.

She chose The Downs out at the interstate junction, with its phony Edwardian decor and a cuisine that was nearly as unenticing as authentic British fare. I had the bangers which resembled sausage in superficial ways and came with mealy cauliflower swamped in oily cheese-food sauce. Mona went in for some manner of savory pudding served in a ye olde pot with waffle-cut potatoes and a nuggety slick of chutney.

We chatted like civilized well-meaning people, were cordial with each other which, on Mona's part, was probably even virtually sincere. But I'd called her, I knew, with acidic intentions and in the spirit of latent resentment which I was having to pay for with bangers and cheese food and cauliflower for lunch.

Naturally, Mona looked good the way women were prone to once they'd thrown me over. She'd lost a little weight for her cruise (I decided) and had taken sun on the deck while Murry was down below cozying up to the toilet. I didn't want her back exactly, but I felt from where I sat the queasy suspicion some desperate night I might.

For her part, Mona was precisely where she'd hoped to be, having, that is, a pleasant lunch with a former romantic attachment as proof that no feelings were damaged and affections remained intact. She told me all about Dinky's progress at the primitive Episcopalian preschool, relayed a couple of Murry's life-affirming aphorisms, and then she revealed the scare that she and Murry had endured together on the occasion of Murry's prostate swelling to twice its normal size. The remedy had come in the form of anabolic steroids and some manner of Eastern prostate massage which Mona had taken instruction in and mastered.

She demonstrated the technique with her upraised foremost finger, and I tried my damnedest not to envision Murry in mid-massage.

"You must love him very much," I said to Mona, and I was going for glib and corrosive, but it came out like a sentiment from afternoon TV.

Mona's eyes grew misty. She touched me, for Godsakes, with her massaging hand. "You know," she told me, "I think I really do."

That's when I shifted to look around the restaurant in a bid to clear my head and saw Maud Hooper at the register paying the checkout girl for food to go. Now it didn't at the time occur to me that the only thing likely worse than a meal from The Downs served tepid at an actual restaurant table was one eaten cold and coagulated at home. I might, that is, have taken the sight of that Hooper and what she was about as input into the true course of her nature, but instead I fixed on the welt directly underneath her eye.

I guess it would be more accurate to call the thing a mouse. It was only slightly lumpy and yellowing about the edges, had at its core a blood-encrusted broken inch of skin. Straightaway I decided how that Hooper had likely come by the thing, and I kept on her until she'd shifted around and caught me in full study when I tried to convey the outrage I was enduring on her behalf.

I have to think anymore I'm probably not adept at conveying outrage, most particularly wordlessly with just my pinched dyspeptic face since that Hooper merely took up her sack and favored me as she passed with what was plainly her creep-from-the-remnant-shop look back.

Mona watched her go as well and troubled herself to ask me, "Who's that?"

In the spirit of heartfelt honesty between two former lovers, I poked at a scrap of banger and told Mona, "I don't know."

5 So we found ourselves in Stoney's van parked upon manicured gravel. I had laid such a solid foundation, had orchestrated to such an extent that Stoney had required the merest of nudges to set him into motion. He'd needed but a description of that Hooper's injury that I'd supplied across his prune-fouled ditch with modest elaboration. I'd ventured, that is, to guess aloud what the woman had run into to come by the lump underneath her eye, the scabbed-over tear in her skin.

I'd schooled Stoney already in the abiding moral duty I'd feel were I the image of an avenging saint in a lacquered painting, had speculated as to the deplorable state of the Hoopers' holy union, had interpreted Stoney's own Hooper exposure to best hostile effect. So I'd laid the various charges before touching off the fuse, and I felt gratified watching Stoney stalking hotly towards his van.

He'd opened the driver's door before he shouted back, "Come on."

Active involvement has never truly held much appeal for me. I prefer loitering in the middle distance and, once the trouble is over, wishing loudly I'd been called upon to help. So I had intended to fuel and dispatch Stoney and greet him on his return to learn what use he'd made of the righteous rage I had incited.

Stoney, however, insisted. Or rather he stood there looking at me until I'd vaulted his ditch and had crossed to join him beside his Econoline van from where I meant to acquaint him with the virtues of a lone avenger, but it appeared to me that clutter would serve to keep me where I was. Stoney, you see, was not in the habit of carrying passengers in his van, so the seat and the floorboard next to his were heaped both with those items he'd not discovered anywhere else to put.

Pipe joints, in large part, and stray carriage bolts. Hook eyes and wrenches, strap hinges and brown sacks with slits in their bottoms that nails had spilled out through. Stoney was carting around what looked, perhaps, ten years' worth of receipts and a lifetime supply of Dairy-O burger wrappers. He had a necklace of molding samples strung on mechanic's wire, an unspooled snarl of bulk lamp cord, two pairs of rubber boots, mallets and snips and galvanized washers, a fractured length of chimney flue.

Since the back of the van was already clotted and choked to capacity, I assumed Stoney would see the great good sense of leaving me behind, and I tried to steer him with word I'd be as much use one place as the other which Stoney hardly heard me at due to the racket he was making raking all of the junk on the passenger seat out onto the ground.

"Get in," he said in a tone that hardly left room for rebuttal.

I'd never previously ridden with Stoney and was surprised at the way he drove, most particularly given the circumstances and the pitch of his irritation. We crept out of his driveway and rolled up the road at twenty-five miles an hour, and Stoney kept after me to buckle my seat belt until I'd untangled and unspooled the thing. It proved gritty enough to leave an immediate stain across my shirt.

As I labored to buckle it, Stoney sat stopped at the blacktop junction and waited for an approaching car he could have crossed in front of a half dozen times.

It seemed odd to me that Stoney would be so prissy behind the wheel given what I knew of his unruly domestic circumstances or could see at the moment of his haphazard nature in his van. With just a degree or two more of neglect, he might have been suffocated by clutter, and yet there he was a connoisseur of the lawful four-point stop. Out on the open highway with no witnesses but cattle, Stoney equally divided his attention between the road and his speedometer needle, checked his mirrors like a man with multiple federal warrants to his name.

After we'd reached in fifteen minutes where I would have been in five, I feared by the time we'd made the Hoopers' executive estate, we would likely have both forgotten why we'd come.

Stoney, however, employed our leisurely excursion to pertinent effect. He acquainted me with an episode of domestic upset in his family as we crawled across the county, signaling at every turn. I learned that Stoney had witnessed a spot of household violence as a child and the experience had left an indelible mark upon him. The trouble had not been between Stoney's parents but his uncle and his aunt. The very woman, it turned out, I'd seen sitting with Stoney in his yard, that unattractive creature with ankles about the girth of number-ten cans who'd looked to me a little too thick and placid to drive a man to violence.

Of course, from my house I couldn't hear what she was nattering about, and she might well have been equipped with just the sort of rancid tongue to promote in a mate the consuming need to tap her with a shovel. Stoney didn't touch upon causes and potential justifications. Instead he told me how he'd happened to see, through a crack at an ill-fitting door, his uncle swat his aunt across the jaw with the back of his hand, hit her with force enough to knock her sprawling on the bedstead.

"Her dress flew up," Stoney told me. "I can still hear the squeak of the springs."

Stoney confessed he'd made a promise to himself that very instant, had sworn about the only oath he could remember having sworn. "That was not the stripe of thing," he said, "I'd tolerate again."

So I guess Saint George had suited Stoney as a personal pledge adornment, and while we eased across the county, I wrapped my mind around the fact that I had done less orchestrating than I'd initially imagined. Stoney had come equipped with a blood relation to avenge and had probably taken everything I'd told him over time and reduced it to "The bastard went and hit her."

I don't mind saying I was disappointed to think that the sight of a sprawling aunt did competition in Stoney's mind with his resemblance to Saint George. The notion that we were embarked together on a cracker family errand bathed the whole enterprise in the low-rent taint of movie of the week. As Stoney's enabler, I felt qualified for a tap with a shovel myself.

Some of the thrill, consequently, had ebbed entirely away from the undertaking by the time we'd spoiled the corduroy finish of that Hooper's graveled drive all the way from the road clean up to the front-porch landing. Stoney shut off his van and sat for a moment glaring at the Hoopers' front door, collecting himself (I guess) for the destiny he'd long imagined while in my capacity as his sidekick I plundered through the floorboard leavings and fished out what I learned only later was the handle of an adze. The thing was a foot and a half long at most, with heft enough to brain a squirrel, not nearly so imposing as the one Murry had carried.

I raised that handle to show it off to Stoney as I asked him, "Hmm?" He snorted once and grabbed it like a child might take his slicker from his mother on a cloudy day.

He knocked politely, Stoney did. He didn't appear to be agitated but looked resolute, determined, devoted serenely to his oath. From the van, I couldn't quite make out which of them answered the door or hear beyond the murmur what Stoney had to say to gain his entry. Then the door swung shut, and I was left to imagine what might be transpiring inside.

I didn't bother myself about it to any extravagant length, guessed Stoney and Douglas were disagreeing as to whose business precisely was whose while willowy Maud looked on in silence, shrinking in a corner. Beyond that, I failed to expend further energy upon the matter since I'm not the sort to harbor much native interest in follow-through. I'm mostly an idle schemer and occasional instigator, am hardly accustomed to much of anything coming from groundwork I have laid. So I was geared to suppose that Stoney and Douglas were conducting a makeshift summit. I'd anticipated shouting, but when I couldn't make out any, I occupied myself by rooting through the glove box of the van.

Stoney had accumulated an ambitious sheaf of tissuey pink homewares-store tickets, and I couldn't imagine he enjoyed the full benefit of his lawful deductions given his haphazard filing technique. Consequently, I was making a mental note to myself to recommend to Stoney a ledger, something compact and portable for Stoney to enter his homewares expenditures in. I seemed to recall that I'd seen one lately in the drug- or the dollar store, and I was trying to sort out in my mind which of them it had been when I heard from inside the house what even I knew for a shotgun blast.

I sat there for a moment looking slack-jawed at the Hooper doorway before I mustered the breath to tell myself ever so lowly, "Oh, Christ."

I am a retroactive genius, a hindsight prodigy. I tend to recognize all that I should have seen coming after it has already passed. Sitting alone in Stoney's van out on the Hoopers' manicured drive, I believe I might even have said aloud, "Yes. Of course. Guns."

He was just the sort, that Hooper. Not to have a pistol in the bedroom drawer or a .22 in a closet somewhere for groundhogs and marauding vermin. No, he was all affectation from his reptile loafers up, and I had sudden certain knowledge that the man owned shooting pieces. Twenty-gauge, probably, with walnut stock and scrolled receiver plates, breechloaders made to order of Italian pedigree. I could picture him in shooting togs, tweedy and bespoke, fine English boots, a Barbour birding jacket. He was the sort to be off to The Borders a couple of times each year where he'd pretend to a taste for Irish whiskey and call the beaters "chaps."

I knew all of this decisively sitting there in Stoney's van but only following the discharge of a barrel. The savvy achieving type, I chose to believe, would have suspected it long before.

I had no clear sense of just what I ought to do, would have preferred to have vanished in a cloud of vapor, but every time I closed and opened my eyes, I was still in Stoney's van. I'll admit now I glanced at the switch, but Stoney had carried off the keys. He was particular in odd ways, and that turned out to be one of them. So I just sat and strained to listen. There was little, however, to hear except for the birds in the trees and laboring diesels on the highway in the neighboring crease of terrain.

I crept at last up onto the front porch and tried to peek in through a window. When I couldn't penetrate the ivory sheers, I approached instead the door where I caught my breath and pressed my ear full upon the stile. I took a moment to reason what suitable etiquette for such a situation might be and settled on tapping upon the door as I pushed it open.

I stuck my head into the empty foyer and fairly chirped, "Hello," in the hopeful cheery tone of a man who'd only happened by. Hardly an orchestrator and not remotely a conniver, a fellow awash in responsibility. When I failed to get a reply, I tried an "Anybody here?" and then drew a steadying breath and stepped inside.

They were in the parlor, as it turned out, to the right off of the foyer. Maud Hooper was perched upon the floor, her legs folded beneath her, and she was rocking and chewing a finger end, looked for all the world like a child. She had settled on a floor joint that complained each time she moved. Douglas was stretched out just before her, was sprawled upon his back. I saw his tongue tip flit across his lips, watched as his eyelids fluttered. Stoney was over by the fine black-leather Chesterfield settee, had dropped down between the sofa and the Queen Anne cocktail table. He'd napped and splattered the surrounding furnishings with effluvia and pulp. I eased as close to him as I dared, given my stomach for such things. He'd taken the blast full in his chest and neck and looked to me masticated, appeared about halfway along to being inside out. The adze handle lay beside him on the fine hand-knotted rug. Splintered and frayed on the business end, it was richly studded with shot.

I choose to believe these days that Douglas recognized me as I approached. His index finger twitched and fluttered. He seemed to shiver where he lay. It hardly took much forensic expertise to decipher what had happened. Douglas had visited on Stoney at enormously close range a barrel of bird shot which had led to a practical illustration of Newton's First Law of Motion. Douglas had given Stoney pellets, had gotten adze-handle splinters back. One of them had speared a vein in his neck. It was about the size of a golf tee, and blood spurted around the stem of it in rhythm with Douglas's heart. The thing was like a cork in a cask, the proverbial finger in the dike. With swift and certain action, I suppose we might have saved him.

Instead I sat down on a patch of unrugged hardwood just beside Maud Hooper. She didn't appear to me frantic as she rocked and gnawed her finger, looked more like a woman who couldn't decide precisely what to do. She allowed me to take her hand in mine, the damp one she'd been chewing, and she turned upon me a gaze I was equipped to understand. It was forlorn and needy, in search of council, readily articulate. I took it to mean "Oh, creep from the remnant shop, help me if you will."

Maud Hooper watched without objection as I plucked that splinter out.

It took far longer than I would have imagined for Douglas Hooper to expire, and he was louder at it than I'd hoped he'd be. He groaned and sputtered and mewed a little like a feral cat, kept it up even after he'd seeped out what impressed me as sheer gallons. He saturated the rug he'd collapsed onto until blood had wicked up the adjacent chair ruffle. He nearly swamped and floated his shotgun, handcrafted (I noticed) in Milan. When he left us at last, he went with a snort and a husky humid sigh.

Maud Hooper was full in my arms by then, her head upon my shoulder. It turned out that she was, by constitution, a migratory sort. Viral. Parasitic. Not the type to go unmoored. She moved from harbor to harbor, man to man, controlling pillar to post, a thing I couldn't have hoped to know without fit cause to find it out.

It occurred to me there in the midst of the carnage in the Hooper parlor as I consoled (I guess I'll call it) Maud Hooper in the crook of my arm that I was likely a better orchestrator than I'd dared to think. That or a flesh-and-bone monstrosity.

I lightly laid a fingertip upon Maud Hooper's broken skin. It was some weeks later before I learned she'd ridden into a branch.

6—✦ There was solace in believing Douglas Hooper had it coming, if not generally for the life he'd led then specifically for Stoney who'd merely shown up with Douglas's wife's domestic interests at heart. That, a pestering lifelong sense of mission and the handle of an adze which hardly seemed freight enough for a man to get shotgunned about. So Douglas's splinter was steeped in justice and not merely encrusted with blood which I decided was why I'd chosen to keep it, had shoved it into my pocket.

I told them that gory business was all about a bill, a payment Douglas had failed to make for work Stoney had performed. They were the usual specimens, the standard county-police type. Former marines. State-patrol washouts. Thugs without portfolio and powers of deduction scanter than their bristly hair. It helped that people in those parts were accustomed to quarrels about money and could readily come to grips with the notion of bloodletting over cash.

Noble oaths and righteous indignation meant virtually nothing to them. There was no lingering manly local sense of courtly imperative. So while I could have informed the police what Stoney had been about and why, I elected to spare them the disorienting upset of the facts and went instead with the homely comfort of a simple failure to pay.

Maud Hooper required no instruction from me, proved the soul of misty-eyed discretion and responded to every nettlesome official police inquiry by working her features into a grimace and dissolving into tears. Even those occasions when we were alone together, I never managed to distill exactly what the woman had come to know of Stoney's guiding intentions, if she was even aware he'd not shown up to quarrel about a bill.

Maud was incapable, I discovered, of being decisive and emphatic. Without vigorous encouragement and freshets of instruction, she could never seem to settle on exactly what she thought. Her preference was for dithering, for noncommittal shrugs, and even in private she couldn't quite tell me what Stoney had said to Douglas to induce a man of such a tidy constipated nature to employ the sort of weapon guaranteed to make a mess.

She'd half-form words with her lips. She'd drop her head and shrug. The investigation was led by Skip who owned a brown suit and a blue one. Each looked to have been stitched together with low-test monofilament line. Skip wore square-toed boots and a fat black belt with a Dale Earnhardt memorial buckle. He favored daisy-yellow button-down shirts and bolos instead of ties. I kept waiting for Skip to be clever somewhere underneath it all, to have a subtle cagey streak mixed with the suet, but it turned out he was merely married to the police chief's sister's child.

Skip's interview technique consisted primarily of freeform reminiscence. In asking a question of me, Skip would usually be reminded of something else, pricked to recall a thing he'd seen somewhere, an episode from his past which he would inform me of at length, indulging every trifling tangent. He'd generally carry on for a quarter hour at a stretch before noticing just how far he'd strayed from the official matter at hand.

Then he'd say dreamily, "Well, anyway," and lick his pencil lead as prelude usually to wandering into the narrative wilderness again.

Douglas's funeral service was rather grand, as things in those parts went. It was held in the liberal unapocalyptic Episcopalian sanctuary where the Hoopers had never been affiliated, but the church was of a size that it could easily accommodate all of Douglas's Baltimore-hoodlum clientele. They showed up in Armani profusion, and I sat for my safety well in the back, as far removed as possible from the vicinity of the widow who shared her pew with two women who turned out to be Douglas's former wives.

I'd seen one of them approach the casket before the proceedings had begun, the oldest of the lot, whose dress (I noticed) was floral and pastel. She'd muttered a word or two over Douglas before, with her foremost finger, jabbing him to satisfy herself that he was dead.

During the eulogy delivered by the Episcopalian priest—a full half hour of wholly generic uplift—I scanned the congregation in hopes of spying out the Baltimore thug who'd previously driven down to menace Stoney. I'd expected to recognize him by his monumental girth, but he had such appreciable blubbery competition that I concluded the leading rewards of crime up on the Chesapeake were very probably polyunsaturated.

Back at the Hoopers' executive estate following the service, I chatted up a local woman, a Kyle from over by the quarry, who attended funerals in a recreational sort of way. Maud sat on the sofa with Douglas's former wives and entertained condolences while a trio of Douglas's clients—I saw them go into his study—forced the lock on Douglas's gun case and spirited his various firearms away.

Stoney's service was held at his grave site on the hill behind his house. He was buried between his mother and his sister, Helen Marie, who according to her headstone had been called back home to Jesus in 1958 when she was two. There was a woman in attendance whose toilet Stoney had replaced, a man whose driveway Stoney had sealed, another whose ductwork Stoney had mended. Stoney's last living relation, his thick unsightly aunt, was too infirm to make the trek up to the graveside proper and sat instead in her Chrysler with the door flung open at the bottom of the hill.

She got Stoney's house since there wasn't, I guess, anybody else to have it, and I imagine she'd waited years for the chance to tidy the place up. A Saturday not two weeks after Stoney had been buried, she showed up in her sedan followed by two black men in a truck who carted Stoney's periodicals out into the yard, doused them with gasoline from a mower can and burned them in the ditch while the aunt sat in a folding chair and carped and oversaw.

I passed the afternoon on my glider soaking in my handiwork.

I suspected I was transitional, sensed Maud Hooper would migrate from me in time even if, at first, she knew some use for a down-at-heel bookkeeper. I stood ready to drape, when encouraged, a comforting arm around the woman, and we enjoyed between us our spot of gaudy traumatic bother to share which we grew content together to think a tragic misadventure. Yet another case of a loaded firearm merely going off. Maud Hooper took my hand sometimes and patted the back of it fondly as a sign, I believe anymore, I was the gentleman she required to do duty between the gentlemen she'd get worked up about. The sort with the pluck and means to make her what she took for content.

It was her idea to go on holiday, her privilege (she told me) to pay since Douglas had seen well after her needs and had ensured her lasting comfort. My role would be both porter and chaste brotherly companion. As recompense, she let me pick where we'd end up.

7 —◦→ Our decor is Euro-Marriott. Our upholstery leatherette. We have milky pickled finishes on our nightstands and our tables. The floor is ancient icy terrazzo. There are timbers in the ceiling that look fuzzy and unsanitary in the morning light. Our apartment walls are hung with sundry views of the lagoon. Torcello in a snow spit. San Michele at sunset. A small-scale model of a *motoscafo* sits on the TV. Ghastly hook-nosed carnival masks all but infest the place.

The British owners have kindly typed and laminated assorted instructions. The shower taps require a surgical touch to regulate. The washing machine in the kitchen is insidiously complicated. Maud and I needed two full days to master the coffeepot. There is an entire sheaf of directions given over to the windows which are Swiss and snug and stout and open probably fourteen ways.

We are deep in Dorsoduro along a meagerly traveled canal and fall asleep at night in separate beds to the gentle slosh of water. The estuarial tang of the place. The odd melancholy footfall on the stones.

Since Maud had never been before, I was of use to her at first, was qualified to squire her about to the sights and the legendary attractions. I let on to have favorites among the cafés, a special knowledge of routes and shortcuts, made out to have traveled to Venice far more often than I'd come. When we were lost back in the narrow neck of some dreary sunless *calle*, I never failed to insist I knew exactly where we were.

I needed a good half dozen attempts over three consecutive days to locate the Dalmatian guildhall with Stoney's painting inside. Admission had jumped a thousand lire, but otherwise little had changed. The place was dark and musty, and the same sullen guard lazed about in his dandruffy blazer. Saint George transfixed his dragon in amber-lacquered splendor across the entire breadth of the near wall.

Somehow I'd failed to worry that Maud Hooper might recognize Stoney, doubted the woman had been exposed to him enough. I was more there on a pilgrimage than to show that painting off. So I left Maud to soak in the thing on her own, sidled down to a murky corner as I fished my relic out from among my change and my Cavalier keys. I laid that splinter on the lip of the wainscoting where I felt sure it would go undetected given the grit and the soot I came away with on my finger ends.

Maud had found him by the time I'd returned to her, had worked her way along his lance, had settled upon his pasty profile above his horse's mane. The sharp breath she drew stopped for a moment and stayed our fellow tourists, attracted even the lumbering bovine notice of the dandruffy guard.

When Maud complained of feeling faint, I escorted her outside where she leaned against the railing of the bridge just up the *calle*. I offered her the crisp white handkerchief it is my custom to carry. I asked her, "What is it?" but Maud shook her head. She shrugged and declined to say.

We've taken to eating in a restaurant I can find reliably. It's probably no more than fifty yards removed from our apartment but requires still modest orienteering skills to come across. The food is indifferent. The waiters obsequious. The patrons predominantly German. The music piped in through the ceiling is heavily contaminated with selections from that Florentine tenor who pitched off of his Vespa.

Maud sticks to the branzino. I'm an anguilla ai ferri man. If we traffic in three or four dozen words throughout a meal, then we've been chatty. We each know the other is living for the day the lease expires.

Maud located a stable out on the Lido and goes there afternoons to ride. It was my habit at first to walk her to the *vaporetto* stop, but anymore she merely slips away and simply disappears. I've grown partial to a bench on the Zattere that faces the afternoon sun. I carry usually one of the volumes from the apartment shelves which are freighted with dry Venetian histories, wretched novels of intrigue, an ornate gilt-edged set of the complete Tobias Smollett. My book of the moment reliably lies neglected on my knee.

There are boats to watch fighting the wind and chop along the Giudecca Canal, massive ships from the Stazione Marittima steaming towards the sea. There are impeccably dressed Venetian women in hats and hose and heels who come away from the grocery and perch to rest on my bench with their yellow sacks. They visit pleasantries upon me in the soft local dialect. I disappoint them (I can tell) with English back.

There are personal regrets to catalog, misadventures to sift and rue. Absolution to agitate for with the fervor of a calling. Self-reproach to settle into as a fresh choice in careers. Come twilight when the sea breeze flags and the lamps light on the quay, I take my unread book in hand, rise from my bench and go.

New in Paperback from Penguin

Polar

With this bittersweet tale of Deputy Ray Tatum's search for a missing child in the wilds of the Virginia Blue Ridge, T. R. Pearson once again blends high humor with pensive melancholy in a vivid portrayal of American life in the rural South. Among the local eccentric citizens is Clayton, the town ne'er-do-well, notorious for his devotion to pornography, who suddenly turns into the town prophet. As Ray unravels the mystery of Clayton's condition, he embarks on an elaborate quest to solve the disappearance of the missing girl. In this wickedly funny and peerless novel, T. R. Pearson confirms what many of his fans have long known—that his is a unique voice in contemporary fiction.　　　　　　　　　　　*ISBN 0-14-200172-4*

Also Available in Paperback from Penguin

"Pearson is a master of what jazz musicians call riffs, improvisations that in his hands are almost unfailingly funny."

　　　　　　　　　　　　　　　　　　—The Washington Post

A *New York Times* Notable Book

Blue Ridge

In T. R. Pearson's eccentric, double-barreled story of crime and intrigue he intertwines two murders—one in the wilds of Virginia and one in the streets of Manhattan. Ray Tatum is the new deputy sheriff of Hogarth, Virginia, a peaceful, backwoods town until the discovery of a complete set of human bones on the Appalachian Trail. Meanwhile, Ray's cousin Paul is summoned to New York to identify another body—the corpse of his son, whom he scarcely knew. As the facts behind the two deaths unfold, Pearson weaves an unforgettable and utterly entrancing story; this is southern storytelling at its best.　　　　　　　　　　*ISBN 0-14-100216-6*

FOR THE BEST IN PAPERBACKS, LOOK FOR THE

In every corner of the world, on every subject under the sun, Penguin represents quality and variety—the very best in publishing today.

For complete information about books available from Penguin—including Penguin Classics, Penguin Compass, and Puffins—and how to order them, write to us at the appropriate address below. Please note that for copyright reasons the selection of books varies from country to country.

In the United States: Please write to *Penguin Group (USA), P.O. Box 12289 Dept. B, Newark, New Jersey 07101-5289* or call 1-800-788-6262.

In the United Kingdom: Please write to *Dept. EP, Penguin Books Ltd, Bath Road, Harmondsworth, West Drayton, Middlesex UB7 0DA.*

In Canada: Please write to *Penguin Books Canada Ltd, 10 Alcorn Avenue, Suite 300, Toronto, Ontario M4V 3B2.*

In Australia: Please write to *Penguin Books Australia Ltd, P.O. Box 257, Ringwood, Victoria 3134.*

In New Zealand: Please write to *Penguin Books (NZ) Ltd, Private Bag 102902, North Shore Mail Centre, Auckland 10.*

In India: Please write to *Penguin Books India Pvt Ltd, 11 Panchsheel Shopping Centre, Panchsheel Park, New Delhi 110 017.*

In the Netherlands: Please write to *Penguin Books Netherlands bv, Postbus 3507, NL-1001 AH Amsterdam.*

In Germany: Please write to *Penguin Books Deutschland GmbH, Metzlerstrasse 26, 60594 Frankfurt am Main.*

In Spain: Please write to *Penguin Books S. A., Bravo Murillo 19, 1° B, 28015 Madrid.*

In Italy: Please write to *Penguin Italia s.r.l., Via Benedetto Croce 2, 20094 Corsico, Milano.*

In France: Please write to *Penguin France, Le Carré Wilson, 62 rue Benjamin Baillaud, 31500 Toulouse.*

In Japan: Please write to *Penguin Books Japan Ltd, Kaneko Building, 2-3-25 Koraku, Bunkyo-Ku, Tokyo 112.*

In South Africa: Please write to *Penguin Books South Africa (Pty) Ltd, Private Bag X14, Parkview, 2122 Johannesburg.*